The
Spanish
Daughter

BOOKS BY SORAYA LANE

Soraya
LANE

The
Spanish
Daughter

bookouture

Published by Bookouture in 2025

An imprint of Storyfire Ltd.
Carmelite House
50 Victoria Embankment
London EC4Y 0DZ

The authorised representative in the EEA is Hachette Ireland
8 Castlecourt Centre
Dublin 15 D15 XTP3
Ireland
(email: info@hbgi.ie)

ISBN: 978-1-83618-539-0
eBook ISBN: 978-1-83618-538-3

PROLOGUE

THE SANTIAGO FAMILY ESTATE, ARGENTINA, 1939

Valentina lay beneath the ceibo tree, gazing up at the green leaves as she nestled in closer to Felipe, the sunlight barely able to filter through the thick canopy above. Their horses were tethered nearby, happy to rest in the morning sun while their young riders stretched out on the grass at the farthest corner of the sprawling farm.

'I wish we didn't have to go back,' Valentina murmured, turning on her side and staring at Felipe. She propped herself up on one elbow, her long dark hair sliding over her shoulder and brushing his face. 'I wish we could stay here all day.'

He lifted his hand and skimmed his fingers across the bare skin of her arm, trailing from her shoulder all the way down to her wrist. Felipe didn't say anything straightaway, instead choosing to lean towards her, catching her lips against his, kissing her so softly she felt she might melt into his arms as they wrapped around her.

'If your father caught us—'

Valentina reached down and stroked his hair away from his cocoa-brown eyes. 'Then why don't we just tell him? Wouldn't it be better for him to know?'

Felipe's eyes widened. 'Tell him?'

She stole another kiss as one of the horses whinnied, starting to become restless after waiting so long to be ridden back. They'd been out for longer than they should have, which meant they'd probably have to gallop home now so she didn't get into trouble. Sometimes Valentina dreamed about not returning in secrecy, of telling her family about Felipe and the love she felt for him. After all these years of loving him, she was ready.

'Yes, I think we should tell him. I think you should ask for his permission,' she whispered against his cheek.

'And what if he says no?' Felipe asked.

'He won't, I'm certain of it. All he wants is for me to be happy.'

So long as Felipe didn't ask her mother's permission, because she knew that she would rather lock Valentina in her bedroom for the rest of her life than accept that she was in love with a boy like Felipe. Her mother had much grander ambitions for her only daughter, was always talking of the matches she'd like to make for her, tempered only by the fact that her father insisted they wait until Valentina was older, so that she could have a say in whom she married. Deep down, she guessed that her father wanted to keep her at home for as long as possible, and she was only too happy to oblige.

'We'd best get back,' Felipe said. 'Basilio won't forgive me if he has to send out a search party to look for us. It'll put an end to us before I even gather the courage to tell him.'

Valentina sighed and let Felipe pull her to her feet, their fingers interlinked, wishing they could have their morning all over again. But as she was smoothing her hands down her blouse to brush away the creases, not wanting anyone to guess that they'd been rolling around on the grass, she heard galloping hooves, and her heart began to race as a lone rider came into view.

No one other than her and Felipe galloped around the farm like that, which meant that something was wrong. Something was very, very wrong.

'Miss Valentina,' the breathless rider called as he approached. 'Come quickly!'

Valentina looked helplessly to Felipe, who quickly leapt up and readied the horses for their ride back.

Please don't be Papa. Let it be anyone but my darling papa.

1

LONDON, 2022

Rose pushed through the glass door and emerged onto the pavement, walking away from the lawyer's office and wondering if she was dreaming. None of what she'd just heard seemed real and she could only imagine how confused she must have looked in the meeting. She slipped her hand into her pocket to feel for the little box she'd been given, her fingers moving back and forth against the smooth wood.

How is any of this real?

She stood and looked around, tilting her face up slightly to feel the sunshine on her skin—something she hadn't enjoyed for days, or maybe even weeks. The past few months had merged into a blur for her, and she could scarcely remember what day of the week it was or when she'd last taken a moment to just breathe in the fresh air. Someone knocked into her then, making her stumble, and Rose blinked as she looked around, almost blinded by the sunlight as she remembered where she was. The city street was bustling with people going about their day, and she was nothing short of a hindrance just standing there.

Rose's phone vibrated in her bag and she quickly reached

for it, almost dropping it in her hurry to read the message when she saw it was from her mother's carer.

All is well here. Your mother is sleeping. Take your time.

She was tempted to hurry home regardless, but she'd barely left the house of late and she still had another two hours before the carer was scheduled to leave. Rose decided to set off on foot and see if she couldn't find a café, and she'd hardly been walking five minutes before she saw one. She headed straight in, smiling immediately at the inviting smell of coffee and happy to be away from the crowded street. It was heavenly and also exactly what she needed.

'You look as if you're in desperate need of caffeine.'

Rose glanced up and saw that the barista was watching her as he reached for a takeaway cup and placed it beneath the machine.

'Is it that obvious?' she asked.

'Painfully so.'

Rose laughed. It hadn't only been a long time since she'd had coffee, it had been a long time since she'd laughed, and it felt good.

'Let's just say I've been living on instant coffee these past few weeks,' she said.

'Let me guess,' he said, making a face as if he was deep in concentration, before grinning. 'Skinny flat white?'

She wasn't sure if she was impressed or annoyed that she was so easy to read, but she decided to go with impressed. 'You got me.'

Rose paid for the coffee and ordered an eggs Benedict to placate her growling stomach when the barista came back to the counter. And if she hadn't been so curious to find out what was in the little box in her bag, she would have stood and flirted with the cute barista for longer. When she'd been working, she'd stopped every morning at the café closest to her office on the way in, enjoying the morning banter and always going to work with a smile on her face and a coffee in her hand. It wasn't so much that she missed the routine of her old life, it was more that she craved the social interaction.

She eventually sat down at a little table in the corner and held the box she'd been given at the lawyer's office, turning it left and then right in her hands as she studied the handwritten name tag attached to it. The string holding it together was old, with little fibres coming away and floating into the air as she worked on the knot with her fingernails. It didn't take long until she was able to pull the string though, discarding it on the table and slowly opening the tiny box, the wood smooth against her skin. She paused, staring down at it for a moment before opening it, nervous about lifting the lid as a wave of sadness passed over her. *I wish you were here to open it with me, Grandma.*

It was only small, and she had no idea what to expect, but what she saw inside when she finally opened it took her by surprise. There was a piece of sky-blue silk, which appeared as if it had been cut or even gently torn from a larger piece of fabric, and as she lifted it out, she saw that a delicate figurine of a horse was nestled at the bottom of the box. She placed the silk down and carefully took out the horse, running her fingertips over the soft edges of the wood, admiring the intricate carving. It was so small and so carefully made, something she guessed a person would have to labour over for hours and hours to create by hand.

'Flat white?'

Rose nodded at the server when she stopped at her table, not even looking up as she murmured thank you, unable to take her eyes from the figurine as she tried to understand what she was looking at—imagining who might have made it and how it might have come to be left for her grandma. The woman at the meeting, Mia, had claimed that the box had been left behind at a place called Hope's House for Rose's grandmother at her birth, before she'd been placed for adoption. Rose couldn't fathom that this had been hidden for decades, just waiting to be discovered.

Eventually she put the horse down and looked in the box again, tipping it upside down, certain she'd missed something, wondering if there was supposed to be a letter or some explanation for what she'd found. But there was nothing. Just two tiny items that held the key to discovering her family's true past.

Rose took the piece of silk in one hand and the horse in the other and stared between the two things, forgetting all about her coffee and closing her fingers over them as if perhaps just by feeling them she might have an answer.

But the truth was, she'd never been so puzzled in her life, and she also couldn't help but wonder what it all meant for her, when she was on the cusp of losing the only family she'd ever known. A shiver ran through Rose as she stared down at the clues. Her grandmother had only recently passed away, barely six months before Rose's mother had been diagnosed, which made finding this connection to the past bittersweet. She'd grown up an only child, living in her grandmother's home after her father had left to work abroad. It had been a multigenerational house—with her, her mum and her grandmother all living together, and she'd grown up feeling as if she had two mothers who'd adored her instead of one.

Rose quickly blinked away tears, not wanting to become emotional in the middle of a café; yet she felt the most overwhelming sense of loneliness. She would have done anything to have her grandmother seated beside her, her soft, weathered hand in hers, glancing over and seeing her bright eyes looking back at her. Or the sense of her mother's warm gaze settling on her as they exchanged a surprised glance at the discovery. It was almost impossible to believe that within the space of a year, she'd have lost both of them. And without them, did she even want to dig up the past? She sighed. *Maybe some things are better left undiscovered.*

But the discovery did bring a smile to her lips, remembering her grandmother's favourite saying, which seemed most appropriate now.

'Let sleeping dogs lie, my darling. Nothing ever came from poking one's nose where it doesn't belong.'

But would I be doing that if someone had intentionally left this behind for you, Grandma? Don't I owe it to you, to find out about your past?

Rose brushed another tear from her cheek and repositioned the clues on the other side of the table before beginning her meal. She was curious, of course she was curious, but with everything she had going on right now, the timing couldn't have been worse.

2

TWO MONTHS LATER

Rose sat in a heap of her mother's belongings, a glass of half-drunk prosecco in one hand, watching her best friend move with an energy that exhausted her. If she'd been alone, she'd have been holding a tissue rather than a glass, but Jessica had blown into Rose's flat like a storm, sweeping her into her arms and refusing to let her wallow. They'd cried together for the first hour, and then Jessica had taken over, immediately ordering groceries and tidying the place as if she were a professional housekeeper rather than a diplomat who'd just flown in from New York.

And now, six hours later, they were sitting in her mother's room and Jessica still hadn't slowed down.

'Would you like my opinion?' Jessica asked.

Rose watched as her friend scooped her long hair up and tied it on top of her head. 'When have you ever not shared your opinion with me?'

Jessica's smile was warm, her eyes soft as she looked back at her. 'You've just lost your mum, Rose. I'm not going to do anything without asking first.'

Rose sipped her prosecco. At first it had seemed almost

rude to drink a celebratory beverage within forty-eight hours of her mother's passing, but Jessica had reminded her of all the times they'd sat and shared a bottle of wine with her mother when she'd visited from New York. It was as good as a tradition. The two of them had been best friends since their first day of high school, and Jessica had dropped everything and caught a red-eye flight from New York as soon as she'd heard the news.

'I think you shouldn't be in a hurry to deal with all her things,' Jessica said. 'There's no reason I can see to rush this part of the grieving process.'

Rose nodded, blinking away tears as she looked around the room. Jessica was right. She didn't want to erase her mother's memory; she was only doing all this because she'd thought it was what was expected of her.

'I think, in a few months from now when it's not all so fresh, you'll be more comfortable coming in here and going through all her things.' Jessica paused. '*When you're ready.*'

'So, what do we do now?' Rose asked, looking around the room and knowing how lucky she was to have a friend like Jessica. 'I hate the thought of being idle.'

'We cook!' Jessica announced, as if it were the most straightforward decision in the world.

Rose laughed, despite it all, following her friend to the kitchen where she unpacked the groceries Jessica had ordered earlier, pouring them another glass each as she sat at the kitchen bench to watch her friend cook, listening to her talk about her four-year-old twin daughters, to whom Rose was godmother.

'It looks like you have a stack of unopened mail there,' Jessica said, gesturing towards the large pile at the end of the bench. 'Would you like me to go through it in the morning, so you don't have to? I'm here to do whatever you need me to do.'

Rose sighed and stood to retrieve it. 'No, I'll do it now. Between the letters from the lawyers, the hospital and the insurance company, it was all starting to get a bit much, but I can't ignore it forever.'

'I know this is a touchy subject,' Jessica said as Rose began to flick through the envelopes, 'but have you heard from Luke?'

Rose glanced up. 'I think I made it pretty clear to him that I didn't want to hear from him ever again, so I shouldn't be surprised, but no. He hasn't even sent me a text since I moved out.' *Not even to see if I'd lost Mum yet.*

Jessica grimaced. 'He seemed so nice in the beginning,' she said. 'Clearly I'm a terrible judge of character though, because he turned out to be an absolute arsehole.'

'I'd be lying if I said I didn't think he was the one, so I guess we're both terrible judges of character.' Luke had been perfect on paper, in fact he'd been rather perfect in general, until he'd criticised her for taking a sabbatical from her job and then given her an ultimatum when she'd told him she'd be moving in with her mother to nurse her until she passed away. It had become immediately clear that he was seriously lacking in compassion, and she wouldn't have swapped the last few months she'd spent with her mum for anything—and certainly not for him.

'And what about work?' Jessica asked. 'How long do you have to decide whether you're going back or not?'

As they talked, Rose sorted the envelopes into piles.

'I have two weeks from now to give them my answer,' she replied. 'They've been incredibly understanding, but they can only let me stay on leave for so long.'

'And the hesitation in your voice is because...'

'Because I don't know if I even want to be a lawyer anymore,' she said, surprised at how easily her thoughts had rolled off her tongue. 'I keep imagining going back to work, practising again, being part of that world, and there's not even a glimmer of excitement inside me at the thought of it. I just don't know if it's for me.'

'You've just lost your mum, so it's probably completely

normal to feel like this, but then again, maybe everything you've been through has made you see things more clearly. If you don't love what you do...'

'It's like my heart isn't in it anymore. I think maybe I need a change of scene, or perhaps I just need a proper break after everything that's happened, to catch my breath.' Rose had been going over and over in her mind whether she wanted to go back or not, whether she was brave enough to turn her back on the career she'd spent so long studying and working for.

'Perhaps I could tempt you to come to New York then? The girls and I would love having you close, and it might be just the change you need.'

'And I would love seeing them more, but...' Rose murmured, holding up the last envelope from the pile and staring at the return address, which clearly stated that it was from Argentina. 'What *is* this?'

Rose forgot entirely what they'd been talking about and slid her fingernail beneath the seal, surprised at the thick weight of the envelope and the matching cream paper inside. She'd managed her mum's affairs for some time now, but she'd never had anything unusual like this arrive before. It was usually correspondence about her banking or insurance, but this... Rose unfolded it and skimmed over the words, one hand lifting to her mouth as she gasped, not believing the words that were printed on the page.

'What is it?' Jessica asked, coming to stand beside her. 'You know my husband will fight the insurance company for you if they're refusing to   '

'It's not that,' Rose murmured, as she read it again before passing it to Jessica. 'It's from a law firm, in Buenos Aires. It's addressed to my mother.'

'Buenos Aires? Are you sure?'

Rose nodded and reached for her drink, taking a large sip and then another, trying to stop the shake in her hand.

'What business did your mother have in Argentina?' Jessica asked, taking the letter from her. 'Why would a law firm from another country be writing to her?'

Rose didn't answer; she just sat there and tried to digest what she'd just read, waiting for her friend to catch up. Jessica had gone silent as she read.

'Rose, this says that your mother is the sole beneficiary of a large estate in Argentina,' Jessica said, her eyes wide as she stared back at her. 'It says that the family matriarch has passed away, and that—'

'My mother has inherited her expansive polo property and the balance of her fortune, as heiress to the Santiago family estate,' Rose finished for her, having already committed the words to heart. 'That it was intended to be left to my grandmother from her biological mother, but that because she's no longer alive, it goes to my mother.'

Jessica met her gaze. 'Which means that now your mother isn't here...'

Rose blinked, hardly able to comprehend the reality of what they were discussing.

'Rose, it means that *you* will inherit this now. *You're* the sole beneficiary of your mother's estate, correct?'

Rose nodded. 'Yes,' she said, her voice so raspy it barely came out as a whisper. 'I am.'

'And you knew nothing about any of this?' Jessica asked, her eyebrows arched in surprise. 'About this family connection? Because it doesn't sound like this is an old lady with a few euros to her name, it sounds much, much more substantial. It sounds like...' She shook her head. 'Rose, this sounds like something that could change a person's life. Have you ever even heard of the Santiago family? Have you been to Buenos Aires before?'

'I knew nothing of it, and I would bet that my mother knew nothing, either. This isn't the sort of thing she'd have kept from me, especially when we had so long together before she passed

away. We told each other everything these past few months.'
Rose closed her eyes, suddenly remembering the little box with
the horse figurine inside; how confused she'd been about the
clues. So much had happened since then that she hadn't had
time to think about them, but this brought it all back. She'd
received unexpected correspondence from lawyers twice now
in the space of a few months. 'Actually...' Rose leapt to her feet
and ran to her bedroom, reaching around in her bedside drawer
until her fingers connected with the wooden box. When she
returned, Jessica had a knife in her hand again and was chop-
ping up mushrooms for her famous carbonara, but she stopped
and washed her hands when Rose returned.

'I think it might have something to do with this,' Rose said,
breathless all of a sudden, the rush of what it had felt like
discovering these clues for the first time coming back to her. 'It
has to be connected, otherwise it's all just too much of a coincidence.'

Jessica took the box from her and opened it, taking out the
figurine and the piece of silk and looking bewildered as she
lifted her gaze.

'What are these?' Jessica asked. 'Rose, where did you get
them from, and why are they in this little box?'

'I think,' Rose said, looking up into Jessica's wide eyes, 'that
these things are connected to my grandmother and her inheritance in Argentina. I found out just a couple of months ago that
my grandmother was born at a place called Hope's House, here
in London, and until now, I had no way of knowing what they
meant.' She paused. 'But this letter? It could explain
everything.'

3

'I'd say that I can't believe you didn't tell me about this, but you've had a lot on your mind,' Jessica said.

Rose stared down at the horse figurine. 'The day I arrived home from being given these things was the day we found out Mum's final test results,' she said. 'I got home, excited to show everything to her and tell her about the meeting, but life fell apart before I had the chance. I put the box in a drawer, and as the days went past, I honestly never thought about it again. There was just too much to deal with.'

Jessica touched her shoulder as she passed, resuming her position in the kitchen. 'Start at the very beginning. I want to hear it all.'

Rose sat back and told Jessica everything—the letter that had arrived, the meeting at the lawyer's office, the other women who'd been summoned at the same time as her—and when she finished, Jessica was spooning her creamy chicken and mushroom carbonara into two bowls.

'So just to get this straight: we're to presume that your grandmother was born at this Hope's House for unmarried mothers, but that she possibly had no idea that she was adopt-

ed?' Jessica asked. 'And then we're also to presume that your mother had no idea about the adoption, the little box that was left behind, or the letter that just arrived? It was all a complete secret?'

'I can't conceive that either of them would have kept anything like this from me. We just weren't a secret-keeping type of family. I mean, you know what we were like, we didn't hold much back. We were three women living in one house, and we talked about everything.'

'Did your grandmother talk about her childhood at all when you were growing up? Did she give any indication that she might have been adopted?'

'She always said that her parents were very strict and expected a lot from their only daughter, which seemed to me just part and parcel of that generation, but that's all. I don't even know if families would have even talked about adoption back then. Wouldn't they have just pretended they'd had her naturally, given the time?' Although now she thought about it, there wouldn't have been many families with only one child at that time, either. Perhaps that was telling in itself?

They sat in silence, eating, and Rose couldn't help but think of the difference that food could make. There was something about a bowl of home-made, creamy Italian food that made her feel as if someone was wrapping their arms around her in a big hug. It was exactly what she'd needed.

'I have a feeling that you haven't decided whether or not to go back to your old job because you've been waiting for a sign,' Jessica said.

Rose sighed. 'You think this is my sign from the universe?'

'Maybe,' Jessica said. 'I mean, if you wanted an excuse not to go back to your old life, then this is it. We're both intelligent, educated women and I know that means we should be all about reason and logic, but sometimes we have to believe that there is something else at play, that the universe really is trying to tell us something. You have a choice here, Rose, and you don't have to do anything you don't want to do.'

Rose twirled the fettucine around her fork before looking up. 'You think I should go to Argentina and meet with this law firm, don't you?'

Jessica's bright blue eyes met hers. 'I think we should start by doing our research, but if everything adds up, then yes, I think you should go to Argentina. I think it would be crazy not to, given what's at stake here.'

Rose nodded, turning her attention back to her food even though she'd almost entirely lost her appetite. Suddenly all she could think about was her mum, and how much she wished she was sitting in the kitchen with them, discussing the mystery, her eyes wide at the secret they were uncovering. *She would have loved it*. If Rose shut her eyes, she could hear her mother's soft laugh, could imagine her throwing her head back when Jessica entertained them with a hilarious story, or watching her eyes widen as they googled Argentina. The three of them had always had so much fun together.

She opened her eyes when Jessica's hand found hers, her fingers squeezing Rose's and bringing her back to the present, her voice soft and full of understanding.

'You're going to get through this,' Jessica whispered, but her eyes were glassy with unshed tears. 'Every day will get a little bit easier, and eventually you'll realise just how strong you are.'

'I know. I just...' Rose cleared her throat and wiped her tears from her cheeks with her fingertips. She was already so tired of crying all the time. 'I just wish she was here, that's all. I wish she was part of this. I wish we'd had longer together.'

'What do you say we finish eating and snuggle up on the sofa to do some research or watch a film?' Jessica asked. 'I'm thinking chocolate or ice cream...'

Rose smiled through her tears. 'I think that sounds perfect.

Although if you stay any longer than three days, I'm not going to be able to fit into my jeans.'

Thirty minutes later, they'd decided to curl up in Rose's bed instead of on the sofa, snuggled up in their pyjamas, each with a laptop balanced on their knees. And despite the chocolate being open between them, Rose was too busy trying to stop her jaw from falling open to even consider eating it.

'Jess,' she said, nudging her friend with her elbow. 'It can't be this place, can it?'

Jessica leaned over, her glasses perched on her nose. '*That's* the place you found?'

'I mean, surely not, right?' Rose scrolled back through the photos to the place she'd stumbled upon as soon as she'd started her search. The Santiago family featured in plenty of articles that dated back decades, but the one that she was most interested in was an article ranking the most beautiful privately owned properties in Argentina. It appeared that their family residence was number three on the list. 'It's breathtaking.'

Jessica took Rose's laptop from her and held it close to her face, as if she couldn't believe what she was seeing either. 'This is the place? *This* is the Santiago family estate?'

Rose nodded and took it back from her, scrolling through the photos depicting a large, low-slung Spanish-style house with a red terracotta roof, surrounded by a group of huge stable blocks and endless fields where horses were grazing. If someone had asked her to imagine the most picturesque, stunning property in Argentina, it might well have been this one. It was also as different as it possibly could be from the architecture and landscape she was used to in England.

'I mean, there could be another Santiago family,' Rose mused. 'It might be a common name in Argentina. Perhaps it's not this one? It's probably just a modest home with a few stables.'

Jessica shook her head. 'Even if you were right, how many families with the last name Santiago would own polo estates? I don't think you've made a mistake—this is the property. I mean, it says it has facilities for literally hundreds of horses. It has to be the one.'

Rose chewed on her lip as she kept scrolling. 'You know, people are fooled by things like this every day. How many times have you received an email saying that if you enter your bank details, you'll inherit millions? These photos are probably all part of the scam.'

Jessica gave her a withering stare. 'Rose, this is not a scam email, just like that meeting you went to here in London wasn't a scam. And if you're truly not sure, then you can take your own lawyer with you, or at the very least have one write back on your behalf. I'm convinced it's real.'

Rose hesitated. Her mum had had insurance to cover most of her extra care over the past few months, and she owned her flat, but Rose was still worried about money. Her own savings had started to dwindle and if she didn't go back to work, she was going to have to be more careful than ever about her finances. But she was a lawyer. She was more than capable of representing herself and dealing with the law firm in Argentina; it was just that with everything that had happened lately, she simply wasn't sure she was emotionally capable right now. Or that she trusted her own judgement.

'Rose?'

'You're right. I'm too close to this to manage it all on my own, so in the morning, you can call them.'

Jessica laughed. 'Me? I'm not a lawyer.'

'No, but you've always been great at detecting bullshit.'

At that they both laughed, and when Jessica leaned her head closer to Rose's, she fought a fresh wave of tears.

'And if I don't detect bullshit and the whole thing seems legitimate, I think we should book you a ticket to Buenos Aires.'

Rose's heart almost stopped. 'I'm not convinced that's your best idea.'

Jessica pushed her laptop back a little, angling it so they could both see the screen. 'Do you see this beautiful property? Do you see how dreamy it is? Not to mention that there are actual horses there. *Horses*, Rose.'

'I don't even know if I like horses!'

Jessica laughed. 'Trust me, you'll like horses.'

Rose wasn't so convinced. She liked animals, but horses just seemed so... huge.

Rose looked around at her childhood bedroom, the place that had been her haven since she'd come back to live with her mum. She wasn't so sure she could leave it behind, not yet. It all just felt too soon.

'I'm not so sure,' she began.

'You know, you could meet a gorgeous Argentinian man while you're there who sweeps you off your feet.'

Rose brushed away tears and laughed. Trust Jessica. 'Luke put me off men for good,' she said. 'But I like the sentiment.'

'So you'll go then?' Jessica asked.

Rose took a deep breath.

'You know, you could come home via New York.'

'It's not exactly on the way, but—'

'Please,' Jessica said. 'Come to New York afterwards and let me look after you. The girls will be so excited, and we can go out for dinners and just spend time together, like this. It'll be just what you need, I promise.'

'You're sure Ryan won't mind?'

'You know he won't, he loves you.'

Rose closed her eyes for a moment, trying to process what she was agreeing to. All she wanted was to curl up and stay at home for the foreseeable future, but Jessica was right. It would do her the world of good to go away and do something that didn't remind her of what she'd lost, even if it did feel too soon. Besides, she'd spent the last six months at home. It was time to do something for herself and try to live her life again.

'Okay, I'll do it,' she said.

Jessica's eyebrows shot up. 'You will?'

Rose groaned, already wanting to change her mind. 'I will.'

'Brilliant! Now come on, let's do more googling. I want to see what the Santiago family looked like,' Jessica said, pulling her laptop closer again. 'And I want to see if we can find any clues about the piece of blue silk that you were left.'

Rose leaned into Jessica as she scrolled through photos, trying to see her grandmother in any of the faces on the screen, to see some resemblance that showed her a connection.

'I wonder if the lawyer will understand what was left behind in the box,' Rose mused out loud. 'Wouldn't he know all about the adoption, if he's the one charged with contacting my family? Wouldn't he have the answers?'

'Maybe. I mean, I would hope so, but perhaps it was all shrouded in secrecy?'

Jessica went silent for a moment, as she clicked on a photo showing a smiling, extremely handsome polo player sitting astride a horse.

'Is he a Santiago? He's very handsome.'

'No, this is Nacho Figueras, the most famous polo player in the world. I just wanted to ogle him for a moment, since he comes up in almost every search for Argentine polo families.'

Rose swatted at her. 'I asked you a serious question!'

'Sorry, I did hear you, but no. I don't think it'll be that simple.'

'You don't?'

'I think family secrets like that take forever to untangle, and that someone who was used in a professional capacity might not be aware of the more personal details,' Jessica said, closing the laptop and turning to face her. 'She might have left her estate to her daughter, or granddaughter in this case, but I'd say there are plenty of things that her lawyer doesn't know. It sounds to me as if this might have been kept a secret for a very, very long time, which means few people will know the truth.'

'Rose, look at this,' Jessica said, pointing to her screen. 'It's a death notice for a Valentina Santiago, dated three months ago.'

Jessica leaned over and read the article, her heart heavy as she realised the sad coincidence of two women from two generations of the one family dying in such a short time span.

Valentina Santiago, the daughter of the late Basilio Santiago, one of the most successful landowners and businessmen in Buenos Aires during the 1930s, has passed away peacefully at home. Known for her lifetime of philanthropy towards polo and women in sport, she will be forever remembered for her significant generosity.

'There's no mention of any surviving family members,' Jessica said.

Rose read the article again, finding it hard to believe that she might be related to the woman she was reading about.

'We can search for more in the morning,' Jessica said with a yawn. 'I think the jet lag is finally catching up with me.'

She kissed Rose on the cheek and shut her laptop, and Rose did the same, finishing up and putting her laptop on her bedside table.

But when they eventually turned the lights out, lying side by side in the bed together, Rose found it impossible to sleep. All she could think about was the call Jessica was going to make in the morning, and whether she was being silly to think of flying to Buenos Aires, even if it was only for a few days.

I wish you were here, Mum.

Which was precisely why she knew she had to go and see

what this lawyer had to say. If there was family out there in the world waiting to meet her, or a heritage that was ready to be discovered, then she owed it to her mother and her grand-mother, in their memory, to find out everything she could.

She glanced at Jessica's sleeping form in the dark, making out the silhouette of her body, lying on her side, turned away from Rose. Jessica was like the sister she'd never had, and she knew that if all else failed, she could always move to be nearer to her.

But first she needed to see what awaited her in Argentina. She could worry about the rest of her life after that.

4

THE SANTIAGO FAMILY ESTATE, ARGENTINA, 1930

Valentina smiled at her father as she ate the last of her breakfast, careful to dab the crumbs at the side of her mouth so that she didn't invoke the wrath of her mother. Her father was sitting across from her, with his newspaper held just low enough that he could look at her.

'It's time for your lessons,' Valentina's mother said, her tone clipped as she gestured for their maid to take her plate. 'Hurry along, please.'

Valentina nodded, averting her gaze from her father for fear that she might smile. Because he'd already told her that she wouldn't be taking her lessons this morning. Today, she was to accompany him to work, and she couldn't wait.

When he cleared his throat, she stared down at her lap.

'Camilla, not today. I'm taking Valentina with me.'

Her mother was silent for a moment, and silence was always more terrifying than raised voices, at least where her mama was concerned.

'Take Bruno with you instead,' she said. 'There's no point in taking Valentina. If you continue to indulge her, she'll start to think—'

'That she will one day inherit my great fortune and need the skills to continue building the empire I've created?' he asked, his voice slightly raised. Her papa didn't get angry often, but Valentina could tell his temper was flaring 'You think I don't understand what I'm doing?'

Valentina glanced at Bruno, who didn't seem to care at all that he was being overlooked. He was her step-sibling, and eight years older than her, but they'd always got along just fine. It was their mother who liked to pit them against each other, always making it clear to Valentina that her firstborn son was her most important child. It was something that Valentina had never understood.

'Basilio,' her mother said, her voice softer now as she tried to soothe him. 'I was only meaning that I don't think she's—'

'I don't intend on discussing the matter. Valentina is coming with me,' he said, folding his paper and then rising. 'Darling, our driver will be here soon. Please go and finish getting ready.'

'Yes, Papa,' Valentina said, demurely so as not to anger her mother. She even paused after standing to kiss her mother's cheek, but the affection was not returned.

Her mother was kind to her at times, but Valentina had always been made to feel as if they were competing for her father's affections. Sometimes she'd wondered if she was even her real mother, the way she made her feel as if she wasn't worthy of her father's love, but she knew how ridiculous that was. She was Valentina Santiago, and her parents' love story had been retold to her countless times over her childhood, including how cherished her birth was after three years of their hoping and praying to have a family. But for some reason, at times her mother didn't seem to even want her.

'Valentina,' her maid, Ana, said, hurrying her away. 'Let me do your hair and get you changed. Your father told me that you would need your best clothes today.'

A shiver of excitement ran through Valentina and she raced

up the stairs, taking them two at a time as her maid clucked her tongue behind her. But she didn't tell her off, Ana never did; she was more maternal to her than her own mother, and other than telling Valentina that she prayed for her, she never scolded her for her enthusiasm. Quite the contrary, she seemed to enjoy it.

'Did he tell you where he was taking me?' Valentina asked, breathless as she sat down on the stool in front of the mirror.

Ana brushed out Valentina's long hair, securing it with delicate pins so that it didn't fall to her face.

'No, *mi pequeño*,' she said. 'But from the look on your face, I can tell you're excited.'

Valentina grinned, trying not to wriggle. 'I am. I love it when he takes me to work with him. I'm going to see his offices again and meet all the people who work for him.'

Ana sighed, but Valentina ignored it and bounced from the stool when she was finished, kissing her maid on the cheek and receiving a quick hug in return.

'Let me get your best coat, just in case you need it. It sounds like you have a very special day planned.'

Valentina took it and bounded back down the stairs, finding her father at the door. He'd been frowning, she could see the lines on his face, but he gave her an easy smile the moment he saw her, as if she'd just brightened his day. That's the way they always were together, as if nothing else mattered—the two of them against the world.

'I'm ready, Papa,' she said.

Her hand slipped into his as they stepped outside, into the sunshine. But he was quick to guide her past the waiting car, leading her by the hand.

'I thought we were going to your office?' she asked, glancing back at the driver who was still waiting for them. She wouldn't have worn her best dress otherwise.

'We are,' he said. 'But first, we are going to walk through the stables. Do you feel the way the weather is changing, Valentina? The slight coolness in the air?'

She nodded, lifting her face to let the breeze touch her skin.

'It's time for my horses to come back to work,' he said. 'The polo season is almost upon us.'

She nodded, loving an excuse to be around her father's beloved polo ponies. Because if there was one thing that brought her father joy, it was playing polo, which meant that she loved the sport almost as much as he did, even if it was only as a spectator.

'Valentina, do you know that something very special is happening this year?' he asked.

She stopped when he did, looking up at him and blinking the sun from her eyes. 'No, Papa. What's happening?'

'The Pingüinos Club is hosting the very first game of women's polo,' he said. 'I am going to take you, so that you can see what women can do. I think it's important for you to see how brave and capable young women can be, that nothing can stop you from achieving whatever you set your mind to.'

Valentina beamed at the idea of going anywhere with her father. 'Will Mama change her mind and let me play polo?'

He laughed and placed a hand on her head. 'No, *cariño*, I don't think so. But perhaps it could be our little secret that we're going?'

Valentina hurried after him when he began to walk again, struggling to keep up with his long stride as she dreamed of what it would feel like to ride on the back of one of his magnificent ponies.

A few minutes later, as Valentina walked up and down the stables and touched the velvety nose of each horse as they peered out at her, their heads hanging over their doors, her father called her name.

'Valentina, there's someone I'd like you to meet.'

She turned immediately and went to join her father and another man who was dressed in riding gear.

'This is José,' her father said, and she held out her hand as he'd shown her to do. 'José, this is my daughter, Valentina.' The man seemed surprised to be introduced to her, but carefully took her hand and gently shook it, as if he was holding something breakable. 'He has recently moved here from Spain to be my stable manager. José is very important to me.'

'Pleased to meet you,' Valentina said. She knew what her father was trying to tell her—if José was important to him, then he was important to her, also.

A movement caught her eye then, and she saw a boy step out from behind one of the stable doors. He had a mop of thick black hair, and when she smiled at him, he poked his tongue out and made her laugh, and she had to quickly bite down on her lip to stop from making any noise.

'Ahh, Basilio, this is my son, Felipe,' José said. 'Felipe, come and say hello to Mr Santiago.'

Valentina watched as the boy wiped his hands on his jeans before shaking hands with her father, his dark eyes meeting hers for a fleeting second before he stood back. She could tell he was older than her, maybe by a year or two, and she liked the way he went to one of the horses who was whinnying and appeared unsettled as he pressed his hand against the horse's cheek to calm him.

'Your son is also a gifted horseman?' her father asked, watching him.

'He is,' José replied. 'We like to say that it runs in the blood in our family. We've been horsemen for generations.'

'And how old is he?'

'Almost twelve years old,' José said, and Valentina saw the way his eyes twinkled when he spoke of his son, the same way her father's did when he introduced her to someone new.

'Well, let the boy ride as a reward for all his hard work. I like to see young people enjoy the sport. Who knows, he might be riding for my team before long, just like his papa.'

As her father turned to leave, Valentina spoke, her soft voice stopping the men from walking away.

'Papa, perhaps Felipe could teach me to ride one day?' she asked.

Her father laughed, as did José, but she saw that Felipe was looking earnestly back at her, as if he didn't think it was a silly idea at all.

The car journey to her papa's office took forty minutes, and she stared out of the window and looked at the scenery as they passed. Her father was busy reading documents, and she found that she couldn't stop thinking about the boy, Felipe. There had been something about him, a manner he had with the horses, or the way he'd looked at her, that made her wonder about his life.

'Papa, what was it like growing up in Spain?' she asked.

He set his papers down and turned to her, his smile kind. 'It was where I learnt everything there is to know about olives and olive oil,' he said. 'I shall take you there one day soon, to see our old farm. It's been too long since we last travelled there, and I want you to remember your heritage.'

He placed his hand gently to her chest. 'You're Spanish in here. Just as I am.'

She nodded, but he didn't turn away from her.

'You have something on your mind?' her father asked.

'I was only wondering what it must have been like for Felipe to move to Argentina from Spain,' she said. 'I wouldn't like to leave my home.'

'Ahh,' he said, smiling as he angled his body towards her. 'You have a kind heart, *mi hija*, it's one of the things I love most about you. And it's true, it must have been very hard for Felipe and his family to move here, but I offered his father a very good job, earning more money than he could have ever dreamed of making where he was working in Spain. It made sense for them to come here, to live a different kind of life.'

Valentina sat silently for a moment, considering what her father had just told her.

'If you want the very best people to work for you, and you want them to be loyal to you, you must pay them well and treat them with respect. It's why my employees feel like family, and one day, when it is you making the decisions about the business, Valentina, I want you to remember that. It's one of the most important lessons that my father taught me as a boy.'

'I will, Papa,' she said, with a fierceness that surprised her. Because she wanted to be just like her papa. She saw how people looked at him, at the respect he commanded, but also the way no one was afraid to talk to him. He shared his easy smile with everyone around him, remembering names and always seeming interested in the families of those who worked for him.

As the car slowed and then stopped, he placed his hand on hers and looked into her eyes. 'Valentina, everything that's mine will be yours one day, do you understand? I am leaving every-thing to you, *mi dulce chica*, because I can tell you have the heart and strength of a lion. I know you won't let me down.'

She loved it when he called her his sweet girl, and she beamed back at him.

'I promise, Papa,' she said, as their driver opened the door. 'I won't let you down.'

Valentina adored her father, and even though she was only ten years old, she knew with every beat of her heart that she would spend her life proving that she was just like him, that she could follow in his footsteps in any way that he wanted her to.

They stepped out and he held out his hand for her, waiting for her to press her palm against his as they walked into the building bearing the Santiago family name.

5

PRESENT DAY

Rose held Jessica as her friend wrapped her arms around her, engulfing her in a long hug as they stood near her departure gate. They'd managed to get flights that left Heathrow within ninety minutes of each other, which meant they'd been able to go through security together and have dinner at the airport, before it was time to say goodbye.

'I'll see you in five days,' Jessica said, taking a step back but keeping both hands on Rose's shoulders. 'I can't wait to show you around New York.'

Rose smiled, hating how emotional she felt at saying goodbye to Jessica. She'd managed to not feel alone while she was staying, but saying farewell was even harder than expected. She wished they were boarding a plane together.

'Thank you for being here. I don't know how you just managed to drop everything to—'

'Tell me you wouldn't do the same if the shoe was on the other foot,' Jessica interrupted.

Rose sighed. 'You know I would. But still, I know it can't have been easy, especially with the girls.'

'Well then stop thanking me. I did what any friend would

do,' Jessica said, picking up her carry-on bag and taking a step back. 'Remember to text me as soon as you land, and send over any documents you want Ryan to cast an eye over.'

Rose nodded.

'But most of all, *enjoy* it,' Jessica said. 'It's not every day you get to travel to a beautiful country and uncover family secrets. It's going to be great.'

Jessica finally turned away and walked to the gate, looking back before heading down the air bridge and blowing her a kiss one last time. Rose watched until she disappeared completely and then went in search of coffee. She felt as if she'd barely slept for weeks, and she was hoping that another shot of caffeine would at least keep her going until her flight boarded.

After she'd ordered, she reached into her bag and took out the little box she'd brought with her. Rose opened it, reaching for the now-familiar piece of silk and rubbing it between her forefinger and thumb, wondering whether to show the clues to the lawyer or not when she arrived.

Just have the meeting, see what he has to say, and take it hour by hour, day by day, she said inside her head, giving herself a little pep talk. *You can do this, Rose. This is what Mum would have wanted.*

Almost fifteen hours later, Rose wheeled her suitcase through the doors into the arrivals area of the airport, still bleary-eyed from sleeping for half the flight.

A man with a whiteboard held high caught her eye, and she stopped when she saw that his sign had ROSE BELLAMY written in capitals across it. She'd expected to catch a taxi to the lawyer's offices, but it seemed a car had been sent for her instead.

'*Hola*,' Rose said, saying one of the only Spanish words she knew as she stood in front of the man.

'You are Rose?' he asked, in heavily accented English.

'I am,' she said. 'I wasn't expecting a driver.'

He nodded enthusiastically and lifted her bag from her shoulder, despite her protests at how heavy it was, and took her suitcase from her other hand, wheeling it ahead of him.

'Let me,' he said, smiling and gesturing that she follow him. 'Please, come.'

She was going to apologise and tell him that she'd had to pack for a few weeks away from home, but decided better of it and just followed him instead. She figured she wasn't the only person he'd chauffeured who'd overpacked.

When they stepped outside, Rose was surprised at how different the air felt in Argentina. It was hot, but not stiflingly so, but it just smelt more... *alive.* Her skin felt almost immediately moist and she was breathing differently, and there just seemed to be a different kind of energy around her than at home.

'Have you read tourist guides about Buenos Aires?' the driver asked, as he bundled her things into his car and opened the rear passenger door for her.

'Ahh, no, not really. This was an unexpected trip, so I didn't have long to plan.'

He ran around and got into the driver's seat, starting the car and pulling out into the slow-moving traffic. 'Everything you read will tell you that it's dangerous here, but it's not. The only thing that's true in the tourist guides is when they say we're the Paris of South America.'

She smiled as she looked out of the window. 'I hadn't heard that one.' *The Paris of South America.* It had a nice ring to it, and she hoped it was true.

'Are you taking me directly to the office?' she asked.

'No, I've been asked to take you to the Santiago estate,' he said. 'It's a forty-five-minute drive from the city.'

Rose startled. 'I had arranged to meet the lawyer at his office,' she said. 'I think it's best if you just take me there. Please give me a moment to find the address.'

'No,' he said, shaking his head. 'I work for Mr Gonzalez, and he told me that his instructions had changed. He will be waiting for you at the property.'

Rose took her phone from her bag, feeling a little uncomfortable and wondering whether she'd been naive in getting into a car with a driver just because he knew her name. She was in a foreign country heading out of Buenos Aires, to meet someone she didn't know, in a car with a total stranger. She closed her eyes and tried to clear her head, but opened them when her phone vibrated in her hand, telling her she had a message.

Hey! Safely at home. Hope you've landed. Text me xx

Rose quickly typed a message back to Jessica, before sitting up a little straighter and deciding to watch the scenery as it whizzed past, to at least get a feeling for where she was if anything did happen. But she knew what Jessica would tell her if she was there: don't overthink everything, just have your wits about you and don't panic.

Which was precisely what she was doing when she found the address to the Santiago property and entered it into Google Maps so she could check they were going where her driver said they were. She had no reason not to trust him, he'd been perfectly polite to her after all, but she also had no reason to trust him, either.

Just over forty minutes later, and with her phone back in her bag after she'd realised that he was most definitely taking her directly to the Santiago estate, Rose had to stop her jaw from falling open. They were entering a long driveway that was flanked by fields on each side, and she admired the endless trees and the wooden railings that seemed to go on for miles. Up ahead, she could see a large Spanish-style house with a terra-cotta roof, familiar to her from the photos she'd seen online, and farther out to the right there was a set of low-slung buildings that were harder to make out.

Her door was opened almost immediately when the car stopped, and the man who'd opened it took a step back, waiting for her to get out. When she did, he held out his hand and gave her a wide smile.

'*Señorita* Rose,' he said, gently shaking her hand and placing his other hand over it, as if he was already familiar with her. 'It's such a pleasure to finally meet you. We spoke on the phone. I am Luis Gonzalez.'

She nodded, put immediately at ease by his warm manner. 'It's very nice to meet you, too.' Rose wasn't sure why he'd said *finally* when they hadn't even been in communication with each other for longer than a week, but he seemed even more friendly than he had been on the phone.

'Welcome to the Santiago estate,' he said, holding his arm wide and gesturing around. 'I am honoured to be the one to show the property to you for the first time. It's one of the largest private estates in Buenos Aires, and one of the largest polo farms in all of Argentina. It was once home to more than a hundred and fifty polo ponies.'

Rose felt as if she were about to wilt under the sun, and yet the lawyer didn't have so much as a bead of sweat on his fore-head, despite wearing a suit. She gently dabbed her upper lip with her finger. Her tourist guide had said springtime wouldn't be too hot, but compared to London it was positively tropical and she wasn't used to it.

The lawyer seemed unworried by her silence, or if he was, he was excellent at hiding it.

'Rose, your great-grandmother was represented by my law firm for over seventy years,' he continued. 'First by my grandfather, then my father and then me. So you see, it was very important to me to fulfil her wishes upon her death, especially when these documents had been filed so many decades ago in preparation for this day. They were sealed and held in my office until her passing.'

'I just, well, this all seems like a dream to me,' Rose said, turning and looking around, taking in the surroundings, seeing horses grazing in a nearby field. 'I'm finding it very hard to believe that I have a connection to this land—to any of the things you've told me, if I'm honest. It has certainly all come as a complete surprise.'

He smiled as if he understood, but she was certain that he didn't. He couldn't possibly understand how she felt after the upheaval she'd experienced over the past year.

'Your great-grandmother was a very private woman,' he said. 'She was fiercely independent, and she knew her mind right up until the end. There is no disputing that your grandmother was the rightful heiress to this estate, then your mother, and now you. *Señora* Santiago had watched your grandmother from afar for many years, and it was always her intention to leave everything to her when she passed away. It's only sad that you never had the chance to meet her.'

Rose followed him as he began to walk, trying to process what he was telling her. She could barely imagine that this woman, the owner of the beautiful property she was standing on, had been watching her family from afar as he'd described. With such resources at her disposal, why hadn't she come forward and tried to make contact with them? Or perhaps the question was, *how* had she not come forward? Rose didn't have children of her own, but she couldn't conceive of staying hidden from her own biological child for all those years, if she'd known where she was.

'There are no other relatives who will lay claim to the estate?' Rose found herself asking. 'No one else who might be expecting to inherit the Santiago property?'

Luis shrugged. 'If there are, we will represent you and make sure they go away. Our client was very firm in her instructions, and she was of sound mind when we drew up her will. You, your mother or your grandmother were to inherit it all, with smaller provisions made for her staff and friends.'

Rose stopped when they rounded a corner and came to the other side of the house. There was an expansive paved court-yard with an enormous wooden table set below an overgrown pergola, with ten chairs placed around it, and a large swimming pool that made her want to dive in. She could already visualise the long summer lunches and relaxed afternoons that it must have played host to, and it made her yearn to have her mother or grandmother with her, so they were seeing it, too. Even the way a green vine with tiny white flowers crept over the pergola was magical.

'This property has been in the Santiago family for well over a hundred years,' he said, his voice soft now as he came to stand beside her. 'And whether you want to be or not, *you* are a Santi-ago, too. The blood of this family, of this land, runs in your veins, and I believe that after spending time here, you will feel the connection. It's what Valentina would have wanted, for you to belong here.'

When Rose turned and met his gaze, she could see that he meant every word, that it wasn't simply a rehearsed speech said to make her feel better.

'Unfortunately, I know nothing about Argentina or horses or polo...' Rose began, her voice trailing off as she tried but failed to explain how out of her depth she felt.

But the lawyer only grinned. 'You have heard of Nacho Figueras, yes?' he asked.

'Nacho who?' she asked, having no idea who or what he was talking about.

'Never mind,' he said with a laugh. 'You will have polo fever like the rest of us before you know it. Our firm will take you as our guest to the Argentine Open while you're here, and you will see for yourself why we are obsessed with the sport, why the love of polo spread across the pampas so easily when it was first played here.'

Rose nodded politely, feeling foolish as she realised whom he'd been referring to. Nacho Figueras was the gorgeous polo player Jessica had been googling back in London. 'I'm only planning on staying for a couple of days, but I do appreciate the invitation. It would have been lovely.'

The lawyer frowned. 'But that is not anywhere near long enough. And you have a property to care for now, a name to uphold, you have—'

'You're expecting me to stay?' Rose asked, unable to hide the surprise in her tone. 'For longer than it takes us to settle any paperwork? Is that a condition of the inheritance?'

'Look around you, *señorita*. See the land you are standing on, open your eyes to what has been preserved for you. Who would inherit a property such as this and not stay to enjoy it?' Luis paused. 'This is home to you now. This, this is where you belong.'

Rose nodded politely, not wanting to offend him, but as beautiful as the estate was, it wasn't home to her. Home was the flat she'd shared with her mum in London; home was the city of her birth, where she'd spent her whole life up until now. Home was... she turned her face away, not wanting him to see her tears.

Home was with you, Mum.

'*Señorita?*'

Rose quickly brushed away her tears and turned back to the lawyer. 'What am I expected to do next?' she asked. 'There must be some formalities to attend to.'

'I would like to give you some time to look around the property for yourself, so that I can answer any questions you might have, and then I will accompany you back to the city so we can sign the requisite paperwork in my office. We have arranged a hotel for you to stay in tonight, but you can return here once everything is settled.'

'Oh, I can arrange my own accommodation, I—'

'Everything is taken care of,' he assured her, and she presumed that he understood her hesitation, because he was quick to allay her worries. '*Señora* Santiago made certain that there was a plan in place for every eventuality, so you don't need to worry about anything. She'd been planning this for decades.'

'She had?'

'Yes, she had. She was determined to ensure her family inherited her estate, and that there were no roadblocks to seeing that her wishes were followed.'

'You said I could take a look around before we go?' Rose asked, surprised at how meticulously everything had been organised and needing a moment with her own thoughts.

'Of course. I'll be here should you have any questions.'

Rose thanked him and then began to walk. She wanted to look inside the house, but it felt too personal somehow to walk inside, especially when none of this felt real to her yet, so instead she walked towards the other buildings she'd seen when they'd first arrived. It didn't take long for her to realise they were stables, and she passed a few horses who blinked back at her, their noble heads over the half-doors, looking at her as if she was the most exciting thing they'd seen all day. She resisted the urge to go over and pat one of them, not even knowing how to approach a horse, and instead stood back and admired them.

Despite Jessica telling her they were like oversized dogs, she wasn't convinced.

Rose took her phone from her pocket then, needing to hear her friend's voice. Jessica answered on the second ring.

'Tell me it's all real and you're a bona fide heiress,' she said.

'Oh, it's real,' Rose replied, keeping her voice low even though she was certain there was no one around. Although she presumed that there must be groundspeople employed to work on the property, to look after the horses and keep it all so well maintained. 'I'm at the estate now.'

'Is it as amazing in real life as it looked in the photos? Or has it become run-down since? I had horrible thoughts that it might be in a complete state of disrepair and need millions spent on it.'

'I don't even know how to describe it, Jess. It's like something from another world,' Rose told her. 'It's one of the most beautiful places I've ever been to, but it's like there's been some mistake. I mean, it doesn't seem real. It's easily as stunning as the images online.'

'Send me some photos, and stop saying that it's not real, because it is,' Jessica said, before groaning. 'I'm so sorry but I have to go, I'm heading into a meeting. Can we talk later?'

'Before you go...'

There was silence on the other end of the line as Jessica waited.

'Thanks for making me come here. I would never have booked that flight if you hadn't pushed me, and then I never would have seen this place with my own eyes.' *This place that feels magical, it's so stunning.*

'You're welcome. Talk soon.'

Rose put the phone back in her pocket, but before she turned to walk away from the stables, she saw someone tall with broad shoulders, wearing a large cowboy-style hat, leading a horse beside him. She watched until she couldn't see him anymore, wondering who he might be as she heard the lawyer call out her name from afar.

'I saw a man by the stables just now,' Rose said when she got back to him. 'Does he work here?'

'That will be Benjamin. He was sponsored by *Señora* Santiago, and you'll see him coming and going most days, until the end of the season anyway. After that, you will have to decide whether or not you share your great-grandmother's love of polo. She wasn't afraid to spend her money on what she loved, and there are many people hoping you will continue her traditions.'

Rose followed him to his car, noticing that her bag was waiting for her in the passenger seat.

'Luis, do you have any idea how Valentina came to leave her child, my grandmother, at a place called Hope's House in London? Do you know anything about her younger years?'

Luis met her gaze over the roof of the car and shook his head, before speaking earnestly. 'No, *señorita*, I don't. It has always been a mystery to me how she came to be estranged from her daughter, or that she even had a daughter at all, but we respected *Señora* Santiago too much to ever ask. If I'm honest, I fear that her secrets have died with her.'

Rose nodded and looked back at the property, her eyes slowly roving across the landscape, taking in the towering trees in the distance that she guessed had stood for even longer than the Santiago family had owned the land. And she had the most overwhelming sense that perhaps whatever secrets her great-grandmother had, had not been taken with her to her grave, but were in fact waiting to be discovered. Why else would she have left her estate to a daughter and granddaughter who'd been kept hidden for so many decades?

'*Señorita* Rose?'

She turned, already deciding that she would come back the following morning to at least look around, or try to find the man she'd glimpsed by the stables to see what he knew. She had three days until her flight to New York, and she would need to make the most of it.

There's no harm in trying to find out more while I'm here.

Rose sat in the car and reached for the little box in her bag, wrapping her fingers around it as she tried to understand how all this had come about, how a woman who cared enough to look from afar and leave a little box of clues behind had stayed hidden for so long instead of just coming forward.

'This place, it will find its way into your soul,' the lawyer said, as he turned the car around. 'I have a feeling that you won't want to leave now that you're here.'

Rose stared at the trees in the distance, at the perfect wooden fences and endless acres of grass, and she had the distinct feeling that he was right. Part of her couldn't wait to return in the morning. But the other part was terrified that she might fall in love with the property and never want to leave.

6

THE SANTIAGO FAMILY ESTATE,
ARGENTINA, 1931

Valentina found every excuse to go near the horses when her mother wasn't watching her. She leaned on the fence post and watched her father ride, showing interest in his training, but really it was Felipe whom she was there for. Even if she only caught a glimpse of him, it was worth it.

At the weekend, it was Felipe who held her father's ponies in preparation for their ride, it was Felipe who would lead them around afterwards when they were hot and breathing hard, and he always made sure to walk the horses past where she was standing. It was in those moments, when he would smile and give her a little wave, or say hello, that her heart would leap, leaving her breathing almost as heavily as the animals he was walking.

But he would never stop. His eyes always met hers and they stared at each other until he could turn his head no longer, until the next time he passed, and Valentina was never brave enough to say anything more than hello. Perhaps if her father hadn't been so near, or Felipe's father hadn't been keeping such a close eye on his son, they might have, but for now she was content to just see him. Especially when he seemed as happy to see her as she was him.

But today when Felipe walked past her, he stopped. Valentina dug her nails nervously into the wooden fence post, her heart pounding.

'Morning,' he said.

'Good morning,' she replied, although it came out as barely a whisper.

But Felipe's grin was contagious, and she found herself grinning straight back at him, her nerves almost immediately disappearing. He ducked his head under the horse's neck, looking back at their fathers, but from where Valentina was standing, she could see they were having a heated exchange about something and weren't looking in their direction. They hadn't even noticed he'd stopped.

'What are they arguing about?' Valentina asked.

'Game strategies,' Felipe said with a shrug. 'It's not a real argument, they just both get very passionate when it comes to polo.'

Valentina laughed, and then Felipe laughed, and she had a warm sensation pass through her as their eyes caught again. She couldn't have looked away from him if she'd tried.

'I like it when you come to watch,' he said.

She nodded. 'I like it, too.'

'Felipe!' came a shout from across the field. 'Keep that horse walking!'

'I'd better go,' he said with a grin. 'See you next weekend?'

Valentina bit her bottom lip to stop her smile from becoming too big before saying, 'I'll be here.'

He shook his head as if he couldn't believe they'd finally spoken as he walked away, glancing back at her, and she felt as if her legs might give out from beneath her.

'Hey, Valentina,' he called out.

Her eyes met his again.

'You look really pretty today.'

She burst out laughing, her hand across her heart. If this wasn't what falling in love felt like, then she couldn't imagine what was.

7

PRESENT DAY

This time when Rose stepped out onto the gravel driveway at the Santiago estate, she didn't feel quite so out of place. She'd woken up in a beautiful hotel, discovered upon checking out that the entire bill, including room service from the night before, had already been taken care of, and now she was getting out of a taxi and bringing her suitcase and bag with her.

After paying the driver, Rose stood for a moment and watched the car go, wanting to wait until she was alone to walk up to the front door of the house. She fumbled in her bag for the key, which was hanging from a ring with a small silver horse on it, and lugged her things up the three steps. She almost knocked, just to make sure no one was inside, but the lawyer's words from the day before kept echoing through her mind.

'All of it is yours, Rose,' he'd said, pointing to the map that was spread over his desk as they sat in his office. 'This property is almost one hundred hectares, and you can see the boundary clearly marked here. With it comes the homestead and the stables, as well as a small holding of land in Mendoza that Valentina bought back some years ago, which I can arrange to have shown to you at your earliest convenience.'

'*Mendoza?*' *she'd asked.*

'*It's where the Santiago family continued to build upon their great fortune when they arrived here from Spain. They once owned the largest property in the region but that, my dear, is a story for another day. Perhaps we can meet for dinner before you go, so that I can share more of the family's history with you?*'

Rose had agreed to meet with him for dinner before her flight to New York, curious to hear everything she could about the mysterious Santiago family, but for now she was looking forward to discovering the property and the house that came with it.

She turned the handle, resisting the urge to call out 'hello,' which was as hard not to do as knocking had been. But it was obvious once she was inside that there was nobody in the house. Rose had been told that there was still a housekeeper who called in twice a week, and who'd made up the main bedroom for her as well as a downstairs room in case she preferred it, and she was surprised at how lived-in the house felt. She'd presumed it would feel dusty or stifling inside, given that no one had lived there for some months now, but it felt as if it had just been aired out. And when she walked down the hallway, she could see fresh flowers on the table at the end. Someone had clearly gone to some effort to make the house feel welcoming to her ahead of her arrival.

Rose left her luggage in the hallway as she kept walking, heading into the kitchen and finding a large space with huge windows that faced out over the property. She could see horses grazing in the distance, the windows framing a view that looked like an artist had painted it, which made her realise just how easy it would be to fall head over heels with the property.

She stood for a moment, her hands splayed on the granite kitchen counter as she stared outside, wondering how she'd gone from looking out of the small windows of her London flat one day, staring at a gloomy sky, to being here today.

Rose turned on her heel then, suddenly feeling melancholy as her mind filled with thoughts of home, and in turn her mother. She ran her fingertips beneath her eyes to brush away tears as she looked into the living room and then another room that she guessed might once have been used to host parties, but was now full of furniture and paintings propped against walls—a storage room of sorts.

She walked up the stairs, loving how cool the house felt despite the warmth outside. Everything about the architecture felt Spanish in style, from the high ceilings to the terracotta tiles in the foyer, and as she found her way to the bedrooms, she immediately saw the billowing white drapes in the room at the farthest end of the hall.

Rose walked slowly towards the room, feeling welcomed by it somehow, glancing into every other bedroom as she passed, counting five in total. But when she walked into the room ahead of her, she immediately felt at home.

There was a small jar of flowers on the bedside table, along with a note, and as she read it she sat on the white bedcovers, glancing up and admiring the wooden four-poster bed that somehow felt as if it came from another age.

Dear Miss Santiago,

I have worked for Valentina Santiago for the past twelve years, and the more time that passed, the more she talked about the daughter she was forced to part with. Her guilt over the years has become immeasurable, but her only comfort was that one day she could leave everything to her biological granddaughter or great-granddaughter. Valentina was a kind, wonderful woman who would do anything for anyone, and I will never forget our spirited conversations, or the way I would find her sometimes staring out of the window, lost in thought, as she imagined how her life might have turned out if things had been different.

   I've left fresh towels in the bathroom for you, and there is enough food in the pantry to last a few days, as well as coffee and other things you might find yourself in need of. I've also put some meals in the fridge that you can heat up. I hope to meet you on Friday, when I'm scheduled to work next.

Yours truly,

Clara

Rose set the note back down on the bedside table, appreciating the kind gesture but finding it hard not to be disappointed. When she'd seen it sitting there, her heart had leapt for a moment, thinking it might have been left by Valentina herself.

She stood then, looking in at the adjoining beautifully tiled bathroom before going to stand at the bedroom window, loving the gentle breeze that whispered through the just-open frames. Rose wished that she could have brought Jessica with her, so that at least one other person in her life could have seen what she was seeing. Perhaps then, it might have been easier to believe that she wasn't dreaming.

Just as she was about to take her phone from her pocket to call Jessica and insist that she and the children schedule a holiday there soon, a figure in the distance caught her eye. There was a man on horseback heading towards the stables, and she couldn't be sure, but she thought it might have been the same man whom she'd glimpsed the day before.

Rose decided to leave her exploration of the house until later, walking quickly back downstairs and stopping only to find the small wooden box that was in her handbag, reaching in and taking out the little horse figurine and slipping it into the pocket of her jeans. She left her hand there, liking the way the figurine fitted into her palm as she hurried through the house to another door that was positioned much more closely to the stables.

She kicked off her sandals there and slipped her feet into a pair of brown leather boots that were only slightly too big for her, closing the door behind her and crossing the expanse of grass that separated the two buildings. Trees had been cleverly planted to provide shade, and she saw that a large tabby cat was lounging beneath one of them.

Rose made a mental note to check whether she'd also inherited a cat along with the countless retired and current polo ponies that were on the list she'd been presented with, before clearing her throat to call out to the man who'd just disappeared ahead of her.

'*Hola!*' she called, raising her voice when she didn't receive a response. 'Hello there!'

She wished she'd spent her time the night before looking up Spanish phrases rather than falling asleep watching Netflix on her phone, but as she was trying to think of what else to call out, the man turned.

Rose quickened her step to catch up with him, surprised that he was scowling at her rather than smiling. He was incredibly handsome, with ink-black hair and eyes to match, his skin tanned bronze from working outside under the sun, but he would have looked better if his face wasn't dragged down into a frown.

'You must be Benjamin,' she said, a little breathless from rushing after him.

He folded his arms across his chest. 'You're late.'

She went to laugh, but noticed that he seemed very serious, and she felt her eyes widen. This was not quite the welcome she'd expected.

'Late?' she finally said. 'I didn't know we'd arranged—'

'Thank you for coming, but you're not right for the position. I don't accept tardiness. Please see yourself off the property.'

He turned on his heel and began to walk away again, and Rose found herself hurrying after him once more, only this time she touched his arm to force him to stop, not sure whether to laugh or be offended.

'I think we're at cross-purposes here,' she said. 'I'm Rose, Rose Bellamy. Valentina Santiago was my great-grandmother, and I've just arrived in Argentina from London.'

Benjamin went from staring at the fingers still touching his arm, to lifting his gaze to meet hers, taking a step back as he raised one hand to his head and muttered something in Spanish that she guessed contained an expletive.

'Please accept my sincerest apologies,' he said, his face creasing as he lowered his hand and offered her a smile. 'I was expecting someone else.'

'Someone who was late for a job interview, perhaps?' she asked, finding herself grinning at how embarrassed he looked. 'It seems you have very high expectations.'

'Something like that,' he muttered, before groaning and extending his hand. 'Can we start again?'

'Of course,' Rose replied, pressing her palm to his, before repeating what she'd said earlier. 'You must be Benjamin.'

'And you must be the long-lost Rose Santiago,' he said. 'It's a pleasure to finally meet you.'

She didn't correct him on her surname; she figured there would be plenty of time to explain it all to him later, and she was too busy enjoying the feel of his rough, slightly calloused fingers against hers to disagree with him. He was far more handsome when he was smiling.

'You've caught me in between rides, and I'd be more than happy to show you around, if that's what you'd like?' He paused and seemed to study her face. 'I've been desperately hoping that whoever inherited this place would have a deep-seated love of polo. Please tell me I was correct?'

Rose grimaced. 'I hate to disappoint you, but I know

nothing about horses, so this is very much outside of my knowledge base.' She hesitated at the hopeful look on his face. 'But I can see that polo is the lifeblood of this property, so I will do my best to learn quickly. It's fair to say that I'm a little overwhelmed at this point.'

'I understand, it's a lot to take in.' He nodded and gestured for her to follow him. 'This property was once home to Basilio Santiago, Valentina's father, who was a very gifted polo player. My great-great-grandfather was his right-hand man, so our families have a very long history that stretches back generations.'

'He worked for the family?'

'He not so much worked as lived and breathed polo with your Basilio. The story goes that they bonded over playing polo together in Spain, and Basilio offered him a generous salary to return to Argentina with him and run his stables. He trusted him with everything when it came to his horses, and they became very close friends over the years.'

Rose nodded, fascinated with the little slice of family history Benjamin had bestowed upon her. She'd expected it to be difficult to glean the information she sought, but it seemed that Benjamin knew a lot about the property, and her heritage.

'Clearly polo runs in your family then,' she said, smiling.

He laughed, his eyes meeting hers as if she'd said something funny. 'I could say the same thing of yours,' he said. 'Valentina might not have ridden in recent years, but, Rose, polo runs in your blood just as deeply as it does in mine.'

She hesitated, not sure how much to tell him. There was a chance he knew more than he was letting on, but there was also a chance that he knew nothing about how she was connected to the family. She wondered if he was as curious about how she'd come to inherit the estate as she was herself.

'Benjamin, did you know that Valentina had a daughter? I mean, my assumption is that most people would have presumed that she was a spinster.'

He laughed. 'A spinster? Valentina Santiago?'

Rose wasn't sure whether to laugh with him or not, but it was so strange to her that the man she'd just met possibly knew more about her family history than she did.

'I wouldn't call her a spinster as such. I'm sure the whole story will unravel itself once you've been here a while, but you're right: we never knew she had a family of her own. I just associate the word spinster with a helpless old woman who never found the life she wanted, and that's not how I would describe the woman I knew. Valentina was full of life, and she's the only eighty-year-old woman I've ever seen riding a polo pony.'

'So my grandmother, Valentina's daughter, wasn't ever mentioned, or—'

'Come this way,' Benjamin said, cutting her off and placing his hand to her back as he guided her. 'I have some very special residents for you to meet.'

Rose didn't like the way he'd interrupted her, but then she also understood that he might not want to talk about his former employer with her yet. She was asking him personal questions about a woman he'd clearly admired despite her old age—she would have to contact the lawyer to see what more she could uncover.

'These are my polo ponies,' Benjamin said, gesturing with his arm for her to look at all the horses blinking back at them, their heads over the half-doors of their stables. 'Well, in fact some of them are *your* polo ponies that I have the privilege of riding, and I'm very much hoping to continue riding them.'

Rose nodded. She couldn't get her head around the fact that she now owned the land they were standing on, let alone the horses that lived there. The past weeks and months were like a blur to her, and combined with the whirlwind trip to Argentina, it was all feeling more dream than reality.

'There are so many of them,' she said, counting a dozen as

she looked up and down the row. 'You need this many to play the sport?'

'Some of them are old favourites, my high-goal ponies who've already proved themselves, and others are having their first season. It's a busy stable.'

'And the ones that are outside in the fields?' she asked. 'You don't ride those ones?'

'Some of them are youngstock that aren't ready to be ridden yet, carefully bred with generations-old bloodlines, but Valentina also had a soft spot for the older horses, the ones that were retired from the game,' he said, reaching out to touch the cheek of one of the equines as he stood beside the stall. 'Many of the retired horses are rehomed privately, but those that were injured or simply too old would come back here to live out their days. She earmarked a significant amount of the property to be an equine retirement home of sorts.'

'And if those older horses didn't come here?' she asked. 'What would happen to them?'

Benjamin made a face and shook his head. 'You don't want to know. To many people, horses are too expensive to be cared for once they have no purpose. The ones that see out their days here are the lucky ones.'

Rose nodded. She was impressed with what she'd heard so far—she couldn't not be—but she was also starting to realise just what she'd taken on when she'd signed the inheritance papers. Once the property was transferred into her name, her responsibilities would stretch further than just property maintenance, and the thought terrified her as much as it thrilled her. She now had fields full of retired ponies who would rely on her for their ongoing care.

'Would you like me to give you a tour on horseback or on foot this afternoon?' Benjamin asked, his smile impossible to look away from.

'On foot,' she replied. 'Polo might be in my blood, but this girl likes to keep her feet firmly on the ground.'

It was then that she thought of her mum, a memory that hit her without warning as she remembered the last time she'd said those exact words, when her mother was trying to convince her to have a go at skiing. Rose had been too nervous to learn as an adult, but now when she looked back, she wished she'd said yes, just because it would have meant they'd spent even more time doing something together.

She looked away and pretended to be studying one of the horses, even reaching out to lift her hand to its muzzle. She was surprised how gently the horse touched her back, its breath warm against her outstretched palm.

'Actually,' Rose said, quickly wiping at her eyes before turning back to Benjamin. 'If we can go slow, perhaps—'

'Horseback it is then,' Benjamin said, looking delighted with her answer even though she hadn't even finished her sentence.

'So long as we go *very* slow. This is all new to me, remember,' she said.

He nodded, his smile reaching his eyes and making her so pleased that she'd run after him to say hello. Even though she'd just arrived, she hated the thought of being alone in the large house, so to know that someone was on the property was reassuring. And she had the feeling that the more time she spent with him, the more she'd find out about the Santiago family.

'I need to go and exercise some of the ponies before it gets too hot,' he said, 'but if there's anything else I can help you with while you're here...'

'No, thank you,' she said. 'I'll just make my way back to the house and read through the endless pages of documents the lawyer gave me yesterday.'

'I'll come by the house later this afternoon for that tour,' he said, nodding before taking a step backward. 'And please, I hope you've already forgotten all about our first encounter, but if not,

I hope you'll accept my apology. I'm not usually so unfriendly to strangers.'

Rose believed him; she could see how warm and charming he was, and she returned his easy smile.

'Actually, Benjamin,' Rose said, as he was turning to walk away. She studied him for a moment, not sure whether to show it to him but knowing that she'd regret it later if she didn't. She reached into her pocket and took out the horse figurine that she'd been carrying around all morning, rubbing her thumb over the groove of its body as she always did when it was in her hand. 'Before you go, there's something I'd like to show you.'

'Show me?' he asked.

Rose slowly opened her palm, looking from the figurine to his face as she asked the question. 'I wondered if you might recognise this.'

His sharp intake of breath and the way he immediately reached for it told her that he more than recognised it. Benjamin's face had drained of colour, and part of her wished she hadn't shown him.

'Recognise it?' he said, as if she'd asked him a joke, his eyes meeting hers. 'Of course I recognise it. Rose, this was carved by my great-grandfather.'

She watched as he stared down at it, silent until he slowly looked back up at her.

'What I'd like to know is exactly how this came to be in your possession.'

8

THE SANTIAGO OLIVE GROVE, MENDOZA, ARGENTINA, 1934

For Valentina, nothing was more exhilarating than harvest time. She stood back and watched as her father rolled up the sleeves of his white linen shirt, his tanned forearms on display as he stood in front of all the workers gathered. Each year he invited as many of the locals as possible, whoever needed the seasonal work, paying them to harvest the olives by beating the trees with sticks while other workers held large nets below to catch the falling fruit.

Her mother always sat in the shade, never venturing far enough to say hello to all the people gathered, but suffering through the day at her husband's demand. Bruno was a more willing participant, taking whatever job he was given, and this year for the very first time, Valentina had been given permission to help. She was already holding the stick her father had chosen for her, and she knew that it wouldn't take long for her slender arms to become sore from raising it above her head. But she didn't care—she was part of the harvest this year, and that was all that mattered.

'Basilio!' she heard her mother call.

He finished speaking to the group before sending them on

their way, and Valentina hovered, not sure whether she was to wait or not, too scared to go near her mother for fear she might send her home early.

'You're too old to be doing this,' her mother scolded. 'Please, Basilio, why did you insist on getting your hands dirty?'

Her papa winked at her, and Valentina stifled a laugh. 'Because it would be bad luck if a Santiago didn't shake one of the first trees,' he said. 'Besides, it's good to keep my arms strong, for holding the polo mallet.'

Valentina did giggle at that, quickly lifting her hand to cover her mouth so her mother didn't see.

'Felipe!' her father suddenly called, and her cheeks stained a deep pink when she turned and saw the boy standing barely ten feet from her. 'Take Valentina with you and show her what to do.'

They stared at each other for an awkward moment, as Valentina heard her mother mutter something about appropriate-ness, before Felipe cleared his throat and gestured for her to follow him. She did, trying not to smile and falling into step beside him as she looked at the net he was carrying. Even if she'd wanted to say anything, all words had left her mind at suddenly being this close to him so she just walked silently, trying not to scuff her shoes into the dry ground beneath. This felt very different to the stolen moments they were used to as he walked past her with the horses.

'You never came for polo lessons,' Felipe said, glancing at her as he spoke.

Valentina felt her cheeks colour again. 'I was never brave enough to ask.'

When Felipe smiled at her, her stomach did a little dance and she found it impossible not to smile back at him. The truth was that she'd wanted to ask her parents many times, but her father had never mentioned it again, and she'd been too nervous to even think of being alone with him. Her mother kept her busy with her lessons, and she'd only seen glimpses of Felipe from the window when she had her nose pressed to it, or in their fleeting moments when she watched her father train his polo ponies.

'I've always found it hard to believe that you don't have your own pony,' he said. 'Your father has dozens of horses.'

'My mother doesn't think it's ladylike,' Valentina found herself saying. 'Papa allows me to do almost everything—he believes that women can do anything that men can...'

'But he's never asked if you'd like to learn to ride?'

She let go a little breath that she hadn't realised she was holding. 'Maybe I haven't wanted it badly enough.'

'And now?'

Valentina looked away. Felipe had a confidence about him that she wasn't used to in boys his age. The young men she met through her family were always polite and confident, but the boys and men who worked for her father would never usually even make eye contact with her, let alone talk so openly. And her mother had only become stricter about who her daughter spent time with in recent months, always reminding her that she expected her to be smarter and better read than any of her peers, to play pianoforte more exquisitely than anyone else her age, even though she knew how much her daughter hated to play.

'Now, I think that I'm ready for those lessons,' Valentina said, sounding braver than she felt. 'When do we start?'

'Will your papa allow it?' Felipe asked.

Her lips twisted into a smile. 'My papa is easy to convince, if I want something badly enough, but I might have to keep it secret from my mama.'

'Felipe, hurry up!'

They both started to walk faster when Felipe's father called, and she nodded to the older man, slightly breathless when they reached the tree he was standing beside. She wasn't used to having to move so quickly.

'Miss Santiago, I'm sorry, I wouldn't have ordered you to run like that if I'd known it was you.'

She glanced at Felipe and they both laughed. 'Please, you're to call me Valentina. Both of you,' she said. 'You're also to set me a task, on orders of my papa. I don't want to stand around while others do all the hard work.' She secretly loved that Felipe's father had barked at them to run, as if she were just a regular girl helping with the harvest.

Felipe caught her hand then, holding it up and turning it over, his skin warm and slightly rough against hers. She'd imagined what it would feel like to have his palm against hers for years, and it was even better than she'd thought it might be.

'These soft hands are going to be covered in blisters by the end of the day,' he said, his eyes catching hers for just a second. 'Are you certain you want to work with us?'

Felipe's father cleared his throat, and she saw the stern way he looked at his son, as if to reprimand him for touching her or perhaps for being too familiar. But Felipe only grinned and held up his net, as if he didn't know what his father was trying to tell him, which only made Valentina like him more.

'You've seen how to do this before?' he asked.

'Of course,' she said, lifting her stick and beginning to prod at the tree, surprised by the soft grunt that sounded from her chest as she realised just how hard the job was going to be. 'I've watched the harvest every year since I was a little girl.'

She was only thirteen and already almost as tall as her mother, her long legs making her appear older than she was. But it was soon clear to her that she was nowhere near as strong as the other young people who were working at the harvest, which only made her more determined to try.

'You'll get used to it, Valentina,' Felipe said. 'But I promise you, your arms will feel as if they're screaming come morning.'

She took her stick from the tree and prodded Felipe with it instead, which made him laugh, and she only wished that she hadn't seen the dismay in his father's eyes when she glanced over at him and saw him making the sign of the holy cross on his chest.

———

Hours later, as the light began to fade, Valentina sat beneath a tree, her back pressed to the rough bark, her eyes shut. She was exhausted. Her shoulders and back ached, her hands were throbbing from the sores that Felipe described as blisters at the base of her fingers, and her skin was sticky with sweat. But she'd never before felt so exhilarated and proud of herself in her entire life.

'Valentina?'

She looked up and saw her father standing before her. He smiled down at her.

'You look exhausted.'

Valentina smiled. 'I am.'

'Your mother is very cross that I allowed you to stay all day,' he said, lowering himself so that he was on his haunches. 'But I told her that you're a Santiago. This is like a rite of passage.'

'I loved it, Papa,' she said earnestly. 'It was such hard work, but—'

'But it made you feel alive?'

She sighed. He understood exactly how she felt. 'I want to do this every harvest, to be part of the process, to see the olives tumble into the nets and stand shoulder to shoulder with our workers.'

He reached out to touch her cheek, his big hand warm against her damp skin. 'You make me proud, *mi hija*,' he said. 'I knew you would love this. Didn't I tell you that you were just like your papa?'

The first harvest was a special one, and she knew that many more would take place all over her family's properties in Argentina and Spain, but this was the one her father had always attended, and this was the one she wanted to attend for the rest of her life, too.

'You may stay and enjoy the festivities,' he said as he rose. 'Just don't tell your mama I gave you so much freedom.'

Valentina nodded, stretching out her arms and watching as her father walked away, taking a glass of wine that was offered to him and laughing easily with a group of men. He would be going back to oversee the *asado*, and the smoky smell of the meat cooking over the open flames filled the air around her. But her attention was quickly diverted when she saw a familiar figure approaching. *Felipe*.

'You look tired,' he said.

'So do you.'

He laughed and sat down beside her, holding out a bottle of cold Coca-Cola, which she took gratefully.

'Today was fun,' Felipe said. 'I hope you'll come back again tomorrow.'

Valentina took a long sip of soda, realising how parched she'd been, before smiling over at Felipe. He was so handsome, but she started to giggle when she saw how much dirt was smeared on his face. She reached out without thinking, gently rubbing her thumb across his skin to remove it, but the moment she did so, she realised that she shouldn't have touched him so brazenly.

His eyes widened and she felt as if she'd stopped breathing, and they just sat there together, him not moving and her fingers still against his cheek. Until Felipe nudged forward and pressed his lips against hers without warning.

His mouth was warm and soft as it bumped into hers, but it was over as quickly as it had begun, and then he was sitting beside her again, his back against the same tree trunk as hers, as she tried not to think about how brightly she must be blushing. He looked every bit as bashful and embarrassed as she felt.

But as she wondered whether he regretted it or whether she'd done anything wrong, Felipe's little finger touched hers, catching around her knuckle as they sat and watched the adults drinking and celebrating, neither of them saying a thing.

It felt like their little secret, and she never moved her left finger as she held up her cola with the other hand and took another sip, trying her hardest not to grin. Her chest was still rising and falling more heavily than usual as she sought to catch her breath, and all she could think was that she wanted to feel Felipe's lips against hers again and again. But for now, she was content for his finger to be locked over hers, touching each other in a way that no one would notice unless they were standing right in front of them.

Harvest day had changed her life, in more ways than one. She knew now what it was to work hard under the sun, to use her muscles and be part of something bigger, but she also knew what it was like to be kissed, how it felt for a boy to touch his mouth to hers.

She glanced shyly at Felipe, who looked just as uncertain as she felt. And she knew, without a doubt, that she would do anything to see him again. Even if it meant risking the wrath of her mother a hundred times over.

It would be worth it.

9

'I didn't expect you to be up so early,' Felipe said, leaning against the door to one of the stables.

Valentina smiled, a shiver of excitement running through her as she stood before him—the boy she hadn't been able to stop thinking about since the harvest a week earlier. But her attention was quickly diverted when Felipe's father appeared, leading a sweaty-looking horse beside him, its hooves click-clacking over the hard-packed ground.

'Miss Santiago,' José said, his eyebrows peaked in surprise. 'Your papa knows you're here?'

She nodded. 'Valentina, remember? There's no need for such formalities with me,' she said, grinning over at Felipe. 'And yes, he does. But it's to be a secret from my mother.' She doubted any of the outside workers would ever cross paths with her mama, but she wasn't taking any chances.

Valentina saw the look that passed over his face, as if he wasn't at all convinced she should be there, but he simply nodded and kept walking, leading the horse into a stall. Her papa had given consent, and that was all that mattered. She expected he would confirm what she'd told him whenever he next saw Basilio, but she didn't mind—she would never have come if he hadn't given permission, so she had nothing to worry about.

Felipe gestured for her to follow him once they were alone again, and she did, stopping to stand at the open door to one of the stalls, watching as he stood beside a beautiful bay-coloured horse.

'This is Pablo,' he said. 'Come closer and meet him. He won't bite, I promise.'

Valentina did what he instructed, never having been inside the stall with one of the horses before. She'd walked past them countless times and touched their noses each time as she passed, or patted her father's polo ponies on the field, but she'd never been in an enclosed space with one of the large animals before, their bodies so close they could crush her if they so wanted. She eyed up Pablo's strong legs and sturdy hooves, but soon her eyes travelled higher and she marvelled at his sleek, shiny coat and muscled body.

'Come and place your hand on him,' Felipe said. 'Feel his strength.'

Valentina watched for a moment, before stepping forward and finally placing her hand on his shoulders, her palm splayed against his soft hair. The horse felt velvety and soft beneath her touch, and she realised then that despite his size, he was as gentle and calm as any animal could be.

'He will match his heartbeat to yours,' Felipe said, and when she looked up, she realised just how close they were standing now. 'If you're calm, he will be calm. If you're nervous and your heart is beating too fast, then he will feel the same and start to jitter.'

She knew that her heart had begun to hammer in her chest, not because she was scared of the horse, but because she was equal parts nervous and excited about being with Felipe. Valentina loved how relaxed he was with her, the easy way he smiled at her and spoke as if she was just another girl his age. But then she started to think about the kiss all over again, and she couldn't stop her heart from racing. She quickly withdrew her hand from the horse.

'Would you like to ride today?' Felipe asked, stroking the horse's neck as he spoke to her. 'I thought we could saddle up and go for a nice long walk, so you can get the feel of being in the saddle, but if you're not comfortable then we can just groom him to start with.'

Valentina swallowed and hoped she wasn't still blushing. 'I would like to ride,' she replied, hoping she sounded more confident than she felt. 'Very much.'

Barely twenty minutes later, Valentina was sitting astride a horse and feeling more at home in the saddle than she'd ever expected. She'd lived on a polo farm for most of her life, and yet somehow she'd never fought for the privilege to ride before, which suddenly felt like the strangest thing in the world. Sitting high in the air and looking out from such a vantage point, feeling the power of the horse beneath her... she could see why her papa was so addicted to the sport of polo, and so far, she'd only walked.

'Pablo was your father's favourite pony for many years,' Felipe explained, as he indicated that she was to nudge her horse on with her heels to keep him walking. 'He told me to bring him out of retirement for you, so that you could learn on him. We call horses like this one high-goal ponies, because they are the most successful in the stable.'

'My father always loved me coming to watch his matches, but he never offered for me to ride, other than to lead me around when I was a little girl for fun.'

'Perhaps he didn't want you to get hurt?'

She shrugged. 'Perhaps. Or perhaps it was never worth the wrath of my mother. She can be fierce when she's angry.'

Felipe laughed, and she decided not to tell him how serious she was. Her mother had very particular beliefs about what a young lady should and shouldn't do, and Valentina had always wondered why she even cared so much.

'Keep your heels down and your back straight,' he instructed. 'And try to balance yourself without holding the reins too tightly.'

She did as he said, finding that her body moved easily with the horse. She also loved the fact that her papa had hand-picked Pablo for her. He might not have come down to watch her take her first ride, but he'd made sure to organise it for her. She would thank him for it later, when she told him just how much she'd enjoyed her excursion.

'Where I grew up, in Spain, the girls were some of our fiercest riders,' Felipe told her. 'We all trained together at weekends, and they were tough competitors.'

'Were you sad to leave?' she asked, imagining what it must have been like for him.

'Yes, but when I saw this place, I could understand why my father had chosen to move,' he said. 'We have a nice home here, your father is very generous to us, and my father is happy. He's working with the best horses in Argentina, and now, so am I. And it also helps that your father is Spanish. I think it makes my dad feel more at home, if that makes sense.'

Valentina was so curious about Felipe, and she found that she couldn't hold her tongue, asking him all the things she wanted to know as they walked on horseback, side by side.

'Do you go to school?'

'Not anymore. I'm working in the stables all the time now.'

'How old are you?'

He laughed. 'How old are you?'

'Fourteen,' she said. 'It's my birthday today, actually.'

Felipe grinned, and she saw a mischievous glint in his eyes. 'Today?'

She nodded, and when he stopped his horse, hers automatically stopped walking, too.

'Then I suppose I should say happy birthday,' he said. 'Although you're making me feel old. I'm fifteen, almost sixteen.'

As she was digesting the fact that he was almost two years older than her, she didn't even guess what was coming when Felipe suddenly stood out of his stirrups and leaned across, brushing a kiss to her lips. It was soft and warm and as toe-tingling as the first time he'd kissed her, until her horse moved and they bumped teeth, and she almost lost her balance and slipped from the saddle.

'Whoa,' he said, reaching out an arm to steady her. 'Are you all right?'

Valentina knew she was blushing as she nodded and righted herself, but she didn't care. Being with Felipe made her forget about everything else, and the way he was looking at her, she knew that he felt the same way she did.

'I don't think your papa likes me,' she suddenly blurted out, cringing as the words came out of her mouth. She hated how young she sounded, especially with him being older.

But Felipe just smiled. 'My father likes you plenty, he just doesn't want me to get too friendly with you. He likes to remind me that your papa is our employer, which means that I should treat you differently.'

Valentina swallowed. She knew what he meant without his having to explain himself, for it was the same reason her mother wouldn't like her being with Felipe—they were from different worlds, she knew that, but it only made her feel more drawn to him. Because he seemed as curious about her as she was about him, and he also seemed unworried about breaking the rules a little.

'Does it bother you, that he doesn't approve?' she asked.

Felipe shook his head. 'Do you care that your mama wouldn't approve of your riding?'

They both knew that it was more than just her riding she wouldn't approve of, but Valentina didn't point that out.

'I'm tired of doing what she wants all the time,' Valentina admitted. 'So no, I don't care that this would make her unhappy. It's worth any punishment if she finds out.'

Felipe grinned as if he was pleased with her answer, before leaning forward and kissing her again, only this time it was slower, and she kept her fingers tightly wrapped around the reins so she didn't fall. When he finally pulled away, she found herself wishing that he hadn't, or that they were somewhere she could reach up and run her fingers through his thick, dark hair or trace her fingertips against his face.

'How long do we have, before you have to be back at the house?' he asked.

Valentina glanced up at the sky, realising how much time had passed. She needed to get back before her mother rose for the day, because as much as she was prepared to endure her wrath, her finding out would stop Valentina from returning the following morning, and the morning after that. 'Not long.'

'Then let's make the most of it,' he said, settling back in the saddle and looking effortlessly at home there. 'What do you say I teach you how to trot? And then tomorrow morning, I'll take you to my favourite place on the property and you can have your first canter.'

Valentina nodded, doing her best to follow along with his instructions and knowing that she would have agreed to learn how to gallop if it had meant spending longer in the company of Felipe.

10

PRESENT DAY

Rose looked up at Benjamin, struggling over how to explain why she had the horse figurine without opening up and telling him the whole story about Hope's House. But she could see from the way he was staring back at her that he wasn't convinced she was supposed to have it.

'It was actually left for my grandmother,' she said. 'In fact, there's a long story about how I came to have it.'

His expression was hard to read, but she could tell he was surprised. 'Could you tell me about it this afternoon, while we tour the property?'

She nodded. 'I will. I promise.'

Benjamin held out his hand and she opened her palm to take it, closing her fingers around the figurine. And as she stood and watched him go, she experienced the strangest sensation that he had a much deeper connection to the property and what she was searching for than she'd realised.

Then Rose's phone vibrated in her pocket, and she took it out, happy to see that it was Jessica, and even happier that it was a video call. She swiped to answer and held the phone out at arm's length.

'Hello from sunny Argentina,' she said, doing a little circle so her friend could see the stables and grounds behind her.

Rose looked up and saw that Benjamin was standing at the end of the building, watching her, but when she glanced at him, he gave her a tight smile and turned, disappearing behind a door. She pushed him from her mind as she smiled into the screen, grinning harder when she saw that Jessica was at home with the girls.

'Quiet day at home?' Rose asked, waving to the girls as they jumped up and down in the background.

'I spent a few hours in the office this morning, but I just got home and thought I'd call,' Jessica said. 'Tell me everything. What's it like there? Have you discovered anything yet?'

Rose began to walk back to the house, slowly, and making sure to stop often so that Jessica could see the property.

'It's beautiful here,' she said. 'Like a raw, honest kind of beauty. It's all huge fields and sunshine, trees and horses. I don't think I've ever been surrounded by so much space in my life before. It's like something from a film, or a retreat.'

'It sounds like exactly what you need,' Jessica said. 'Hell, it sounds like exactly what *I* need.'

Rose watched as Jessica walked from the living room to the kitchen, pouring herself a coffee before sitting down at the kitchen table. Jessica's home was gorgeous—a New York brownstone that had been extensively renovated, the kind of home that Rose had always imagined herself living in. But as she looked at Jessica's home in the background now, she wondered if perhaps she'd wanted what Jessica had because she hadn't figured out what she actually wanted herself. It had been easier to see herself having the same life as her friend's one day, rather than trying to forge her own path.

'I like it here more than I expected I would,' Rose said, sitting down beneath a tree and leaning against the rough bark of the trunk as her left hand fell to the ground, fingers playing

over the stems of grass below. 'I mean, I can't even remember
the last time I touched actual grass. Part of me wants to hurry
back to the familiarity of London and my flat, but the other part
of me is curious about life here. About how it would feel to
spend some time here and live a different kind of life for a
while.'

Jessica nodded, sipping her coffee, the house sounding quiet
in the background now as if the girls had either gone outside or
perhaps snuck onto their iPads. 'I was hoping you'd say that. I
mean, you've had a year that would have defeated most people.
You deserve some time to recalibrate.'

'I haven't given my firm an answer yet, about returning to
work.'

Jessica stayed silent, and Rose blinked back at her, knowing
what she was thinking.

'You think I should quit, don't you?' Jessica had said as
much when they'd been in London, and Rose had purposely
not been thinking about the decision.

'I think that you need to follow your heart. Do what *you*
want to do rather than what everyone expects of you,' Jessica
said. 'If you need this break before you go back to work, and you
can afford to take that break, then I don't think it would be the
worst thing for you to do. You can always go back to practising
law; a short break isn't going to end your career. I don't think
you need to be afraid of that.'

'But what if it does?' Rose asked, blinking away tears. She
didn't even know why she was so emotional, but even thinking
about the life she'd built and walking away from it was terrifying to her. 'What if I take the time off and nothing is ever the
same again? I already feel like it will be hard to go back, but if I
take even longer...'

'You're scared because everything has changed,' Jessica said.
'You feel like your job is the last link to the way your life used to
be, before the cancer, before your mum passed, but it's not. You

still have your home to go back to, and you still have me, and no one can take your memories away. You might find that you feel even closer to her there, away from everything familiar.'

Rose sighed. 'Maybe I should just move to Argentina then, and start over.'

They both laughed, and Rose felt so much better for having spoken to her friend. She always seemed to know just what to say, just when she needed it.

'Show me around more,' Jessica said, leaning in closer to the screen. 'I want the full tour, and I have to see the house. I still can't believe it's as beautiful as the pictures looked.'

Rose stood, realising the cat she'd seen earlier had come to stand nearby. She reached out and scratched the top of his head, noticing that he followed her as she walked away. She'd wanted a friend, and it seemed that she'd found one, albeit one who looked like he'd seen a few fights, given the tear to one of his ears and a scar that ran down his front leg. Rose gave him one last pat. *We're not so dissimilar, you and me. I feel like I've been through a few rounds in the ring, too.*

'Okay, so this is the house,' Rose said, standing to show her the exterior and leaving the cat to stretch out in the sun. 'It's stunning, and the inside is just as gorgeous. There's something very relaxed and peaceful about it, despite how large it is. Like you can tell it's been loved.'

'I can see why you like it so much.'

'Honestly, it's impossible not to like it, even if I can't see myself staying here.'

'And have you met anyone there? Do they have a groundskeeper or any staff?'

Rose glanced back out at the stables, catching sight of Benjamin leading a horse that was all saddled up for a ride. She watched him again, not quite sure what she thought of him yet. She didn't care about the way he'd first reacted to seeing her; it had been amusing seeing him back-pedal, but there was something she couldn't quite put her finger on yet. 'There is someone here, I'm not sure how to describe him but he rides the polo ponies. It seems that my great-grandmother was his sponsor, which I suppose means that I am now.' She was about to tell Jessica that there was also a housekeeper whom she hadn't met yet, but she was interrupted before she had the chance.

'What's he like? Anything like the gorgeous players we found online?'

She paused. 'He was, well, he's fine. I'm reserving my judgement until we meet again later today.'

'Fine?'

'Okay, he's absolutely gorgeous, I'm not going to lie. I mean, he's an Argentinian sportsman, so use your imagination, but I just wasn't sure about him when we met. I'll let you know what I think when I see him again.'

'All right. But I'll hold you to that. I want to hear *all* about him.'

Jessica let her get away without asking more, for now, and Rose quickly began a proper tour of the house so that she didn't have to answer any more questions about the elusive Benjamin just yet. But her thoughts kept being drawn back to him—there had been something about the look on his face that she just couldn't stop thinking about, and she realised that if she was going to ask him more about the figurine, then she would have to show him the piece of blue silk, too. And tell him exactly how she'd found herself on an unexpected flight from London to Buenos Aires to inherit the infamous Santiago estate.

Rose hadn't been sure whether to walk down to the stables and look for Benjamin, or wait for him to call at the house, so she was happy to see him crossing the lawn barely three hours later. She found herself watching him, noticing the way his long stride covered the ground, his golden forearms on display thanks to his rolled-up shirtsleeves, one hand lifted to shield his eyes from the sun as he approached the house.

'Hi again,' she said as she opened the door. 'Would you like to come in?'

'I have two horses saddled up and ready for us, but I could do with a cold drink if you're offering.'

'Follow me and I'll see what we have,' Rose said. 'Someone was kind enough to stock the fridge and pantry for my arrival, so I'm sure there will be something.'

'Clara,' he said, taking his boots off before following her in his socks. 'She took very good care of Valentina, but I know she's been worried about losing her job. She usually calls in and cleans the house, brings groceries, that sort of thing.'

'Valentina was in the house until the end?' Rose asked, opening the fridge. 'I can't believe someone of her age would want to rattle around such a big place, but it does sound as if she was very well cared for.'

When she turned back around with a bottle of juice in one hand and a Coke in the other, she saw that Benjamin was studying her with a surprised expression on his face.

'You truly don't know anything about Valentina, do you?' he asked.

Rose slowly shook her head from side to side. 'Other than what the lawyer told me and the few articles I managed to find online, I know virtually nothing about her.' She hesitated, not sure how much to tell him. 'I feel as if I've been transported to another place and time, where everyone expects me to know this woman they admired, but I'm honestly just a stranger.'

He took the juice without saying anything, and Rose watched as he unscrewed the top and took a few long sips. His face was brushed with dirt from being outside all day, his hands weathered and his nails clipped short, and she couldn't help but think how different he was to almost every other man she'd ever met in her life before. The men she worked with looked like they lived in their suits, and she couldn't think how they'd ever end up with dirt beneath their nails. Benjamin was not the kind of man she'd ever been around before.

'I think you need to start at the very beginning, so I understand your story,' he finally said, before finishing the juice. 'The figurine you showed me earlier? I don't think anything has ever taken me by surprise like that before. I've been thinking about it all day.'

'I could see that when I showed it to you. You looked like you'd seen a ghost.'

'Honestly? I felt like I had,' he said, settling on one of the high stools at the kitchen counter. 'You see, the only person I know who could carve a small piece of wood into something so intricate was my great-grandfather. My father has one just like it beside his bed to this day, and I have the strangest feeling that if we put them side by side? That they'd be identical.'

Rose swallowed, unscrewing the lid on the glass bottle of Coke she was holding and taking a sip, for something to do. It also gave her an excuse to look away from Benjamin, who was staring at her in a way that made her uncomfortable it was so intense.

'I can't imagine how unusual it must seem, having me turn up here with no knowledge of the woman you all admired,' she began, setting down the bottle on the counter. 'But I need you to understand that it couldn't be more unusual than it is for me. I still can't quite wrap my head around it all.'

'You're asking if it seems strange to have an English woman turn up claiming to be the long-lost descendant of Valentina Santiago?' Benjamin laughed. 'You have no idea.'

Rose sighed. 'The great-granddaughter of Valentina Santiago,' she corrected. 'Or at least, that's what I'm told.'

He frowned, opening his mouth to say something before

closing it. She could tell he had something on his mind but was perhaps too polite to say what he was thinking.

'Just say it,' she said. 'I have a thicker skin than you'd expect, and I'd rather you spoke freely.'

'None of us can believe that Valentina had a daughter, or great-granddaughter in your case,' Benjamin said. 'I mean you no disrespect, but why come now? Why not come before she died? Why wait all this time?'

Rose met his gaze, understanding why he was asking. She would have felt the same if someone had appeared out of thin air after her mother died, and it seemed like he had been very close to Valentina given how protective he was of her.

'Because until last week, I didn't even know she existed.'

Benjamin didn't blink. 'I'm sorry, you—'

'I received a letter from her lawyer in Buenos Aires, notifying me that a large estate had been left to me, and I only came here because my best friend convinced me to. To begin with, I didn't even believe it.'

It was possible she'd never seen another human being look so taken aback in all her life.

Benjamin looked away and rubbed his hand across his jaw, before turning back to her. 'So, you didn't read that she'd passed away and come here to stake your claim once she was gone?'

Rose's eyebrows peaked. 'No, I most certainly did not. But I did come here to try to find out about the woman who was my biological great-grandmother, and I'm hoping you might be able to tell me more about her. I want to know who she was, where my family came from, how I'm connected to Argentina.'

'But the figurine,' he said. 'How did you have that if you didn't know about—'

Rose held up her hand. 'It was left to my grandmother, along with something else.' She stood and walked across the room to the table, returning with the little wooden box and passing it to him. 'Please, open it.'

Benjamin carefully opened the lid, his hands dwarfing the box, and she watched as he took out the little horse, before reaching for the piece of silk.

'A few months ago, I received this little box. It was left for my grandmother by her biological mother, when she placed her for adoption. I'm told it sat hidden, undiscovered until very recently, and they were clues that made no sense to me.' She swallowed, unsure if she'd already told him too much. 'My grandmother never found what was left to her.'

'Until you came here,' he said, putting the two items back into the box and returning it to her.

'Until I came here,' she agreed. 'I never expected to figure out the link between my grandmother and what was left for her, because as far as my family were aware she wasn't even adopted, but when I received the letter from the lawyer here, it suddenly all started to fall into place. The clues that had seemed impossible to make head or tail of suddenly had meaning.'

'Just so I understand correctly, it was Valentina's choice not to make contact with you all these years? She was the one who made that decision?'

Rose could see that Benjamin had already softened towards her. His shoulders were more relaxed now, his smile easier than it had been before. 'That's right. It appears that she watched my grandmother from afar her entire life, and perhaps my mother and me, too. Which makes me think that there was a reason she never tried to make contact.'

He stroked his jawline again, his brow creased as if he were trying to work it all out. 'Valentina was a woman with all the resources a person could need at her disposal, so she must have had a very good reason not to make contact.'

'Or perhaps, despite everything she had, an adoption was a source of shame for her?' Rose said. 'Trust me, I've turned the question over in my mind for days now, and all I can think is that she didn't want to come forward and turn my grandmother's life upside down by revealing such a secret. Or that perhaps she was still trying to hide what had happened in her past? It was different for women then, and she might have still held on to how she felt as a young pregnant woman.'

Benjamin nodded. 'Perhaps you're right,' he said. 'And I'm sorry for ever questioning your right to be here in the first place. We were all very protective of Valentina and of this property. Did anyone tell you that it's been held in the one family for almost a century?'

'Trust me, I feel the weight of that history,' Rose said.

'It's hard to explain what it's like to lose someone, especially someone who meant so much.'

She smiled, refusing to let it slip in front of Benjamin even as she felt herself cracking. 'I understand.' *More than you could possibly imagine.*

'Well, on that note, how about we go for a ride? I'd very much like to show you just how special this property is.'

Rose's stomach did a little flip, and she was grateful for the distraction from her thoughts. 'Let's go now, before I change my mind about this whole riding business.'

11

Rose had never felt so uncomfortable in her life, but she couldn't fault how patient her teacher was being. If she hadn't been sure about him before, then she was now—he might have been gruff in the beginning, but she already admired the gentle way he treated his horses, and the kindness he was showing her.

'Try not to clench your fingers around the reins,' Benjamin said. 'Take a deep breath, relax your shoulders, heels down and breathe.'

'That's too many things at once!' she said, half laughing through her fear. 'You look like you're sitting in your favourite armchair, and I feel like I've just climbed onto a rollercoaster.'

Benjamin's laugh made her laugh, which temporarily distracted her from the terror she was experiencing.

'And now I'm going to fall off because you're making me laugh!'

'You're more likely to fall off all bunched up and nervous than you are now that you're laughing,' he said. 'Just trust me. I wouldn't have put you on a horse that wasn't safe. You just need to roll your shoulders down and relax.'

She took a deep breath and tried to keep her shoulders down like he'd instructed.

'Look around you, Rose,' he said. 'I know I have an ulterior motive in wanting to make you love it here, as does everyone who loves this place, but it's one of the most special properties I've ever known. Just focus on the view and try to forget about the horse beneath you. It will make riding all the more enjoyable.'

Rose did as he said and looked around, and even though she was still gripping the reins as if her life depended upon it, she found herself breathing more deeply. He was right, it was stunning, and the fields seemed to stretch farther than her eye could see.

'How do you feel?' he asked.

She glanced over at him, taking in his one hand on the reins, the other resting on his thigh. He was so at ease, so relaxed, that it made it hard for her not to feel at least a little relaxed, too.

'You honestly want to know?'

'I do.'

'I feel as if the weight of the world is resting on my shoulders.'

Benjamin rode beside her in silence.

'I was referring to being on horseback, but if you want to go straight to the tough talk, then sure.'

Rose groaned. Of course he'd meant the horse riding.

'But since you brought it up, this is a very special place, Rose. I honestly can't imagine that a more beautiful property exists anywhere, and there's something pretty special about being the first to show it to you.'

'If I'm honest, I feel completely out of my depth here. I can't even comprehend that I'm connected to this land, or that this isn't just some kind of fantasy.'

Benjamin looked at her as if he understood, but she wasn't sure that he could even if he wanted to. 'Then just enjoy the fantasy. Explore the property, get to know the place, spend some time with the horses here. I promise that you'll fall in love.'

She blushed, knowing that he was talking about the property but imagining that it might not be so hard to fall in love with the man showing her around, either. Or at least fall in lust, perhaps.

He gestured for her to keep walking.

'Let me show you the rest of the estate,' he said.

She was happy to follow, wishing she was videoing the view so she could look back later and know that it hadn't been a dream.

'This is the polo field,' he said, gesturing to an immaculately maintained stretch of grass that appeared to her much, much bigger than a football pitch. 'We host some very special games here.'

'Did Valentina play polo herself?' Rose asked.

'Not that I know of. But she was passionate about women playing the sport, which always made me wonder if she wished she had,' he said. 'Sometimes she'd talk about her father, and how much he'd influenced her love of the sport, but they were rare times because she wasn't often nostalgic. She liked riding around the property though, when I was a boy, exercising some of the older horses.'

Rose sat and looked around, wishing she'd been able to travel to Argentina to see the property with Valentina before she'd passed away. It was on the tip of her tongue to tell Benjamin that she'd recently lost her mother, to explain to him how difficult all this was for her to process right now after everything she'd been through, but something stopped her.

'I want you to fall in love with this place, Rose,' Benjamin said, leaning back in the saddle as she watched him, his hand resting on the horse's rump. 'I know this is going to sound crazy, but I feel like it's my job to sell this place to you, to convince you of how special it is so that you never want to leave.'

She sighed as her horse stopped walking, taking the time to look around and drink in the scenery around them. It was beautiful, there was no denying that.

'I'm sure you feel like there's a lot resting on your shoulders, Rose, and there is. But just let the next few days be about getting to know Argentina and the people here.'

Rose glanced away, used to blinking away tears by now, but somehow still not used to the gut punch of pain when she thought about the past few months and what she'd lost.

'I'm sorry, did I say the wrong thing?' he asked, looking concerned as his eyes seemed to study her face.

'I recently lost someone,' she said. 'Someone I loved very much, and every now and again it just hits me. It wasn't anything to do with what you said.'

Benjamin's smile was kind. 'I find that a good gallop makes me forget all about my pain. Perhaps I could tempt you?'

Rose laughed, surprised at how quickly he'd been able to make her smile. 'How about we try a walk again? I think just plodding along should be enough to keep my mind off things.'

'Deal. A walk it is.'

They set off again, and Rose found her gaze travelling back to the man beside her instead of the view. He might not have made the most brilliant first impression on her earlier in the day, but he was certainly redeeming himself now, and she couldn't help but respect how passionately he felt about the land they were riding on.

———

'Is it usual not to feel your legs after riding?' Rose asked as she swung her legs from the stirrups and looked down at the ground. 'And to have no idea how to get off?'

Benjamin dismounted in a way that looked effortless, leaving his horse to stand there as if it also knew exactly what to do somehow, while he came around to her left side.

'Your thighs will hate you in the morning, but you'll get used to it,' he said, before holding his hands out. 'Swing your right leg over and I'll catch you.'

She stared down at him, not quite sure whether she wanted to, and also not sure quite where his hands were going to be catching her.

'Ahh—'

'Trust me. I've got you.'

Rose did as he instructed, swinging her right leg back just as she'd watched him do, well clear of the horse, and his hands caught her around the hips and carefully guided her down. His palms were firm against her jeans, but the moment her feet were on the ground he let go, and she found herself wishing he hadn't removed them quite so quickly.

'Rose, come to the polo with us this weekend,' Benjamin said, his eyes searching hers as he took a step backward. 'You're my patron, after all, even if you didn't intend to be, and I think you'd love it. I'd love for you to see the game of polo first hand.'

She sighed, about to say no but then imagining what fun it might be. 'I'm supposed to be flying to New York on Saturday.'

'What's in New York?'

'My best friend.'

'Can you go to New York another time? I know you'll enjoy it if you give it a chance.'

Rose hesitated. Jessica would understand; so long as she went there to visit eventually, she doubted that it would matter to her at all, but the thought of extending her stay in Argentina unsettled her. None of it felt real still, almost as if she hadn't yet woken from a dream, and as nice as Benjamin was, she felt as if she were intruding on his world rather than being part of it.

'You might find that polo is in your blood, after all, and if you don't spend time here, you might never know,' Benjamin said, his eyes seeming to twinkle as he watched her. 'What do you say? Will you stay, Rose?'

Something ignited inside Rose then, a swirl in her stomach that spiralled through her body as she stood before Benjamin.

'You truly think I'll love it?' she asked.

He grinned, and it was contagious. 'I don't think so, Rose, I *know* you will. Once you've spent a week in Argentina?' he raised his eyebrows as he leaned closer. 'You're never going to want to go home.'

Rose swallowed what felt like a hard lump in her throat, having a feeling that he might be absolutely right. Because right now, as she looked out at the sprawling fields around her, she could very much see herself staying in Argentina forever.

12

ARGENTINE OPEN POLO CHAMPIONSHIP,
BUENOS AIRES, 1938

'How are you feeling about the game this weekend?' Valentina asked her father as they strolled past the stables.

He reached for her hand, holding it in his for a moment as he smiled across at her. She wasn't a little girl anymore, but she still loved to hold her father's hand, to bask in his attention like this when it was just the two of them.

'I'm feeling good. Polo is what I live for.' He laughed. 'Other than you and your mother, of course.'

Only the day before, she'd visited the olive grove with him, and today he'd asked her to meet him after her lessons, which made her think there was something he wanted to tell her. It turned out that she wasn't wrong.

'Valentina, you asked me some time ago about Spain,' he said. 'It was one of the hardest decisions of my life to move here, to leave behind my country and start somewhere afresh, but I did it to prove myself. I wanted to move away from my family and show that I was a self-made man, and Argentina was a country I'd always loved. I'd played polo here before and I had a feeling it was the right place for me to make my mark.'

She nodded, listening carefully to him.

'My heart is divided these days, though. I am Spanish but I'm also an Argentine now, just as you are. But no matter how much I fall in love with Argentina, we must remember our Spanish heritage, always.'

It was Valentina reaching for his hand then, and he clasped it back, drawing her in close so she could lean her head into him. She was tall now, taller than her mother, but she doubted she would ever reach her father's height.

'Promise me that you'll always take care of this property, Valentina. Your mother doesn't have the connection to the land that you and I do, which is why it's up to you to ensure it's never sold,' her father said. 'One day, you will raise your own children here, and you must never let anyone take your birthright from you. This is to be Santiago land forever.'

Valentina squeezed his hand. 'I won't ever leave here, Papa. I promise.'

He lifted her hand and placed a kiss to it. 'My beautiful girl, what would I ever do without you?'

It wasn't often her father became emotional, but Valentina saw tears shining in his eyes then, and as they kept walking, she had the strangest feeling that something was wrong, that he was keeping something from her.

'Papa, is anything troubling you? Is there a reason you wanted to walk with me today?'

'Does a father need a reason to spend time with his daughter?'

'No, Papa, of course not.'

Valentina dropped her head so that it fell against his shoulder. She only wished they could spend more time together like this, just the two of them. They were the moments she loved the most, more than anything, and she cherished every single one of them.

Valentina had always loved attending the polo and watching her father play, but today she had more reason than usual to be excited. Her father was playing, but so was Felipe's father, which meant that Felipe was there as his groom, preparing all the ponies and even riding them to warm them up before the game. She was currently watching him cantering back and forth on one horse at the same time as leading another, and despite his young age, he made it all look effortless. Valentina's father had said he was a natural horseman, and she could see that he hadn't been exaggerating. It wouldn't be long before he was the one playing.

In the beginning, she hadn't been able to understand why her father had brought a stable manager all the way from Spain instead of finding someone already in Argentina, but she could see now that they were friends more than anything. It was impossible to miss the easy manner they had with each other, and clearly Felipe's father was well respected by the other players. Only last week, she'd heard that it was he who'd helped them win a tournament, which had of course made her father all the more fond of him.

When it was almost time for the match to begin, Valentina watched as Felipe swung around, going to tend to the horses waiting on the sidelines for their turn. She found it fascinating how often the players switched horses throughout a game, and how excited the horses seemed when it was their turn. She was still very much looking forward to her father taking her to watch a women's game one day—she could barely believe it was true that women's games even existed—to see young ladies swinging mallets and showing off their skills, and if it was as exciting and fast-paced as watching the men.

Felipe caught her eye then, giving her a wave, and she quickly looked around to make sure her mother wasn't watching before waving back. Even from where she was standing, she could see the way his eyes lit up when he saw her, and she knew that if someone was looking at her, they'd have seen the same look on her face. She was always pleased to see him.

Valentina would have done anything to go and stand with him, but she knew her mother would never forgive her. She was in a pretty dress that her mama had chosen for her, white with light blue dots, and although she didn't mind it, she would have much preferred to be in breeches and boots, helping to prepare the horses for when they were next needed.

'Valentina, come and meet some of the ladies,' her mother called out, beckoning her over.

She exchanged a quick glance with her brother, who looked thankful that the attention had been diverted away from him. Valentina fixed a smile and stood close to her mother, knowing what was expected of her.

'My Valentina is seventeen now. Before I know it, she'll be all grown up and married.'

Valentina was grateful when a waiter came past holding a tray of drinks, and she happily took a glass of lemonade as the other women all began talking about their children and tittering about finding them husbands or wives. The last thing she wanted to think about was getting married or leaving home; she had no intention of doing either any time soon, and her father had already made it clear how fortunate she was—she would never have to marry for money or security. He wanted her by his side, learning the business so that one day she would be able to take over his position, and if she chose to marry, it was only to be for a love match. She'd been embarrassed when he'd first brought it up, but she understood that he was trying to tell her that she didn't have to follow her mother's well-meaning plan—marriage wasn't the only way for a young woman with means.

Thankfully the first chukka started then, and all the ladies turned to watch the horses galloping down the field, momentarily suspending their conversations. Valentina sipped her lemonade as she watched her father expertly handle the mallet, connecting hard with the ball and sending it flying down the field at speed. Her heart swelled with pride, but as much as she tried to watch the game, her eyes kept dancing over to where Felipe stood.

'Valentina?'

She quickly looked away, her eyes immediately fixed on her father again the moment her mother said her name, as if she might be able to detect whom she was staring at. And when she glanced at her, Valentina knew that she'd been caught. Her mother's eyes were narrowed, and she could tell by the pinched look around her mouth that she wasn't happy.

'Valentina, come and stand closer to me,' her mother said. 'And don't forget, *mi hija*, that there is a reason we stand on this side of the field and that the others stand over there. Make no mistake about whom you are, or where you're supposed to be.'

Valentina's cheeks burnt hot as she kept her head turned towards the game, for she knew precisely what her mother was trying to say. A boy like Felipe would never be good enough for her; not now, not ever, and there would be no changing her mother's mind.

'How are your riding lessons going, Valentina?'

She kept her eyes on the horses in front of her on the field, not wanting to look at her father for fear that he'd somehow be able to read her mind, which was full of thoughts of her morning rides and all the stolen kisses she and Felipe had shared by the stables. She'd managed to escape her mother's clutches once the first game was over, and had been enjoying a few moments alone, away from the crowd, until her father found her.

'They're going very well,' she said. 'Felipe thinks I take after you, actually.'

'Ahh, now why doesn't that surprise me?' Her father laughed, his arm against hers as he leaned forward on the rails beside her. 'I should have let you start riding years ago, Valentina. I'm sorry.'

Valentina didn't know how to tell him that she was grateful he hadn't—if he had, she would never have been able to learn from Felipe, to spend so many mornings in his company, basking in his undivided attention. Learning to ride at precisely the moment she had was one of the best things that had ever happened to her.

'Tell me, are you still enjoying riding Pablo after all this time, or would you like me to buy you a horse of your own?'

'Pablo is perfect for me,' she replied. 'I'm told he was your favourite horse when he was younger?'

'You've heard wrong,' her father said, grinning at her as he turned. 'He is *still* my favourite horse. I've never scored more goals on one pony than I did on him—he was something very special. But if you love him, then he is yours. I'd love to think that my daughter was the one taking care of him and riding him in his retirement from polo.'

Valentina stood on tiptoe and pressed a kiss to his cheek. 'Thank you. I don't know a lot about horses yet, but I think he's enjoying being made a fuss of again. And I promise to retire him properly when he's ready.'

She looked up at her father now, waiting for him to say something else as his eyes twinkled back at her. But as he opened his mouth, he paused and suddenly touched his hand to his chest, looking uncomfortable. She saw that a line on his forehead bulged, as if he were under great stress or fighting a feeling of pain as he stared back at her.

'Papa, are you okay?'

He was silent for a moment, before shaking his head, appearing uneasy, but clearly not wanting her to know how bad it was.

'I'm fine, my love. Just a chest pain. It's nothing to worry about.'

'Should I call for a doctor? Just to be sure?'

He shook his head again, leaning forward and pressing a kiss to her forehead. 'I'm fine. This is what happens when an old man like me tries to play sport with men half his age. A glass of wine and something to eat, and I'll be as good as new.'

Valentina was about to insist he see the doctor when her mother came marching over, looking very annoyed at having to walk in her beautiful cream heels across the grass. She remembered a time when she was a very young child when her mother had been more relaxed, fun almost, but as the years had passed, she'd changed, obsessed with elevating her place in society and wanting her family's status to rise at the same time. Valentina knew it embarrassed her father, but he seemed to go along with it to keep his wife happy, ever the peacemaker.

'Basilio, what are you doing over here? We have people to talk to and—'

'Mama,' Valentina interrupted, receiving a sharp stare in reply. 'Papa wasn't feeling well. I think—'

'Basilio?'

He shook his head and stepped forward to drop another kiss into Valentina's hair. 'Enjoy your afternoon, *mi querida niña*,' he whispered. 'I'll keep your mother busy so you can have fun without her watching you.'

'But Papa,' she whispered back, looking up into his dark eyes. Any other time she would have revelled in being given some time to have fun without her mother hovering, but something about the way he'd touched his chest before, the almost frightened look in his eyes, had scared her.

'I'm fine, Valentina, I promise. If I was worried, I would call for the doctor myself. I take my health very seriously.'

She nodded and watched them walk away, but she couldn't quell the little knot of fear in her stomach even as Felipe waved to her from the other side of the fence and beckoned for her to come and join him and his friends. Valentina glanced back at her father one last time before slipping under the fence rail, waving back to Felipe once she was out of her mother's line of sight and gathering her skirt into her hand so she could run across the grass towards him.

Later that day, when they were all home and her father had fallen asleep, Valentina went to find her mother. She'd felt a void growing between them recently, almost as if she'd done something wrong without knowing what it was, and she hoped that by seeking her mother out, she might soften towards her again. The more she thought about it, the more she felt it might have something to do with her age. She was a young woman now, and she wondered if it was simply because her mother no longer viewed her as a child.

'Mama?' Valentina called out, as she softly knocked on her door. 'May I come in?'

She looked around the half-open door and found her mother sitting in front of her mirror, her face bare of make-up as she brushed out her long dark hair. Valentina shared little of her mother's personality or interests, but she did share her looks, and it was almost as if she were staring into the mirror and seeing how she might look in thirty years' time as she studied her mother's reflection. Their hair was the same—an almost-black mane with a gentle curl at the tips—and they had the same light golden skin with the darkest brown eyes flecked with a hint of gold. And as she stared at her mother's reflection, she was reminded of how beautiful she was, and of all the stories her father had shared of falling in love with her at first sight when he'd seen her across a room.

'Mama, I've been worried about Papa all evening,' she said,

taking a seat in the armchair in the corner of the room. 'He wasn't feeling well this afternoon. Something was wrong.'

'Your father is fine,' she said, brusquely, as if Valentina had moaned to her about the weather rather than her father's health.

'But he was holding his chest, as if he was in pain. I'm worried about him.'

Her mother set her brush down and looked back at Valentina in the mirror, before slowly turning to face her. 'Do you know what would help your father?'

Valentina shook her head.

'It would help if he wasn't having to worry about his only daughter gallivanting around with the hired help,' she said, her voice low. 'If your intention is to bring our good family name into disrepute, then you're doing a fine job of it.'

Valentina swallowed, her face hot as she folded her hands together, palm to palm, opening her mouth but not knowing what to say. If her mother had wanted to hurt her, then she'd done precisely what she'd set out to do. 'Mama, I—'

'You think I didn't know that you've become friends with the stableboy?' she asked. 'That you've been learning to ride, because your father wants to indulge your every whim, even though I expressly forbade you from doing so? You thought you could hide those things from me?'

This time, Valentina didn't even try to reply, keeping her head bowed so she didn't have to meet her mother's angry gaze, her eyes fixed on the floor.

'You will not see that boy anymore, Valentina. It's not appropriate for you to be fraternising with the staff, especially at your age.'

Valentina looked up then, her heart racing in response to her mother's words. 'Mama, you cannot mean that. He's a friend, and he's only teaching me to ride, and—'

'Enough! You speak to me as if I'm going to change my mind, but I'm not your father, Valentina. You don't have me wrapped around your little finger, and I know full well that it's more than learning to ride. I saw the way you looked at each other today. I'm no fool!'

Valentina stood then, but it took every inch of her strength not to burst into tears and run from the room. But if she didn't stand her ground now, she knew that her mother would never respect her.

'I have my father's permission to take riding lessons from Felipe. He's even gifted me his old horse, and I'm thoroughly enjoying my daily rides.' She paused, her breath coming in fast pants. 'I do not intend to stop, just as I do not intend to stop worrying about my father, so please stop treating me like a child and start speaking to me as the young woman I am.'

And even though she felt like a coward for doing so, Valentina quickly turned on her heel and walked away from her mother before she could say anything else. She didn't know what she'd done to earn her mother's wrath, but she did know that she only had one ally in this house, and that was her father.

Her mother acted as if she was nothing more than an inconvenience, and if that's the way she was going to treat her, then Valentina had no intention of being an obedient, placid daughter any longer.

13

PRESENT DAY

Rose had never experienced anything like the Argentine Open. From the moment she'd arrived, she was so pleased that she'd decided to come. She'd had no idea how many people would be attending; the enormous, immaculately prepared field was flanked by stadium seating on both sides, with tents at one end for the VIP guests, of which she was fortunate enough to be one.

'Rose!' came a call from the other side of the tent, just as she was reaching into her purse for the ticket that had been sent to her the day before.

She saw Luis Gonzalez waving to her, and she nodded to the security guard as he stood aside to let her pass.

'I'm so pleased you came,' he said. 'And that you're still in Argentina, of course.'

'Well, I met Benjamin, and let's just say he was very persuasive,' she told him. 'But I'm pleased to be here—it's turning out to be quite the experience.'

'Let me get you a glass of champagne and introduce you to a few people, and then we can watch the game,' he said, taking her arm and walking her across the tent so that they had a view of the field. Rose tried to ignore the feeling that everyone was looking at her and attempting to figure out how she was connected to Valentina Santiago; more likely it was her imagination and no one had even noticed her presence.

Rose admired the glossy horses as the players warmed them up, their coats shining in the sunlight. But it wasn't until Luis touched her arm that she turned to look across to the other side of the field.

'Someone's waving to you.'

She blushed when she realised that Benjamin had his hand raised and was looking straight at her, sitting on horseback and talking to a teammate. He wore white breeches and a dark blue silky polo that clung to his skin, and if Jessica were beside her, she'd have whispered that perhaps Benjamin might take the prize for best-looking polo player.

Rose waved back, her eyes tracking him as he cantered across the field, effortlessly swinging his mallet from one side to the other. He certainly made it look easy, and she very much doubted that it was.

'You seem to have caught my brother's attention.'

Rose turned slightly to see a beautiful young woman standing beside her, holding an almost empty glass of champagne.

'Rose,' she said, holding out her hand. 'And you must be Benjamin's sister.'

'Maya,' she said, giving Rose's hand a quick shake. 'My brother told me this is your first time attending a polo game?'

'It is, but I'm certainly hoping it's not my last.'

'Well, I'm going to let you ladies get to know each other,' Luis said. 'I'll be back with some other people who've been so looking forward to meeting you.'

Rose tried not to appear as panicked as she felt about being left, and she also fought against the desire to drain her glass, for confidence. Maya's smile had disappeared, and Rose had the distinct feeling that she wasn't so pleased to meet her.

'Your family has polo in their blood, so I'm sure you'll enjoy the game today,' Maya said, with a coolness that Rose was certain she hadn't imagined.

'So your brother told me, although I have to admit that I've never really been around horses until yesterday, let alone understood polo,' Rose said. 'It's all new to me, but I'm very interested to see what it's all about.'

Maya gave her a long glance, and Rose had the distinct feeling that Maya didn't trust her.

'May I ask you a question?' said Maya.

'Of course.'

'Is it true that you never met Valentina or visited the Santiago property before? Even when you were a girl?'

'All true,' Rose said, before lifting her glass and deciding that draining half of it sat squarely between a bad decision and a good one. 'And if I look out of place, it's because I am, but Luis and Benjamin both insisted that I stay, so here I am. I'm doing my best to fit in.'

'We're a very close family here, Rose, and we all adored Valentina and felt very protective of her, so I'm sure you can understand how surprised we were when you arrived.'

Rose could feel the words between them that were going unsaid, knew that really Maya wanted to tell her they didn't trust her and wished she'd just go home. 'I can assure you that no one was more surprised by all this than me.'

Maya's eyebrows lifted, as if she were about to ask another question, but Rose was saved by Luis, who came back with an older couple who seemed just as curious about her, only far more friendly than Benjamin's sister.

'It was lovely to meet you, Maya,' Rose said, as Luis commanded her attention. 'I'm sure our paths will cross again.'

But as she turned away, she felt herself hoping that they

didn't. Either Maya was extremely protective of her brother, or perhaps she was worried about Valentina's legacy. Maybe she'd expected something to be left to her? Either way, Rose doubted the other woman was ever going to warm to her.

'Here we go!' Luis declared as the game began, sparing Rose more small talk as everyone turned their attention to the game being played in front of them.

When a waiter wearing all black came past with more champagne, Rose happily took another glass, clapping as Benjamin's team got a goal and gasping when three of the players galloped so close she felt the ground vibrate beneath her feet.

But no matter who had the ball or what was happening on the field, Rose found her eyes permanently drawn to Benjamin. His dark hair curled slightly at the back, damp and clinging to his neck, his face partly obscured by the helmet he wore, but somehow he still looked breathtakingly good.

She smiled to herself as she took another sip of champagne, imagining what it would have been like to have Jessica and her mum there, elbowing her in the side the very second they knew she was attracted to him. They would most definitely have approved of her little crush, and she found that the more champagne she sipped, the more she could fantasise about what it might be like to get to know Benjamin a little more intimately.

'Rose,' Luis said, touching her arm and drawing her from her thoughts. 'That's the end of the chukka. May I take you around the tent to introduce you?'

She smiled politely. 'Of course.'

'There are so many people hoping you'll fall in love with polo,' Luis said, leaning in and speaking in a low voice. 'Without the Santiago sponsorship...'

Rose nodded. She understood what he was trying to tell her. 'Whether I stay here or not, the only thing that matters to me is preserving whatever legacy Valentina left behind. If that means sponsoring polo, which was clearly dear to her heart, and if there's enough money to continue to do so, then I have no intention of letting the polo community down. I sense that they loved her very much.'

'Spoken like a true Santiago,' he said. 'Maria! Lola! Come and meet Rose!'

Rose stifled her groan and took another sip of champagne. If only the next chukka would start so she'd have an excuse to run to the front of the tent and watch the game.

'You look like you're enjoying yourself.'

Benjamin was holding a towel around his neck, and she found her eyes transfixed on him. His hair was curled and damp with sweat, his top clung to his body, and she had the distinct realisation that she needed to be very, very careful where Benjamin was concerned. He was gorgeous, there was no other way to describe him, and he was also proving impossible to look away from.

She reminded herself to blink and forced her eyes back to his, which only worked to embarrass her as he'd clearly seen the way she was looking at him.

'I think I've had too much champagne.'

'I never would have guessed,' he teased, before stepping over the little fence separating the tent from the field and ducking his head low towards her. 'Would you like to get out of here? I always find the small talk at these things very painful.'

'Yes,' she whispered. 'I kept sipping to avoid talking, and now...' Rose wobbled and Benjamin caught her arm, which made her giggle.

'Come with me,' he said. 'Once you get out of here, you'll be fine.'

She clung to his arm and carefully stepped back over the

little white picket fence, kicking off her shoes and carrying them in her hand as they walked together, the grass soft beneath her toes. Rose leaned into him, not caring that he was hot and sweaty. She even dropped her head to his shoulder for a moment, hoping it would ease the pounding that was starting in her head and wishing she'd stopped after one glass. Drinking alcohol in the heat wasn't her smartest idea.

'Where are you taking me?' she asked.

'To where we keep the horses,' he said. 'Away from the crowds.' Benjamin grinned when he glanced down at her. 'I think you'll like it.'

She looked up then and saw the horse trucks lined up and the grooms watering and caring for the ponies. It was as far removed as possible from the tented section where she'd been, and it looked like the perfect place to hide from all the people wanting to talk to her.

'I'd put your shoes on though, if I were you. Unless you don't mind standing in horse dung.'

Rose didn't need to be told twice, leaning heavily into him as she balanced on one foot and then the next to slip her feet back into her shoes.

'You know, you're nothing like I expected,' Benjamin said, catching her wrist when she wobbled.

'What did you expect?' she asked, leaning closer to him so that his head blocked the sun from her eyes.

Benjamin stared down at her, his eyes flickering to her mouth before meeting hers again. 'An uptight English woman who'd never think of getting drunk at her first polo match.'

Rose laughed. 'Well, it turns out that I've managed to surprise both of us.'

'It was all too much over there, huh?' he asked, when they resumed their stroll again.

'This year...' She hesitated, not sure how much to say and feeling a lot more sober all of a sudden. 'I've had a lot of change in my life lately. I'll tell you about it another day, but I just don't feel like meeting new people and making small talk right now, and I know everyone was only being friendly and Luis wants me to feel welcome, but—'

'But sometimes you just don't need all the noise. I get that,' he said. 'It's why I spend more time with horses than people, and it's why I retreat back here so I can just enjoy the peace and have a quiet drink on my own after a game.'

Rose could tell from the tone of his voice that he wasn't just trying to placate her—there was something about the way he'd spoken that told her he actually did understand how she felt.

'One of my closest friends died a few years back,' Benjamin said as they neared a sleek black truck. He opened a compartment on the side and took out two bottles of water, passing her one. 'After that, I kind of closed myself off. I didn't even know if I'd play polo anymore, until Valentina visited me one day. And trust me, when a woman in her nineties pays you a visit and says she needs to talk, you answer the door.'

Rose smiled at the thought, imagining a spindly white-haired woman knocking on the door. Whatever she said had clearly worked to get him back in the saddle.

'Did she help you, or did she order you back?'

'She helped me. Valentina told me that she understood loss more than anyone, but that I had a choice to make,' he said, unscrewing the lid on his water and taking a long sip. Rose found her eyes drawn to his throat, somehow finding even the way he swallowed water mesmerising. 'She said I needed to decide then and there whether I was going to live a full, beautiful life or whether I was going to lose myself to sadness.'

Rose felt a shiver run through her.

'I didn't know what she was referring to at the time, but now I'm guessing that it was placing her daughter for adoption. She appeared to live an incredible life, and I believe she did, but it wasn't because her life was perfect. She wanted me to know that she understood my pain.'

'Your friend, did he die playing polo?'

Benjamin took such a deep breath that his shoulders lifted. 'He was training one of his horses and they both fell. His horse crushed him in a totally freak accident.'

'I'm sorry.'

His smile was tight, but she could see the softness in his eyes that told her how much he cared, how much it still hurt. Which was why it was on the tip of her tongue to tell him about her mother.

'One day you'll tell me about what you've been through?' he asked. 'When you're ready?'

Rose stared at him, almost ready but then suddenly not. She didn't want to talk about what she'd lost, not today. Not with him. 'I will.'

'So, what did you think of the polo?'

He turned away from her and lifted his shirt over his head, leaving her to stare at his golden, muscled back. Rose was suddenly very much in need of her bottle of water. He changed into an identical shirt before turning back to her.

'It was impressive,' she said. 'You were impressive.'

He raised a brow. 'You figured out the rules.'

'I did.'

They stood for a moment, him seeming to consider her as they stared at each other, and when he held out his hand for her now-empty water bottle, she found herself placing her palm against his instead of the bottle.

Benjamin's lips curved at one corner. 'You've had too much to drink,' he murmured.

'I have,' she whispered back. 'Which I'll have you know is very rare for me.'

'If you hadn't,' he said, taking a step closer to her, 'I might kiss you.'

Rose waited, catching her bottom lip beneath her teeth as she stared up at him, waiting, *hoping*, for him to kiss her. But instead of pressing his lips to hers, he leaned in close and whispered against her ear, his breath soft and warm against her skin.

'You know, I'm still hoping to change your mind about Argentina.'

Rose swallowed. 'What are you hoping to make me think?'

A smile teased across his mouth. 'That there's nowhere more in the world you belong.'

14

THE SANTIAGO FAMILY ESTATE, ARGENTINA, 1939

Valentina lay beneath the ceibo tree, gazing up at the green leaves as she nestled closer to Felipe, the sunlight barely able to filter through the thick canopy above. Their horses were tethered nearby, happy to rest in the morning sun while their young riders stretched out on the grass at the farthest corner of the sprawling farm. From the very first morning that she'd learnt to ride with him, it had become a daily occurrence, so long as the weather was fine, and it had become the one thing that Valentina looked forward to the most.

'I wish we didn't have to go back,' Valentina murmured, turning on her side and staring at Felipe. She propped herself up on one elbow, her long dark hair sliding over her shoulder and brushing his face. 'I wish we could stay here all day.'

He lifted his hand and skimmed his fingers across the bare skin of her arm, trailing from her shoulder all the way down to her wrist. Felipe didn't say anything straightaway, instead leaning towards her and catching her lips against his, kissing her so softly she felt she might melt into his arms when they went around her.

'If your father caught us—'

Valentina reached down and stroked his hair from his cocoa-brown eyes. 'Then why don't we just tell him? Wouldn't it be better for him to know? I don't want to keep what we have a secret anymore.'

Felipe's eyes widened. 'Tell him?'

She stole another kiss as one of the horses nickered, starting to become restless after so long waiting to be ridden back. They'd been out for longer than they should have, which meant they'd probably have to gallop home now so she didn't get into trouble, but sometimes she dreamed about not returning in secrecy, of telling her family about Felipe and the love she felt for him. After all these years of loving him, she was ready.

'Yes, I think we should tell him. I think you should ask for his permission,' she whispered against his cheek. 'How long are we supposed to wait?'

'And what if he says no?' Felipe asked. 'What if, once he finds out, we have to put an end to this?'

'He won't, I'm certain of it,' she murmured. 'All he wants is for me to be happy, and if it's you who makes me happy, if he truly understands how we feel, then I think he will give us his blessing.'

So long as Felipe didn't ask her mother's permission, because she knew that she would rather lock her in her bedroom for the rest of her life than accept that Valentina was in love with a boy like Felipe. Her mother had much grander ambitions for her only daughter, was always talking of the matches she'd like to make for her, tempered only by the fact that her father insisted they wait until Valentina was older, so that she could have a say in whom she married. Secretly, she guessed that her father wanted to keep her at home for longer, and she was only too happy to oblige.

'We'd best get back,' Felipe said. 'Basilio won't forgive me if he has to send out a search party to look for us. It'll put an end to us before I ever gather the courage to tell him.'

Valentina sighed and let Felipe pull her to her feet, their fingers interlinked, wishing they could have their morning all over again. But as she was smoothing her hands down her blouse to brush away the creases, not wanting anyone to guess that they'd been rolling around on the grass, she heard galloping hooves and her heart began to race as a lone rider came into view.

No one other than her and Felipe galloped around the farm like that, especially this early in the morning, which meant that something was wrong. Something was very, very wrong.

'Miss Valentina,' the breathless rider called as he approached. 'Come quickly!'

Valentina looked helplessly to Felipe, who quickly leapt up and readied the horses for their ride back.

Please don't be Papa. Let it be anyone but my darling papa.

'Papa!' Valentina called as she ran into the house, throwing her leather gloves to the ground and shrugging out of her jacket, hot from the fast ride back. Her heart was beating so hard it felt as if it might explode out of her chest, her breath coming in heavy pants that made it almost impossible to draw enough air into her lungs.

The doctor was already there, but she couldn't see or hear her mother, only their staff scurrying around as if they weren't sure where they should be. Their maid, Ana, was sobbing near the door, and the worker who'd come to fetch her stood now with his hat folded in his hands, as tears trickled down his cheeks, but it was the doctor to whom Valentina gave her full attention, her heart racing even faster as she clocked his solemn expression.

She already knew what the news was going to be.

'What happened?' she asked, as she entered the ground-floor bedroom where he must have been taken, sitting down on the edge of the four-poster bed and staring at her father's ashen face. She reached for her father's hand, but quickly withdrew it when she felt his cool, damp skin. It didn't feel like her papa's hand, and if this was the last time she held it, that wasn't how she wanted to remember his touch. This wasn't how she wanted to remember *him*.

'Miss Santiago, I regret to inform you that there was nothing I could do for your father.'

'He's gone?' she whispered, looking back at her father. 'But we had breakfast together this morning, I just saw him, I—'

The doctor reached out and placed his hand gently over her arm, and she found herself staring down at where he touched her. She could hear his words but they made absolutely no sense, and she wasn't sure whether she wanted to scream at him that he was wrong or slide to the ground and beg him to tell her different news. Because this couldn't be true—none of it could be true!

'Your father suffered a heart attack,' he explained, his voice low and soft. 'There was nothing anyone could have done to save him, it happened so quickly and so unexpectedly. I'm sorry. Your father was a wonderful man.'

Valentina began to nod, and she wished Felipe had come with her, holding her hand as she'd received the news, so that she hadn't been alone. Only minutes ago, she'd been imploring him to tell her beloved papa about their relationship, and now he was gone. Felipe was never going to be able to ask him for her hand, and she was never going to have the chance to tell him that she'd loved Felipe since she was a young girl at her very first harvest. That she'd found the love match he'd been so determined that she find.

She blinked away her tears, trying her best to stay composed in front of the doctor even as her body began to tremble. Her mother should have been here, by her side, but instead Valentina was alone.

'Thank you, for coming so promptly,' she said, trying to find the right words. 'I appreciate what you did to try to save my father, that you came here, that...' It didn't matter how hard Valentina tried—she simply didn't know what else to say.

The doctor nodded and let go of her as she lost her words, reaching for his black leather bag and doing up the zip as she watched on, keeping her gaze fixed on him so that she didn't have to see her father. A shudder ran through her as she realised that someone would have to decide what to do with his body, that the doctor was leaving and there was no one else there to tell her what to do next. Her mother clearly hadn't been able to cope and had taken to her bedroom or sought refuge somewhere else in the house.

'He was a great man, Miss Santiago, one of the very best,' the doctor said. 'I'm truly sorry for your loss. Please pay my respects to your mother when she returns.'

'You haven't seen my mother?' Valentina asked, confused. Where would her mother be at this time of the day?

'Unfortunately, I have not. Your maid let me in when I arrived.'

Valentina nodded and waited for him to leave the room, before she rushed back to her father and collapsed over him, her tears coming in powerful sobs as she cried over the body of the man she'd loved more than life itself, still not believing that he was gone.

Why did you have to leave me? Papa, it can't be true, you can't be gone.

'Mama,' Valentina gasped, rising and holding her arms out to fold herself against her mother when she heard her return.

She'd been sitting beside the bed with her father for hours, wait-ing, not wanting her mother to discover what had happened without being there to break the news. 'I've been waiting for you. Something terrible has happened.'

But instead of the embrace she'd been expecting after so many hours of holding vigil alone, her mother's body was rigid, her arms not even moving from her sides to return her embrace. Instead, she was as stiff and cold as the body lying on the bed.

'Did you know?'

Valentina blinked back at her mother, wrapping her arms around herself as she stared into her cold eyes. She glanced back at her father, wishing that he was still there, that he'd reprimand her mother for being so cold towards her, that he could see the way his daughter was being treated in his absence. But her father was gone; it was just her against the world now.

'That he was unwell?' Valentina asked, confused. 'That he was going to die?' She didn't know what her mother was asking her. 'If you're asking whether I knew he might die, then of course the answer is no! But I begged him to see a doctor the day of the polo. Mama, I begged *you* to make him see a doctor, but you wouldn't listen! No one would listen to me.' She was breathless, her hand over her chest now as if her own heart might give out from the pain.

'Valentina, I want to know why he did this. I want to know what sorcery you used to make your father do this to me!'

Tears began to slip down Valentina's cheeks as she stared back at her mother, registering the coldness of her gaze. 'Mama, I don't know what you're talking about,' Valentina whispered. 'But Papa is dead, Papa—'

'Left you almost everything!' her mother erupted, her cry echoing through the room, loud enough for anyone else in the house to hear. 'Our home, the business, most of his fortune... *everything*! The only mention of me in his last will and testament is to ensure that I'm not left destitute by having a roof over my head and a monthly stipend, a request that he implores his beloved daughter to uphold. And my Bruno has received nothing more than a collection of watches and the house in Buenos Aires!'

Valentina swallowed, quickly wiping at her cheeks with her fingertips. But it didn't help, because more only fell, making her skin slick with tears as she realised where her mother had been and why she hadn't been there to sit with her father's body. Why she had already left the house before the doctor arrived. Her father had been deeply in love, he'd told Valentina as much when they'd been together, recounting the story of how he met his wife and how he still adored her, but clearly the same could not be said for her mother.

'You've already met with the lawyer?' Valentina forced herself to ask. *While he was lying here? While I was sitting with his still-warm body? Before the doctor even arrived?* 'You were here when it happened, and instead of staying with him and waiting for the doctor, you just left? You thought it was more important to travel into town to discover the contents of his will than to stay with his body?'

Her mother stared back at her, her gaze still so cold that it sent a shiver through Valentina. And she couldn't help but notice that her mother never even looked at Basilio's body, not once—the man who'd been the heart and lifeblood of their family, who'd meant everything to her, suddenly seemed invisible to her mother. Valentina had expected her mother to be in floods of tears, to appear broken; but instead, she was calculating how much money she expected.

'I didn't know, Mama. How would I have known something like that?' she whispered.

'All those hours you spent with him, the times he took you to the office and you had his ear,' her mother said, 'he must have said something. What did you do to make him turn on me like this? What kind of lies did you tell him?'

Valentina straightened her shoulders, hearing her father's voice in her head, and suddenly knowing in her heart why he'd chosen her. It had always been her—she could see now that he'd been preparing her for this day her entire life—only she'd never expected her mother to be her enemy. And it was likely her father had never expected this day to come so soon, either. He would have thought he had years to prepare her for taking over the family business and managing their affairs, and instead here she was, a girl of only seventeen, facing the most difficult challenge of her life at the same time as grieving the one person in the world that she loved the most.

'Papa wanted me to take over the family business,' she said, forcing her voice to be clear and lifting her head, even though her throat was hoarse and her eyes were so gritty and sore that it hurt just opening them. 'Papa said that I was like him, that I could continue to make our family business prosper, that he was teaching me so that I understood his way, and the way of his father before him. But he never told me that—'

'Bruno will run this family's business!' her mother snapped. 'Your father indulged you your entire life, Valentina, making you believe that you could do anything. But this is a man's world, no matter what he told you, and your brother will be managing our family's affairs from now on. I don't care what his will states, Bruno is the man of the family now that your father is gone, and you will show him the respect he deserves. You're not even an adult, so I'll have no problem taking over from here.'

Valentina lowered her gaze, not about to fight with her mother when her father's body lay behind them. He would not have wanted them to argue, but she also knew that he didn't want her brother to be his successor, either. Basilio had been a wonderful stepfather to Bruno and cared deeply for him, but he'd wanted his own flesh and blood to take over what he'd built, to care for the people in his employ and grow their wealth for generations to come. Someone he trusted to uphold the traditions he'd instilled.

'I will appoint your brother to find a suitable husband for you in the interim, while I arrange everything with the lawyers. I'll have the will overturned immediately, so that it remains a secret.'

'Mama, no,' Valentina said. 'I want to know all the contents of Papa's will. I intend on honouring whatever he—'

'Valentina, he wanted to gift his *stablehand* a house, and all his employees thousands of pesos on his death! He was clearly not in his right mind, and any fool would be able to see that. I won't be giving away any of our fortune to anyone, and if you think I'll let you follow his wishes, then you are very, very wrong.'

No, you're wrong, Mama. He knew exactly what he was doing. He wanted to reward those who'd worked hard for him, and Felipe's father was more than just a stablehand, he was his right-hand man, the person he trusted with his most prized ponies. And he would never have called him his stablehand, either.

'I will not marry,' Valentina said, more boldly than she'd ever said anything to her mother before. 'You cannot simply make me marry any man whom you or Bruno choose. My job—'

'Your *job*?' Her mother laughed. 'Your *job* is to be a respectable daughter, Valentina, who will appropriately mourn her father and then take a husband. You're seventeen years old and I should have had a fiancé arranged for you months ago, instead of letting your father indulge you with his notions of a love match. You'll be your husband's problem after that, and whatever I do allow you to inherit will become his property, not yours.'

'He wanted a love match for me, so that I could have what he had,' she whispered.

'You thought your father and I were a love match?' her

mother laughed again. 'Oh, don't get me wrong, I loved your father. But if he'd been penniless I wouldn't have so much as cast an eye towards him. I loved him because of the life he could give Bruno and me, and I will mourn him with great love because of the fortune he has left behind.'

For me. He left that fortune for me!

Valentina tried not to cry, but it was impossible. She felt like a little girl again as she fell to her knees, her sobs uncontrollable as her shoulders shook, her face buried in her hands. Her papa had insisted that she could choose her own husband one day, that she would have choices in her life, that no one would ever force a Santiago to do anything against their will. *How wrong you were. He's not even cold in the ground and everything is being taken from me.*

She took a deep breath and looked back at her mother, knowing that she couldn't wait any longer to tell her the truth. If she was going to be left penniless, then she was at least going to marry the man she loved. 'Mama, I already know whom I want to marry.' Valentina paused. 'I'm in love with Felipe, and I will leave with him and you'll never have to so much as look at me ever again.'

'Felipe?' she repeated, before her eyes narrowed. 'The stableboy?'

She wanted to tell her that Felipe wasn't just a stableboy—he was the son of her father's most trusted and loved employee—but she didn't get the chance.

'Valentina, your father told you fairy tales your entire life. But you listen to me, and you listen to me very, very carefully,' her mother said, bending down and roughly forcing her fingers beneath Valentina's chin, making her head jut up. 'I make the rules now, and that means there will be no more riding, no more unaccompanied visits to the stables, and no more seeing that stableboy again. Do you hear me? You will marry a respectable young man of my choosing, and you will most certainly not be disappearing. We have a family name to uphold, after all.'

Valentina had never known hate before, but as she stared back into her mother's cold eyes, she understood what it was to despise another human being. Her mother had often been aloof with her; it had always been her father who'd swept her into his arms and showed affection, but she understood now how much her mother had resented their closeness. That she'd never loved Valentina's father so much as she'd loved the life he'd given her, that she'd chosen to bear his child to strengthen their marriage, to provide a life for the son she adored.

'Yes, Mama,' Valentina lied, her voice low, closing her eyes as her mother let go of her, the clack of her heels telling Valentina that she was walking away. There was no point in arguing with her, not now.

But once the room was silent, Valentina pushed herself to her feet and went to her father, bending low over the bed and pressing a final kiss to his cheek, lingering as she did so, inhaling the gentle scent of his cologne and committing the softness of his skin to memory. How such a strong, wonderful man could be taken from the world without warning was beyond her, and even as she gazed down at him, it was almost impossible to believe that he was gone. But he was gone, and she was going to have to learn to live without him.

I won't let her do this, Papa. I won't let her take away everything you wanted, I promise. I will spend the rest of my life making you proud.

And she wouldn't stop seeing Felipe, either. He might not be wealthy or from a landowning family, and he would never live up to her mother's expectations, but he loved her, and right now she needed to be held, to be comforted by someone who'd loved and respected her father. By someone who knew her for whom she truly was, and who knew the man her father had been.

Valentina whispered her goodbyes to her papa and tiptoed from the room, taking off her shoes so she could walk silently through the house and slip out the door, running across the grass barefoot and not stopping until she came to the stables where she knew he would be waiting for her.

Felipe would know what to do, and if he didn't, then they would both find a way to honour her father's name and be together.

15

PRESENT DAY

Rose stood in front of the wardrobe and tried to tell herself that she wasn't doing anything wrong. But it still felt strange to be going through the private things of another without permission.

She gave you permission when she left everything to you in her will.

Rose stood on tiptoe and took the large plastic box down that had been placed on one of the shelves—not hidden away but in full view, almost as if it might have recently been opened. She'd already looked through the clothes and other personal effects that had been left behind, but they were simply the clothes of a petite older woman, as well as some very impressive pieces of jewellery that she presumed had been gifted to Valentina when she was much younger. Rose would have them carefully packed away and stored while she considered what, if anything, to do with them, but her curiosity had been piqued with the discovery of the box.

Holding it, she sat on the bed, opening the lid and gasping when she found a matching piece of blue silk to the one she'd found in her tiny box. She took it out and felt the familiar touch of the soft fabric, before setting it aside and carefully going through the rest of the contents in the box.

There were a handful of photos in an envelope, and she took them out and slowly looked through each one, smiling at the beautiful girl looking back at her. Valentina had been a gorgeous child, with thick almost-black hair that curled down to her waist, and the biggest eyes Rose had ever seen. There was a man beside her in some of the photos, sporting a thick moustache and a smile that always seemed to be directed towards the young girl, presumably her father, and in one of the photos there was a very attractive woman, slender and tall, with enough of a resemblance to the child to make Rose believe she was Valentina's mother.

Rose ran the tip of her index finger over the face of the little girl, studying her before filing the photos back into the envelope. There was another photo that she found once she put the envelope aside, of a young man sitting on a horse and holding a polo mallet. Rose turned the photo over to see if it had anything written on it, and she was pleased to find the name *Felipe* along with the date 1938. She stared at it a while longer before going through the rest of the treasures, knowing in her heart that these were the things that Valentina had held dear, the things that she hadn't wanted to part with, for them to have been kept in the box, separate from her other belongings.

There was a little velvet box, which held a small gold ring, and she ran her thumb over it and held it up, hoping to find an engraving on the inside and smiling when she did.

She held it a while longer, before trying to fit it on her ring finger and failing. Valentina's hands must have been incredibly petite, as the only finger Rose could slip it onto was her little one. She stared at it, wondering who Felipe was and why his name had never come up when the lawyer had given her the name of Valentina's one and only husband, from whom she'd received an annulment. Rose guessed the ring was from her wedding, although she couldn't be sure.

There was a pretty dress with soft blue dots on it at the very bottom of the box, along with a well-loved teddy bear with its arms barely hanging on by a thread. Rose placed the teddy on her bed, propped against the pillows, and took out one of the last things in the box: a small bottle of perfume. She took off the lid and held it to her nose, expecting it to either smell bad or not at all after so many years, but the scent was divine still and reminded Rose of the peonies her mother had had such a penchant for. She dabbed some to her wrists and behind her ears, liking the fact that she had something to connect her to the great-grandmother she'd never known.

But as much as a trip down memory lane she imagined the contents of the box had been for Valentina, to her they only told snippets of a story that failed to provide answers to any of the questions she had. Her only clue to the past was the name Felipe, who must have meant a great deal to Valentina for her to have a ring with their names engraved inside it.

And the piece of silk. She'd left it behind for her daughter all those years ago, and she'd kept a matching piece for herself, which showed just how important it must have been. Rose reached for it again, lifting the silk to her face and inhaling, as if the scent of it might give her another clue. But it smelt of nothing.

Who were you, Valentina, and why, with everything at your disposal, did you choose to place your daughter for adoption? Why did you never come back for her?

Part of Rose wondered if she'd ever find out the answers she sought, and after she'd packed the box away, she tucked herself up in bed, hugging one of the pillows tight to her as she thought about her Mum. She would have given anything to have her to talk to. To tell her about Benjamin and their day at the polo, to ask her about her grandmother and whether she'd even hinted at being adopted, to have her to explore Argentina with and to pore over all the clues from the past, so they could try to figure out the mystery together.

She squeezed her eyes shut tight, knowing that it didn't help to wish for what could never be, but finding it impossible not to when all she wanted was her mum back.

You never did tell me how I was supposed to navigate life without you, Mum.

If only there were a manual for how to deal with losing the single most important person in your life. Because if there was, Rose would have been first in line to buy it.

The next day, Rose was sitting outside in the courtyard, tucked beneath the shade of the pergola looking over the latest round of documents sent from the lawyer, when Benjamin appeared. He looked dusty and hot—the exact opposite of how she felt—and she smiled, putting down what she'd been reading, happy to see him. She'd been hoping to see him since the polo game on Saturday, but other than waving to her from a distance, they hadn't spent any more time together since.

'You've finished for the day?' she asked.

'I have. But I've come to convince you that there's another game of polo you have to attend next weekend.'

'Another game?' she asked. 'I've only just recovered from watching the first one.'

Benjamin laughed, before indicating the seat across from her.

'Please, sit, I'd be happy for the company. I'm so tired of looking through all this paperwork.'

He leaned forward and took the orange juice she'd poured earlier and then forgotten about, taking a long, slow sip. She watched him, drawn to his easy manner and how comfortable she felt around him already. Although she could feel the creep of a blush when she thought about how close they'd come to kissing the other day.

'I'd offer to help, but paperwork isn't my thing.'

'Would you believe that for years it *was* my thing?' she asked.

'For your work?'

She nodded. 'Yes. When I was a lawyer.'

Benjamin took another sip of her drink, ignoring her raised brows. 'You said *was*.'

Rose groaned. 'I'm still turning the decision over and over in my mind, but I officially resigned from my job this morning. I have no idea whether I've done the right thing or not, but I had to give them an answer and I wasn't ready to go back.'

'You're brave,' he said, sitting back and folding his arms behind his head.

'Brave or stupid,' she replied. 'I'm not quite sure which one yet.'

'Well, I'd give you the benefit of the doubt and say brave,' Benjamin said with a wink. 'Does this mean you've decided to stay?'

Rose pretended to ignore his question; she was still so uncertain of how she felt or what she wanted to do. 'So tell me about this next polo game,' she said, happy to turn the subject away from her and back to him. 'You're playing?'

'I am, but it's a friendly match rather than a professional one. We have a long lunch afterwards and drink wine, so it's very relaxed.'

She smiled, liking the sound of it. 'Where is this relaxed polo game? Will I be able to find my own way there?'

Benjamin's grin hinted there was something he wasn't telling her.

'I feel like I'm being tricked, but I have no clue why.'

'Every year we hold a social tournament, for all the local

families to come and watch and be part of,' he said. 'It's some-thing everyone looks forward to, and we play mixed teams of men and women.'

Rose frowned. 'And the catch is?'

'That it's held here,' he said. 'The Santiagos have hosted it for almost eighty years, with a break of a few years during the war. It's quite the tradition.'

'Here? It's held here, at this property?'

'Now you can see why I want you to say yes,' Benjamin said. 'Without your approval...'

'Of course, but please, make it simple for me. I'm not used to being hostess.'

'Everyone is so looking forward to meeting you.'

Her eyes widened. 'Everyone? Who's everyone?'

'Everyone who knew Valentina. They want to meet the hidden granddaughter. They're curious about you, but it won't be like the other day. These are just good local people to whom the Santiagos mean a lot, and I know you'll like them.'

She groaned and shut her eyes for a moment. The reason she was loving it here so much was because it was so peaceful and she didn't have to see anyone except for Benjamin. She'd never spent so much time on her own, but oddly, she'd never felt so content.

'How about we start by you meeting just a few local people then,' he said, and when his fingers brushed hers, her eyes popped back open.

'Neighbours?' she asked.

'I was thinking my family,' he said. 'They're very interested to meet you.'

Rose grimaced. 'Have you asked your sister if she wants to see me again? Because she was the opposite of friendly at the polo.'

'My sister thinks you're here to stake your claim and put everything up for sale,' he said. 'She's loyal to the Santiago family and their legacy, and she needs to spend time with you to get to know you. I think you'll like her.'

'She did her very best to make sure I didn't feel welcome, although I can understand why,' Rose told him, nervous about the idea of seeing his sister again.

'Give them the chance to meet you properly,' Benjamin said, his voice gentle. 'I think you'll enjoy yourself, and my parents might be able to help you with some of your questions about the family. And I'll handle my sister.'

'When?' she found herself asking, despite the thought filling her with horror.

'How about dinner tomorrow night?'

Rose refused to be nervous, and she also refused to be scared of his sister. 'Thank you for the invitation, I'd love to come.' Maya might not have been the friendliest when she'd met her, but Rose was curious to meet the rest of Benjamin's family. 'And you're welcome to host the polo here. I have no intention of changing any traditions.'

Benjamin touched her hand again, and as she looked into his eyes, she wondered for a second whether he was finally going to lean closer and kiss her. But instead, he removed his hand and stood, smiling down at her.

'*Adiós*,' he said. 'Don't sit out here too long with your papers.'

She lifted her hand in a wave and sat back in her chair, reaching for her orange juice and drinking what was left of it. The thought of dinner with his family was oddly terrifying, but part of her was curious, too, about what they would be like. Not to mention that she'd always loved having dinner at the homes of friends with large families—the conversation and banter had always made her wish for siblings of her own.

But staying for dinner and then the polo meant that there was no way she could make her rescheduled flight to New York. She'd come to Argentina thinking it was something she had to do on her way to visit Jessica, but she was quickly starting to realise that there was something about Argentina that was making her want to stay, at least for a little bit longer.

Rose sat back and looked around her, at the citrus trees in big terracotta pots, the pool stretching out before her, the blue sky above. Being here was good for the soul, and as much as she knew this wasn't her real life, she also knew that it would be stupid to leave in a hurry when she had nowhere else to be.

Just stay. Give yourself another week or two. Hell, stay a month. She'd never lived abroad or travelled; she'd jumped straight into her law career without even catching her breath after university, and the past year had drained every last bit of her energy. So long as Jessica didn't mind her changing her flights, it would be stupid not to stay, wouldn't it?

'You're not coming to New York, are you?' said Jessica the moment her face came into view. 'I've actually been waiting for you to call, believe it or not.'

Rose shook her head. 'I can't believe I'm saying this, but no, I'm not.' She took a deep breath. 'I don't know what's happened to me, but the more I find out about my ancestors, the more time I spend at this property and discover the past—'

'Rose, you don't have to explain yourself to me,' Jessica said. 'Just tell me whether this has anything to do with Benjamin, because I feel like you haven't told me enough about the tall dark Argentine who's clearly captured your attention. I have a feeling it's not all about the past.'

She laughed. Trust Jessica. 'Honestly, he is a part of it, but he's not the main reason. I just, I don't know how to even explain, but I already feel like this place is part of me. I'm just not ready to leave yet, and it's the strangest thing to say, but I actually feel like I'm finally discovering who I am.'

'I understand. Trust me,' she said, lowering her voice to a whisper. 'If I had the chance to have some gorgeous man sweep me off my feet in a foreign country...'

'I heard that!'

Ryan's voice in the background made them both burst into laughter, and Rose was so relieved she'd called to say she wasn't coming rather than sending a message. She'd tried to compose it and it had been impossible, and she needed to chat with her friend.

'You've done so much for me, Jess, and I don't know how I'll ever be able to repay you for all your support. I promise I'll come and see you before I go back to London, though. I can't wait to see you and the girls, despite the delay.' She laughed. 'And you, Ryan, because we all know you're still listening.'

Ryan appeared in the frame behind Jessica and gave her a wave, looking guilty as charged.

'You forget that there are so many things I'm going to need you for, Rose. You make it sound like this is a one-way street with me helping you, but it's not,' Jessica said, and when Rose saw tears shining from her friend's eyes, she welled up, too. 'When the girls leave for college, the day they get married, when they move out of home...'

'I'll be the crazy aunt crying with their mum or consoling you with wine and chocolate,' Rose said. 'And I'll be proud to be there for every milestone. You know I'd never miss any of those things, and if there's ever a time you need me, I'll be on a plane to New York before you know it.'

'Well, now we have all that sorted, get off the phone and go and enjoy your evening,' Jessica said, smiling through her tears. 'And know that we love you, and that you're welcome here any time, whether that's next week, next month or even next year. You never have to explain yourself to me, and you never have to ask for permission to arrive on our doorstep.'

Rose blew her a kiss as they said goodbye, setting her phone down and lying back on her bed once the screen was black. Initially when she'd arrived at the house, she'd considered moving into one of the other rooms, but there was something soothing about the main bedroom with its enormous four-poster bed and view out over the property that she felt drawn to.

She lay there a moment and stared up at the white canopy above, the edges caught up for now, and visualised lying there in the middle of the summer with the sides down so that she could sleep with the windows thrown wide open. Initially, the quiet had scared her. She'd yearned for the familiarity of her flat in London—the noises of traffic and the city outside her window. But after her second night here, she'd realised that a change had been what she was truly yearning for, without even knowing it. The silence had been a relief, allowing her to sleep deeply and wake rested, almost as if her body had reset being somewhere different without all the noise of her usual life, and even now there was a peacefulness about how she was feeling that she couldn't quite describe. *It's as if I can finally breathe again. It's as if I can see clearly after months of blinking through fog.*

Eventually Rose sat up and reached for the little wooden box that she'd kept beside her bed ever since she'd arrived. She always returned the piece of silk and the figurine to it whenever she'd had them out, and she took them out again now, lying back down with them clasped in her palm. And not for the first time, she wondered if Valentina had ever lain in this room, or on this bed, holding the horse in her hand as she tried to figure out what to do. Rose was determined to discover what had happened to her and why she'd come to make the decision to leave her baby at Hope's House, and she feared that she might never discover the answers to her questions if Benjamin's family didn't open up to her. Which meant that she had to find a way to connect with them when she met them all, to get them to trust her and talk to her about the Santiago family.

But if his sister's reaction at the polo was anything to go by, she might have her work cut out for her, no matter what he said. Rose sighed and decided to look through the clothes she'd brought with her. It was just dinner, and she knew that she didn't need his family's approval, but if her hunch was right, then Benjamin's family might be the key to her discovering everything she needed to know about Valentina.

16

Rose hadn't realised that Benjamin's house was within walking distance, although given she was wearing heels, she wouldn't have elected to go on foot anyway. She'd taken the Range Rover in the garage, which had felt like stealing when she'd stood in front of it with keys in hand, but logically she knew that the car was hers now, and she'd used Google Maps to navigate the two-minute drive. It had been a while since she'd driven, since she always used public transport at home, but she'd found it was like riding a bicycle, and other than one too-hard press on the brakes, she realised how easy it would be to get used to having her own car.

When Rose got out of the vehicle she ran her palms down her jeans, studying the house and realising it was like a small version of the Santiago estate, built in a Spanish style with off-white plaster and a terracotta roof. She wondered if it had been designed by the same architect, or whether it was just the style of the era. The door swung open while she was studying the house, and Benjamin appeared, wearing jeans and a black T-shirt, his feet bare as he leaned into the frame. She'd become so used to seeing him in his riding gear that it came as a surprise to find him in casual clothing, his hair freshly washed and still damp from the look of it. He was impossible not to admire.

'I see you found the place easily enough,' he said.

'I did,' she replied, smiling as she met his eyes. 'You could have told me it was so close though. I wouldn't have bothered spending so long inputting it into the GPS.'

'I live a little farther away,' he said, 'but this is still home.'

'You grew up here?' she asked, as she stepped forward.

Benjamin stood back so she could pass, closing the door behind him. 'I did. My parents still live here, and my grandparents before that. It's one of those places that I can't see us ever parting with.'

The smell of something delicious wafted out from the kitchen, and Rose's stomach rumbled. 'Something smells amazing.'

'Everything my mother cooks is amazing, it's what brings me home so often. Do you like to cook?'

Rose grimaced. 'I'm an expert at heating things up,' she said. 'My best friend is a fantastic cook, and so was my mother, but for some reason I never quite figured it out.'

Benjamin's smile faded. '*Was?*'

Rose took a deep breath and cleared her throat as tears pricked her eyes. She hadn't meant to tell him like that, but the words had just slipped out, and now she either had to fumble her way out of what she'd said or lie. And she didn't want to lie to Benjamin. 'My mum passed away just before I came here, which has made finding out about our family and travelling here to Argentina so much harder.'

'When you said the other day that you'd had a tough year—'

'You must be Rose,' came a deep, warm voice, before she and Benjamin could finish their conversation.

Benjamin gave her a sad look that made her wish she hadn't told him about her mother at that exact moment, but she turned from him and smiled when a man, with skin even more golden than Benjamin's and a thick head of silver-streaked hair, appeared.

'I am indeed. And you must be Benjamin's father.'

'Please, call me Alvaro,' he said, taking her hand and then leaning in to kiss her cheek. His palm was warm and his cheek was soft with a close-cropped beard. 'It's a pleasure to have you here, Rose.'

'I'm so grateful to be here for dinner. I was just telling your son that I'm not very accomplished in the kitchen, so a home-cooked meal is most welcome. It smells delicious.'

He gave her a conspiratorial smile and a wink. 'You'll find the women in this family take a little longer to accept someone new, but they tend to show their love through their cooking.'

'Alvaro! Stop cloistering the girl,' came a much louder female voice. 'Rose, thank you for joining us tonight. I'm Martina.'

When Rose caught sight of Benjamin's mother, walking through to them as she took off her apron, she knew that she was going to be the one she had to win over. She guessed that she was in her mid-sixties, her dark hair pulled up into a soft bun at the nape of her neck, wearing a navy and white dress. She was beautiful, and Rose could only guess at how stunning she must have been when she was younger.

'Thank you so much for having me. I hope it's not too much trouble.'

'Trouble?' she laughed. 'Trouble are the two men you've just passed in the hallway. You will be no trouble at all, I'm sure of it.'

Rose glanced back over her shoulder at Benjamin, who was following with his father, and although their conversation sounded light, the way he looked at Rose told her that he was worried about her. She only wished she'd held her tongue and told him in private about her mother.

'Rose, I believe you've already met my daughter, Maya.'

She nodded, braving a smile. 'I have, we met at the polo. It's lovely to see you again.'

Maya's smile could have been warmer, but Rose was left feeling grateful that she'd given her a smile at all. Perhaps tonight wasn't going to be as awkward as she'd thought.

'Do you drink wine?' Benjamin's mother asked.

'I do.'

'Alvaro! Wine!'

Rose swapped amused looks with Benjamin as his father jumped to attention and took a bottle of wine from the table.

'This is a Pinot Noir produced here in Argentina,' Alvaro said, as he poured his daughter a glass first. 'It was actually one of your great-grandmother's favourites, which is why we always kept a bottle on hand.'

Rose lifted it to her lips and paused to inhale before taking a sip. 'It's lovely,' she said. 'I can see why it was a favourite.'

Benjamin's mother had her back turned to them as she prepared food, but Rose loved the way their house was designed, with a big wooden table in the kitchen so that they were all able to chat together while she cooked.

'How are you enjoying the Santiago estate?' Alvaro asked. 'Benjamin seems to think you're very much at home there.'

'He does, does he?' she said, glancing over at him and receiving raised eyebrows in response. 'I have to say that I'm loving spending time here, it's a beautiful place. I'm just having a hard time thinking of it as my own, I suppose.'

Benjamin's sister said something in Spanish and received a sharp response from her mother, which turned into a rapid-fire conversation between her and her brother. Rose found herself glancing away, uncomfortable, and decided to rise and offer her assistance.

'Is there anything I can do to help?' she asked his mother.

'Everything is done, and I'm terrible at sharing my kitchen, but you can take this to the table for me.'

'Well, I'm a terrible cook, so I'm rather grateful you didn't ask me to do something complicated.'

'Your mother didn't teach you to cook?' Martina asked, sounding surprised.

'My mother was a fabulous cook, and my grandmother before her. We actually all lived together, just the three of us, and they were both so good at taking care of me that they always shooed me out of the kitchen.' Her heart broke as she spoke of them, wishing again for just one more moment with the three of them together. 'I wish I'd learnt from them when I still could.'

'Ahh, so you had two mothers,' she said. 'They fussed over you like I fuss over my Benjamin. You're a lucky girl.'

Benjamin came to stand behind Rose, placing a warm hand on her shoulder, which earned an enquiring stare from his mother. Rose wouldn't have been surprised if she'd dropped the spoon she was holding at seeing her son touch their guest, but she appreciated the gesture. She'd always felt that a person showed their true colours when faced with sadness or a difficult situation, and Benjamin had shown her that he cared, which meant a lot. He could easily have stood back and let her tell his mother on her own.

'Rose's mother passed away very recently, before she came here,' Benjamin said, his voice soft as he gently squeezed her shoulder.

'You've lost your mother?'

Rose nodded, wishing they weren't having this conversation in front of a woman who was so maternal that it reminded her acutely of her own mum. 'I did. She had a long illness and I lost her only last month, so it's been a very difficult time.'

'You didn't tell me this?' Martina said, shaking her head at her son. 'How could you not tell me this about our guest?'

'Mama, I only just found out tonight,' he replied, in a tone that made it clear she was not to say anymore on the matter. 'It's why I'm telling you now.'

Rose had never been so taken by surprise when Martina put down the spoon she'd been holding and enveloped Rose in the kind of hug that was usually reserved for family or very close friends. She held her tightly, not letting go for a long time as she whispered something in Spanish, before finally standing back and touching her palm to Rose's cheek.

'I'm sorry for your loss, Rose. There is nothing more painful than losing a mother, so I understand what you're going through.'

'Thank you,' Rose said, as unexpected tears caught in her lashes. 'She meant everything to me, which is why coming here has felt so special but also so very hard. I feel like staying here has given me a break from my real life, from everything I've had to deal with, and I suppose I'm searching for a connection to family now that I don't have anyone left.'

'You lost your grandmother, too?'

'I did. She passed away last year.'

His mother nodded, her hand lingering on Rose's before retrieving her apron and putting it back on. Benjamin picked up the bowl Rose had been about to take and indicated for her to follow him.

'Come and sit down,' he said.

Rose stood at the table, glancing back over at his mother, and then at his sister and father, who were still seated. 'I know you were all very close to the Santiago family, and if my being here makes you uncomfortable for any reason, I understand. I can go.'

'Rose, Valentina's family is our family,' Martina said, as she carried an enormous dish of food to the table and placed it in the middle. 'Please, don't leave. I would very much like to get to know you. We all would.'

Rose looked at each of the faces turned towards her. 'Are you sure? Because—'

'Please, stay,' Benjamin said, holding out his hand to her and beckoning for her to sit beside him. 'Or at least don't go until you've tried my mama's famous paella. We can't let you leave on an empty stomach.'

She hesitated.

'Please stay,' Benjamin said. 'It would mean a lot to me if you did.'

Rose looked between them all, at the warm, hopeful expressions on their faces, and slowly sat down. Talking about her mother had stirred her emotions, but she could see that opening up had changed the way his family were looking at her, too, especially his sister. It was clear they all wanted her to stay, not just Benjamin.

'To family,' Alvaro said, holding up his glass.

Rose held hers in the air before taking a sip and settling in her seat as Martina started to serve them all. The food smelt delicious, and she couldn't wait to taste it.

'Rose, Benjamin has told us that you didn't know that Valentina was your great-grandmother,' Alvaro said. 'That must have come as quite a shock.'

'It did. I received the letter regarding the Santiago estate after my mother passed away. All of the correspondence had been addressed to her, you see, and it was very difficult not having her or my grandmother to talk to about any of it.'

'So, you think they might have known about it?' Martina asked.

Rose shook her head. 'In the beginning, I did wonder whether perhaps my grandmother knew, or at least had some inkling about her adoption, but the more I've discovered, the more it appears that all of this was kept a secret. No one in my family knew.'

'That's why you never came here to see Valentina?' Maya asked. 'You truly never knew about her?' She paused. 'Or your inheritance?'

Rose met her gaze. 'Truly. I'd never heard the Santiago

name in my life, and I never knew we had any connection to Argentina. I certainly didn't know I had any inheritance other than the flat in London that my mum owned.'

'Tell them about the little box,' Benjamin said, as everyone began to eat.

Rose took a small forkful, her taste buds exploding. It tasted every bit as good as it smelt.

'For goodness' sake, let the girl eat!' his mother said. 'She won't get a chance to eat any paella if we keep asking her questions.'

She laughed. 'It's fine, I don't mind.' Rose gave them a very short version of how she'd come to be the recipient of the little box with its clues, and how it had made no sense to her until she'd received the letter from the lawyer in Buenos Aires. And when she paused for breath, she saw that they'd all stopped eating.

'A piece of blue silk?' Benjamin's mother said. 'Felipe's polo shirt?' she asked, turning to Benjamin.

'Perhaps,' he said. 'It was the first thing I thought of when I saw it.'

'Rose, do you have the clues with you?'

'I do. I have them in my bag.' She'd had the strangest feeling ever since she'd received them, and she'd rarely left home without them.

She dabbed her mouth with her napkin and went to get her bag, which she'd left by the front door. When she returned, they all stopped talking, and she took out the little box and placed it on the table, pushing it across to Alvaro.

'The lawyer told me that Valentina had watched my grand-mother from afar,' she said. 'But for some reason, she never tried to approach her, deciding instead to leave her fortune to her. And that's the part I'm struggling to understand.' She paused. 'And I came across the name you just said, Felipe, on a photo in Valentina's wardrobe.'

Benjamin's father gasped when he saw the figurine. 'This was made by my grandfather,' he said. 'And this was left for your grandmother? By Valentina?'

She nodded. 'It was.'

The table fell silent then, and Rose was left wondering whether she'd done the right thing in sharing her story or whether she should have stayed silent.

'Rose, has anyone told you how our families are connected?' Benjamin's mother asked. 'Has Valentina's lawyer told you anything?'

She looked to Benjamin. 'I had a feeling that there was more to the connection between your family and the Santiagos than I understood, but no one has explained it to me.'

'Alvaro, I think it's time someone told Rose about our families. She deserves to know the truth.'

'The truth?' Rose asked.

'My great-grandfather worked for Basilio Santiago,' Benjamin's father said. 'He's the reason my family moved here from Spain in the 1930s.'

'Your family moved here so that he could work for the Santiagos?'

'They did. He was given an opportunity for a better life, to work for a man he respected and came to call a great friend, but as wonderful as that was for the years they worked together, everything changed when Basilio died.'

'I've seen Basilio in Valentina's photos, or at least I presumed the man with her was her father.'

'Valentina was Basilio's only child, and from the stories that were passed down, he adored her more than anything in the world. She was left everything in his will when he died but, unfortunately, she had to fight for what was hers. As did our family.'

Rose tried to process what she was being told. 'With everything you know, does it make any sense to you that Valentina would leave clues that pointed to your grandfather in that little box?'

It was Martina who spoke this time. 'It was no great secret that Valentina was in love with Benjamin's great-grandfather. They tried to hide it, but it was impossible. Even if they thought that no one knew, everyone did.'

'They had a romance?' Rose asked, as she started to realise what Martina was telling her. 'You don't think that we're...' Rose took a breath, looking at Benjamin and hoping that she was wrong. Her stomach felt as if it was doing somersaults. 'You don't think we're all related, do you?'

Alvaro shook his head. 'They were in love, but Valentina didn't marry Felipe, and as far as we're aware they never had a child. He was an honourable man, and we don't believe they would have had a child outside of marriage.'

'Then why leave clues that pointed to him, for her daughter to find?'

Alvaro sighed. 'I don't know. Perhaps she wished that he was the father?'

'Or perhaps,' Benjamin's mother said, 'she simply left the two things that were dearest to her at the time, because she didn't know what else to leave?'

Later that evening, as Benjamin walked her out to the car, his hands in his jeans pockets, Rose stopped beneath the fairy lights his parents had strung up around the pergola and turned to him. Despite being unsure about dinner, she was glad she'd decided to come.

'Thank you for a lovely evening,' she said, sliding her fingers into her pockets for something to do. It also made her less tempted to reach for Benjamin, especially when someone could be watching them from inside.

'I hope you'll forgive my family for taking a while to warm up.'

'There's nothing to forgive. I actually think it's nice they're protective of you, and of my great-grandmother. It sounds as if they truly cared for her, and I've left knowing more than I did before about her past.' It had also been a lovely evening after the bumpy start. 'I had a really nice evening. I'm pleased I came.'

'They did care for her, as did I,' Benjamin said. 'And nothing makes me happier than knowing you enjoyed your night with us.'

'I just...' She breathed out. 'Were you going to tell me about your great-grandfather?'

'That he and Valentina were in love when they were children?'

Rose pushed her shoulders up to her ears, her hands sliding even farther into her pockets. 'Were they children, though? Would she have left clues pointing to him if it was just a girl-hood crush? We're talking about a woman who was old enough to give birth and place her daughter for adoption, so she was hardly a child then.'

Benjamin took a step forward, and before she knew it he'd reached out and brushed some loose hair back from her face. There was something about him that just kept drawing her in, and it wasn't lost on her that Valentina had clearly felt the same way about his great-grandfather.

'All I know is that they had a romance that wasn't meant to be, and that my great-grandmother always believed that her husband was in love with Valentina, even though, as far as I know, they never saw each other. There was no scandal, just two people who once meant something to each other.'

Rose suddenly forgot all about her family mystery as Benjamin moved even closer, his body so close that if she changed the angle she was standing at, they'd be touching.

'I wish I had more answers for you, Rose, but that's all I know.'

'You promise you're not holding anything else back? That there are no family secrets you're keeping?'

He dipped his head a little lower. 'I promise.'

Rose didn't know if it was the wine they'd been drinking or the balmy night air tinged with the smell of flowers, but she found herself slipping her arms around Benjamin's neck. She wasn't sure if he kissed her or if she kissed him, but in the moment, it didn't matter who started it, because neither of them was making any effort to stop.

Benjamin's lips were soft against hers, as if they had all the time in the world for long, lazy kisses that might never end. His fingers skimmed her back and hers brushed the nape of his neck, and they stayed like that for so long that she almost forgot she was supposed to be leaving.

'I feel like a teenager sneaking a kiss on the front porch,' she whispered, when their kiss finally ended and they gently pressed their foreheads together.

'Let's just hope my family aren't watching from behind the blinds like they did when I was fifteen,' he whispered back.

They both laughed, and Rose eventually pulled away. 'Will I see you tomorrow?'

'You will,' he replied. 'I'll be there bright and early to work the horses, and perhaps after I could stop by for lunch?'

Rose took a step backward. 'I'm sure I can figure out lunch, even with my limited skills.' Or more likely she could ask Clara, who was scheduled to come to tidy the house the following day.

She waited a moment, not ready for the night to end but knowing that they couldn't stretch it out any longer.

'Well, I guess it's goodnight then,' she said.

'Rose,' he said, just as she was about to turn away.

Benjamin took her hand, turning her palm over in his.

'Have you thought any more about the polo match next weekend?' he asked.

She laughed. 'Please tell me that's not why you kissed me.'

'It was only *one* of the reasons I kissed you.'

Rose swatted at him but he caught her hand again before she could connect. 'I thought I'd already said yes.'

'So, I can send out the invitations tomorrow?'

When he held her fingers up and kissed her knuckles, she knew it was possible that she would agree to anything he asked in that moment.

'You can.'

Benjamin kept hold of her hand and walked her the rest of the way to the car, opening the door for her and waiting until she started the engine and put the window down. When she did, he leaned in and brushed one last kiss to her lips.

'You taste like paella,' she whispered.

'And you taste like wine,' he whispered back. 'Are you sure you should be driving?'

'I only had one, and I'll be home in less than a minute.'

'Until tomorrow, then,' he said, taking a step back from the vehicle so she could pull away.

'Until tomorrow.'

And as she drove away, Rose's cheeks hurt from smiling so hard, and she realised that the last time she'd been so happy had been when she, Jessica and her mum had enjoyed a long weekend away. But unlike every other time she'd thought of her mother, this time her smile didn't fade. Somehow, here, after the night she'd had, she didn't want to cry.

For the very first time, Rose only wanted to smile.

Benjamin made her feel as if she was alive again, and although she fully expected to burst into tears the next time she thought about her mum, right now she was okay with being happy. She just hoped the feeling would last.

17

SANTIAGO FAMILY ESTATE, ARGENTINA, 1939

Valentina lay in Felipe's arms, tucked into him like a small child as he wrapped himself around her, his strong arms locked across her body. They were in one of the empty stables, curled up against a hay bale, as she cried against his chest.

Felipe released his hold on her as he began to stroke the hair from her forehead, and Valentina did her best to catch her breath, listening to the steady, constant beat of his heart.

'I can't believe he's gone,' Valentina whispered.

Felipe's mouth pressed to the top of her head, and she nestled even closer to him. He didn't say anything, but he didn't need to—his touch was enough. She realised then why she'd been drawn to him for so many years—he might not be a wealthy man like her father had been, but he had the same quiet strength he'd had; the same calm, strong demeanour, and she knew in that moment that her father would have approved. If he could have seen them together, if he'd had the chance to spend time with the two of them, he would have given his blessing, and her deepest regret was not telling him while she had the chance.

'What are we going to do?' Valentina asked, whispering against his chest. 'If my mother forces me into a marriage—'

'She won't,' Felipe said, his voice vibrating through his chest. 'We will leave if we have to. We'll find a way to be together.'

Valentina looked up at him, at the worry etched on his face. 'But we have no money and nowhere to go.'

'Then we will go to Spain,' he said. 'I have extended family there, and your family has business interests there, too. As soon as you turn eighteen, we can marry.'

Valentina stared down at Felipe's hand and linked her fingers through his, imagining them both wearing simple gold bands to acknowledge their union. If they ran away and married, they would have nothing, unless she managed to challenge her mother. But legally, she knew there would be little she could do until she turned eighteen, which was a year away.

'What about your family?' Valentina asked. 'Could you really leave your parents?'

Felipe nodded with a confidence that she didn't believe, because she knew how much he loved both his mother and father—he was used to working with his father every day.

'If we don't go, you'll be taken from me,' he said, pressing a kiss to her forehead. 'We can reunite with my family later, but if you're forced into a marriage...'

She nodded, as a fresh wave of tears threatened to engulf her. He was right—if she was married off to another man, they would never have the chance to be together ever again.

'Papa would have hated this,' she murmured. 'His family ripped apart by money, my mother dismantling all the plans he'd left in place. He'd be turning in his grave.'

'She hasn't succeeded yet,' Felipe said. 'I know nothing about the law or things like this, but surely if a successful man like him left a written will—'

'Valentina!' came a hiss from outside. 'Felipe!'

'That's my father,' Felipe said, nudging her forward and then helping her up to her feet as he stood. 'We're in here,' he called back.

'Valentina, you need to go,' José said, his eyes wide. 'Your mother has threatened my job if I don't send you back to the house, and she's warned me that if she finds out that you and Felipe have been seeing each other without her permission...'

Valentina nodded, understanding what he was trying to say. She wiped at her eyes, itchy and sore from crying, and turned to Felipe. She ignored the fact that his father was standing there, cap in hand as he waited for them to say goodbye, and stood on tiptoe to kiss Felipe, sliding her arms around his shoulders to hold him.

'I love you,' she whispered into his ear.

'I love you, too,' he whispered back, fiercely, holding her fingers in his so tightly it felt as if he might never let go.

When Valentina finally turned away from him, tugging her hands from his hold and nodding to his father as she passed, a wave of emotion caught in her chest and left her fighting to breathe as tears streamed down her cheeks.

No matter what Felipe said or what they planned, she had the most awful, overwhelming feeling that her mother would find a way to put a stop to it all. And if they did succeed in being together, then Felipe's family would be the ones punished for their actions. She didn't know what was worse—a life without Felipe, or knowing that she was responsible for his family's downfall.

———

Valentina stood with her back pressed to the side of the house, before running out into the pouring rain. She'd arranged to meet Felipe that night, and nothing was going to stop her.

She ran in the dark, the rain soaking her dress and dripping from her eyelashes, knowing the way even without lights to guide her. Valentina knew every inch of the property, could have navigated her way around blindfolded if she'd had to, and she counted the steps across the grass to the stables, knowing that she just had to make it there without being seen. Once they were hidden in one of the stalls, no one would know where to look for her on such a stormy night. Or at least she hoped not.

'Valentina?'

Felipe's soft, hesitant call when she pulled open the door made her heart flutter. They hadn't seen each other for two weeks, with Valentina unable to leave the house, but she'd managed to get a note to his father when she'd passed him on her way to the car the day before. She'd kept it in her pocket for days, waiting for her chance, and the moment she saw him she'd run over and quickly slipped it into his hand, telling her mother that she'd heard him call out and wanted to accept his condolences. Other than the one outing into town for a new dress, she'd felt as if she'd been kept prisoner, confined to one wing of the house unless she was summoned for dinner.

But she forgot everything when Felipe emerged from the shadows. He was as handsome as ever, with his dark hair combed back off his face and his eyes immediately searching hers. But he didn't look himself—she could see the same strain echoed on his features as she felt in hers, and she wondered if he had the same deep knot of worry in his belly that she did.

'Felipe,' she murmured, standing in the entranceway with her hair dripping and making a small puddle beneath her.

He ran towards her, folding her in his arms despite how wet she was, his lips to the top of her head, his hands warm around her.

'I didn't think I was going to see you again,' he whispered. 'I've waited every day, hoping you'd come down to find me.'

Valentina squeezed her eyes shut tightly as she tried to stave off her tears. She'd promised herself that she wouldn't cry, that she'd cherish every moment she was with Felipe and save her tears for later. But it was proving easier said than done. Being in his arms again made her realise just how much she'd missed him.

'My mother may as well have me under lock and key,' Valentina said when he held her at arm's length, gently stroking the backs of his fingers down her cheek and smudging away a tear. 'She won't let me do anything without supervision.'

Felipe took her hand and led her into one of the stalls, where he had some hay bales set up and a blanket. She was grateful when he pulled it out and wrapped it around her, keeping his arm there and rubbing her shoulder as her teeth began to chatter from the cold. They sat down, and she tucked her legs up beneath her, grateful for her long dress so the hay couldn't scratch her bare skin.

'Before we say anything else, just in case you have to leave in a hurry,' Felipe said, letting go of her and reaching into his pocket, 'this is for you.'

He held something out to her that was wrapped in soft tissue. Valentina looked up at him, curious about what was inside.

'I was going to wait until your birthday, I've been working on it for months,' he said, his voice huskier than usual. 'If something happens, no matter what, I wanted you to have it.'

'Thank you,' she whispered, as she carefully unwrapped the gift.

In her hands, she held the most intricately carved figurine of a horse. She ran her fingertips over the edges, marvelling at how perfect it was.

'It's beautiful,' she said, looking up at Felipe. 'No one has ever made me anything before.'

'I wish I could have bought you a diamond, or something expensive, but—'

'No,' she said, closing her fingers around it to keep the figurine safe in her palm as she leaned forward to kiss him. 'It's the loveliest thing I've ever seen. I will cherish it forever.'

Felipe kissed her back, and Valentina had the most awful feeling that it might be the last time their lips would meet. The kiss felt sad—*heavy* almost—and she wished they could go back to stolen kisses and whispers of the future they were going to have together.

'Felipe, I need to tell you something,' she said, hesitantly, not wanting to ruin the moment but knowing, just as he had, that she might have to leave at any time if they were caught.

He stared into her eyes as she held the horse figurine in her hand still, somehow finding strength from it.

'I don't think I'm going to like what you have to say,' he said.

Valentina took a deep, shuddering breath. 'My father cared very deeply for your family. In fact, he cared for everyone who worked for him, but your father was very special to him. It seems to me that what they had went deeper, that they were good friends more than employer and worker.'

Felipe nodded, and she continued, 'In his will, my father left specific instructions for what was to happen to his estate. I, for one, was to inherit almost everything, but I wanted you to know that he left provision for your family. Your father was to receive a generous sum of money, along with the choice of whatever horses he would like to keep, and the deeds to the house your family live in were to be transferred to your father, also.'

She watched Felipe's face and saw the disbelief that passed over his features.

'He also made provision for every single employee to receive a sum of money.'

'And you're telling me this because it's not going to happen? Even though your father—'

'*Nothing* my father wanted is going to happen,' Valentina said, hearing the bitter edge to her voice. 'My mother already has her own lawyers involved, and they're threatening to overturn it all. She wants control of everything, and she's trying to say that he wasn't of sound mind, that no man in his right mind would give away so much money.'

Felipe took her hand in his. 'What does this mean for us?'

Tears filled Valentina's eyes again. 'She has plans to marry me to a man I've never met.'

Felipe's mouth formed a hard line.

'I've told her I won't do it, that she cannot force me, but she's adamant that I don't have a choice. And she's also said...' Valentina's voice caught in her throat.

'What? What has she said?' Felipe asked, his eyes searching her face.

'She's said that the only way your father gets to keep his job is if I go along with her wishes. Otherwise she'll make certain that he never gets another job in Argentina ever again. She said that she'll ruin your family by any means necessary.'

'What could she do to ruin us? Who would believe lies and rumours?'

'Felipe, if she inherits everything, then she will be one of the largest landowners in the country. My father took great pains to ensure his wealth never changed who he was, but my mother is different.' She took a breath. 'My mother scares me with her ambitions.'

'Then you need to fight for what's yours,' he said.

Valentina shook her head. 'I can't, not until I'm eighteen. Until then, there's nothing I can do.'

They sat in silence, and she shivered despite the blanket, her skin still damp from the rain.

'If I asked you to leave with me now, to run away and marry me, to never come back here, would you come?' Felipe asked.

Valentina's smile was immediate. 'Without a moment's hesitation,' she said. 'If it was just you and me, I'd tell you that we should run right now, leave before the sun comes up in the morning.'

'But?' he whispered.

'But I don't think you'd ever forgive me,' she whispered back. 'You would miss your family, and I would be the reason you could never go home. It would be my fault that they'd lose everything.'

They sat a while longer, with Valentina leaning into him as Felipe's arms wrapped around her once more, his breath warm against her cheek.

'This can't be the end, Valentina,' he murmured. 'I can't stand by and watch you marry someone else, but I don't know what I'm supposed to do.'

'Then wait for me,' she said, sitting back and cupping his cheeks in her hands. 'Just promise that you'll wait for me.'

'I can do that. I'll wait for you forever if I have to.'

'I promise you that I'll find a way to have my father's will reinstated, and when I do, I'll return for you,' she told him, taking his hands in hers and whispering kisses across his knuckles. 'Nothing can keep us apart, and I'll resist this arranged marriage with every fibre in my body.'

'And until then?' Felipe asked.

'Valentina?'

She froze as she heard her stepbrother's voice. It wasn't as terrifying as if it had been her mother's, but it still sent spirals of fear through her body that they'd been found.

'Valentina, I know you're in here.'

Valentina wrapped her arms tightly around Felipe and kissed him, pressing her lips to his for as long as she could.

'I love you,' she whispered. 'No matter what happens, or what you hear, know that I love you with all my heart and that I always will.'

'I love you, too,' he whispered back.

And as she tucked the figurine carefully into the pocket of her dress, he lifted his coat and tore a piece of blue silk from the top he was wearing.

'Take it,' he said, passing it to her. 'Your father gave me this when I joined the team, the very first time I played.'

She quickly tucked it into the same pocket and slipped from the stable, hoping that Felipe didn't follow her and confront her brother.

'I'm here,' she announced, seeing her stepbrother standing near the door.

'You look terrible.'

She glanced down at her wet clothes and lifted a hand to her damp hair. The blanket she'd had around her shoulders had slipped to the ground, but she left it where it fell.

'Why are you here?' she asked.

'Because you're wanted back at the house,' Bruno said. 'You'll have to clean up before she sees you though.'

By *she*, Valentina knew that he meant their mother.

'You could put an end to all this,' Valentina said. 'Instead of being a coward, you could be grateful for everything my father did for you, for the generosity he showed you. You could refuse to follow through with your mother's plan.'

The stepbrother whom she'd once thought of as an ally instead of an enemy just laughed at her, as cruelly as her mother might.

'And turn down all that money? Don't be a fool, Valentina. I've been overlooked my entire life, but not anymore.' He looked around. 'This is all going to be mine.'

'But he didn't overlook you, Bruno! You never showed any interest in the family business, but he still left you a house and—'

'Enough!' His voice silenced her.

She stood for a moment longer to catch her breath, knowing she had to end the conversation before Felipe appeared behind her, unable to listen in the shadows any longer.

'Why does she want me at the house?' Valentina asked, suddenly suspicious.

'Your intended has arrived to meet his blushing young bride.'

Valentina closed her eyes, not certain if the gasp she'd heard came from her or Felipe, hidden behind the stable door; so close and yet somehow, already, so far away.

18

TWO WEEKS LATER

Valentina closed her eyes. Her entire body had been shaking as she stepped up to the altar, but her mother's sharp prod in her back as she'd arranged her silk train reminded Valentina what was expected of her. If she'd thought she could have escaped, she would have, but she was under no illusions about what lengths her mother would go to, to ensure this marriage went ahead. But as she tried not to cry, her father's words echoed in her mind.

You are my daughter, Valentina. One day this will all be yours. We have the same Spanish blood running through our veins, don't you ever forget that.

She slowly opened her eyes and blinked away tears, repeating the words that were asked of her while at the same time searching for a way to honour her father. It had never been so clear to her as it was now that he'd foreseen something like this happening, that he'd understood that she was the only person who could truly fulfil his legacy. But she doubted he'd ever imagined her mother would force her into marriage, and from the estate that she'd always called home.

Before Valentina knew it, her new husband was leaning

forward to kiss her, and she stood as still as possible, trying not to feel sick when his lips touched hers. And when she glanced out of the window of the little church, her heart shattered into a thousand pieces.

Felipe was standing there, his face forlorn, his eyes catching hers and somehow conveying all his pain and hers in one fated glance as they stared at each other. But he only stood for a moment, long enough for her to let out a sob as her legs wobbled beneath her, before he was gone. Before the man she loved disappeared from sight.

'Ahh, she's weak at the knees from her new husband's kiss,' the stranger beside her said, planting his hand around her waist to keep her upright.

She shuddered; that stranger was the man she was now married to.

The family gathered around them all laughed, and Valentina felt the sharp stare from her mother. But she didn't care. She might be able to force her into marriage, but she couldn't make her smile. She couldn't make her behave or do her bidding.

I wish you were here, Papa.

'The poor girl is still riddled with grief over her father, as are we all,' her mother said, dabbing at her eyes.

'Of course,' Valentina's new husband said. 'Which is why this union is so special. It gives everyone a new beginning, doesn't it, Valentina?'

She nodded, refusing to wilt before them. Valentina forced her shoulders to straighten, her jaw clenched as she wondered how they could all stand there and smile as if her father hadn't just died and her mother hadn't forcibly wed her to a man she had no interest in even speaking to, let alone marrying. She wished she could make herself invisible.

'Smile, Valentina,' he muttered in her ear. 'No one likes the look of a sullen bride, no matter how beautiful she might be.'

Something inside Valentina died in that very moment, and she desperately fixed her eyes on the window, willing Felipe to reappear so that she could catch one last glimpse of him, wishing she'd said yes to him. She'd made promises to her father, and she'd had every intention of honouring them, but she couldn't help but question whether, if he'd known what future she faced without him, he'd have told her to elope with Felipe and never look back.

19

PRESENT DAY

Rose was starting to like polo. It wasn't that she had an affinity with the game itself or even understood it all that well, but she was beginning to see why so many people loved it. Polo had a way of bringing everyone together, and she was so pleased that she'd said yes to hosting the tournament. Benjamin had been right—this was different to attending the Argentine Open. Today was about the local community coming together and enjoying a day under the sun, watching the game.

The field had been meticulously tended to by a groundskeeper, and it appeared to have stripes mowed across it, as perfect as she thought a bowling green might be, and there were white tents erected down one side of the field to provide shade from the midday sun. A catering company had arrived an hour earlier, unpacking countless boxes and setting them up, and although Rose was technically the host, everything was appearing as if by magic. When Benjamin had said he would take care of organising everything, he'd been true to his word. Or perhaps there was a running order every year, painstakingly detailed by Valentina at some stage, that had been adhered to.

Rose had carefully rummaged through Valentina's wardrobe and found a beautiful wide-brimmed straw hat with a soft-blue ribbon tied around it, and she'd decided to wear it with a simple white dress and flat sandals. She had no idea how dressed up everyone would be, but she figured it would cover all bases, and it showed off her lightly tanned arms. Plus, she felt connected to Valentina in a way, wearing her hat and hosting an afternoon that had obviously once been very special to her.

'Hello?'

Rose heard someone call from downstairs and turned away from the window, going down to see who it was. She'd left the front door open in case anyone came looking for her, but so far this had been her only visitor.

'Martina,' she said, surprised to find Benjamin's mother standing in the hallway. 'I wasn't expecting you.'

She smiled. 'I thought perhaps we could walk to the field together,' she said. 'Since we're both here to watch my son.'

Martina winked and Rose found herself laughing. His mother was no fool—clearly she knew why Rose had an interest in watching the game, or Benjamin had been right and his family had seen them kiss outside their home the other night, which had given them away.

'Would you like a drink first?' Rose asked. 'I have a bottle of champagne in the fridge.'

'I'd very much like that,' she said.

'Did you spend much time here with my great-grandmother?'

'I did. Our family were always close to Valentina, and saw a lot of her over the years, but you know, there was always something I couldn't quite put my finger on. But with you being here and asking questions, it's made me wonder if there wasn't something kept secret between our families all this time.'

Rose led the way and went to the fridge, pausing only to set her hat down, as Martina took a seat at the table. From where she sat, Rose knew she'd have a perfect view out to the field, where she expected some of the riders were already warming up.

'I've had a feeling there was a deeper connection, too, if I'm honest, and I've found myself asking if Benjamin knows more than he's telling me,' Rose said.

'If there's something to know, I can assure you that my son doesn't know it,' Martina said, taking the glass that Rose passed her. 'But my husband might, and you've made me very interested in discovering what it is.'

They sat together, clinking their glasses gently before both taking a sip.

'I remember Valentina wearing that hat. I'm sure it will look just as beautiful on you as it did on her.'

Rose reached out to touch the straw edge, smiling as she did so. 'Every day I look through some more of her things. It's strange, because I couldn't bring myself to sort through my own mother's things after she passed, and yet I feel sad that no one is here to touch Valentina's clothes and remember her as they do so. I know that makes no sense saying it out loud.'

'I understand. You want to feel as if you're paying tribute to her memory, even though you didn't know her.'

'And maybe it makes me feel better about not being able to go through my mother's possessions,' Rose said with a shrug.

Martina's smile was warm, and Rose saw the obvious resemblance to Benjamin.

'You being here is a good thing, Rose. This property is so special, and it needs a custodian like you. Someone who feels the connection to the past, but at the same time has the vision and youth to breathe new life into it. So don't let anyone make you feel as if you don't belong.'

'Even if I feel like a fraud most of the time?'

'Darling, you're not a fraud. Valentina Santiago was the kind of woman who had her wits about her at all times. If she left her estate to you? It means she believed that you belonged here, and that's all that matters.'

'You truly believe that?'

'I *know* that, and so does everyone else who was connected with her. So, no matter how you feel or what you think, you belong here.'

'I have a feeling your daughter might disagree,' Rose said with a wry grin, surprised at how at ease she felt talking to Benjamin's mother.

'Maya was rude to you at the polo game, and when you arrived at our home, but she's changed her mind about you. We all have.' She laughed. 'None more so than my son, it would seem.'

Rose blushed, but before she could say anything else, someone called out 'knock, knock' behind them. When she turned, Benjamin was standing there in his white breeches, a dark blue silk polo top that clung to his broad shoulders and tall black leather boots.

'Benjamin! Who brought you up? Take those boots off in the house!'

'*Lo siento, Mama,*' he said, apologising and coming forward to kiss first her cheek and then Rose's. 'I don't think the lady of the house minds, though.'

Rose laughed, feeling the familiar warm sensation she always had when Benjamin was near. They might not have known each other for long, but she somehow felt like it had been months, not weeks. 'She doesn't, but she also knows better than to disagree with your mother!'

He held out his arms to both of them and Rose found herself grinning across at his mother as she slipped her arm through the crook of his elbow. She hadn't expected to have this much fun, and she was so pleased she'd decided to extend her stay, even if it was just to see one more polo game and spend another weekend in Benjamin's company.

'My team never loses a game here,' he said, winking as he led both of them out of the front door, letting Rose go slightly ahead so they could all fit through. 'We have a tradition of winning whenever we play on Santiago soil.'

'Has anyone ever told you how unattractive overconfidence is?' she teased.

But before Benjamin could reply, his mother groaned.

'All the time, Rose, all the time. But he never seems to care.'

The day had passed by in a blur. Rose felt as if she were in a bubble, meeting more people than she could name as they all drank wine and ate delicious food beneath the canopy of the enormous white tent, but the atmosphere was different to the last game she'd attended. Benjamin had been right about it being more relaxed, and it wasn't that she hadn't enjoyed the last game; it was just different. If she'd been with friends, if Jessica had been there or if Benjamin had been a spectator rather than a participant, she would have had a lovely day enjoying the Argentine Open. But today, with his mother introducing her around, and the crowd as relaxed as could be, albeit curious about meeting the new Santiago in residence, she couldn't have been more content. It was almost like being with extended family, and she found that Argentinians were incredibly welcoming.

And watching Benjamin play... well, that was something else entirely. She found herself mesmerised as he galloped up and down the field, transfixed by the sound of the horses' hooves beating on the hard ground as they raced past. It was so physical and dangerous, but at the same time incredibly hard to turn away from.

'I thought I should come and say hello.'

A shoulder bumped into Rose's, and she glanced sideways to see that Benjamin's sister had come to stand beside her.

'Your brother is quite something to watch,' Rose said, turning her attention back to the game.

'He is. I've watched girls fawn over him all his life,' Maya said. 'They all want to bed the gorgeous polo player.'

Rose swallowed, wishing she still had a wine glass in her hand and unable to think of a quick reply. 'I'm not entirely sure what you're trying to tell me,' she eventually said, turning to look at Maya.

'I'm trying to tell you that I've never seen my brother be the one to do the chasing,' Maya said. 'Which tells me that he might be falling for you, and that is not something I ever saw in his future.'

'I'm flattered, but honestly—'

'That was my very drawn-out way of saying that I'm sorry,' she said. 'I hope you can forgive me for being rude when we first met, because if my brother likes you, then I like you. I just never saw him settling down, but suddenly that doesn't seem such a far-fetched idea.'

Rose smiled, relieved that Maya was being so friendly, even if she was embarrassed by her straight talking. 'I can most definitely forgive you. Truce?'

Maya smiled, too, and gave her a quick hug. 'Truce.'

They stood side by side and watched the final chukka, before Maya turned to her, placing a hand on her arm.

'He loves nothing more than a cold beer after the game, and no one will miss you if you disappear for a bit. You should go to him.'

'Thanks for the tip.' Rose watched Maya move away and make small talk with a group of neighbours, before eventually excusing herself and taking two beers from the bar. She slipped from the tent and headed over to where the horses were being unsaddled, seeing Benjamin helping his groom and leading two of his horses over to the water for a drink.

She walked to a nearby tree, leaning against it and taking a sip of beer as she watched Benjamin. There was a quietness about him that she found endearing, a sense of him being comfortable with whom he was, and she was certain it was why the horses were so calm around him. He was kind in the way he handled them, and she watched as he sponged one of their faces, laughing when the horse raised his head and sent water spiralling down on him.

But she didn't have long to observe him before he turned, almost as if he sensed her watching. He didn't wave, but he did find someone to take the horses from him, and she found herself staring at him as he crossed the ground with his usual long stride.

'I see you have beer.'

Rose pushed off from the tree and held one out to him. 'I heard you like one after the game.'

He grinned and took it from her, taking a long sip, the bottle raised high and making him look as if he was being recorded for an advertisement. Her throat went dry just looking at him.

'You enjoyed it?'

'I've enjoyed everything about today,' she said. 'I'm so pleased we went ahead with it.'

'So am I. It would have been a shame to break with tradition.'

She hesitated. 'And it would have been a shame for me not to see how welcoming everyone is. They're just good people, quick to smile and as friendly as can be. Somehow they made me feel very much at home.'

'Maybe it would have been a shame not to see you in that pretty dress, too.'

Rose felt her cheeks ignite, and she didn't have any time to recover before he stepped closer to her and touched her cheek.

'May I kiss you?'

She swallowed. 'Yes.'

Benjamin reached down and cupped the back of her head with his palm as she tipped her head back, her hat falling to the ground behind her as he brushed his mouth to hers. The kiss they'd shared outside his parents' house had been sweet and hopeful, but this kiss was electric—she felt it through every inch of her body.

When he finally pulled away, Rose found herself breathless as he braced himself on the tree behind her head. But she only waited a moment before standing on tiptoe and kissing him again, not caring that he was hot and sweaty as she slipped her arms around his neck, still holding her beer as her lips found his again and again.

'We need to get back to the party,' she eventually whispered, her mouth still hovering over his.

'I'd say by this stage in the afternoon,' he murmured, 'no one would even notice if we didn't return.'

'Your sister knows where we are. She's the one who told me to bring you the beer.'

He winked. 'Well, my sister knows better than to tell on me.'

They both sipped their beer for a moment, and Rose felt a flutter in her stomach that she didn't ever remember feeling before as she leaned back against the tree. He was waiting for her to reply, to make a decision, and when she reached up to touch his cheek, he responded by sliding an arm around her waist and drawing her closer.

Benjamin's lips touched her hair and she snuggled tighter against him.

'You're sure no one will miss us?'

He laughed, and tightened his hold around her waist, whispering in her ear. 'Would it matter if they did?'

Rose laughed with him, tipping her head back to the endless blue sky above, the sun beating down on her shoulders as she leaned into the man beside her. Argentina had been good for her soul, and Benjamin was good for her heart.

And for the first time, she truly imagined what it would be like if she stayed.

20

ARGENTINA, 1939

Valentina felt as if she were living in a nightmare; a nightmare that she woke up to in the morning and lived through until she went to bed each night. Most days she could barely keep the tears from falling from her lashes, which only irritated her new husband all the more. She would always collapse back into bed when he left for the day, only to find out that his maid was telling him about her behaviour in his absence.

It was also the reason for her very first bruise, inflicted by a man she should have been able to trust, that left a blue-green welt so dark that no amount of powder or cream would conceal it.

'Look at me!' he'd roared to Valentina at the dinner table, as she'd whimpered at the other end, her eyes downcast and her napkin furrowed between her fingers.

Valentina had lifted her gaze, bravely meeting his angry stare.

'You look at me like you're scared of me, you spend all day miserable in bed, and you haven't even the decency to greet me properly when I arrive home from work. What is wrong with you?'

'I'm sorry,' Valentina had murmured. 'This marriage, being here with you, it's all a shock. I wasn't prepared for any of it.'

'Come here.'

Valentina froze. She did not want to go to him. She knew what happened when she went to him, what he expected from her, what he *took* from her. Her body began to tremble.

'I told you to come here!' he repeated, but louder now, angry as he stood and marched around the table to her, grabbing her long hair in one fist as he raised the other in an open palm, slapping her so hard across the cheek that she would have fallen had he not been gripping her hair so tightly.

'Your mother warned me that you were a princess, but I want to make this very clear,' he said, his face inches from her own. 'You are my wife now. You are no longer the daughter of Basilio Santiago, you're *my* wife.'

I'm only seventeen. This isn't the life I was supposed to have. I cannot belong to you!

But instead of speaking her mind, Valentina merely nodded, accepting of her fate. The time for defiance had been before she was betrothed to him—now she was resigned to the fact that she had no say in her own life. It would have broken her father to know what had happened to her and the fortune he'd worked so hard to create; her father, who'd treated her with so much love and kindness.

'Now,' her husband said calmly as he hooked his finger beneath her chin and turned her face slowly, inspecting her cheek, 'shall we get back to dinner? It would be a shame to let our food go cold because of your bad behaviour.'

Valentina nodded, swallowing and forcing a small smile even though it made her cheek hurt all the more. But she wouldn't touch it, wouldn't lift her fingers and acknowledge the pain in front of him. She could at least control how he saw her react; she could cry about it later, when she was alone.

'How was your day?' she asked, mimicking the question her

mother had always asked her father when he'd arrived home. 'Would you like me to prepare a drink when you arrive home each evening?'

His smile made her feel sick to the stomach. 'See? You already have the hang of it.' He took a mouthful of his food and she forced herself to pick up her fork and taste a little, even though the last thing she wanted was to eat. 'Fernet and cola, and make sure to give it a good stir.'

Valentina nodded, squeezing her eyes tightly shut for a moment when her husband turned his attention back to his food and trying desperately hard not to cry. She found herself imagining what it would have been like to sit across the table from Felipe when he returned from work each day. They wouldn't have had a meal prepared by a cook or formal silverware, but his smile would have melted her. His eyes meeting hers would have made her want to run into his arms. She could have dealt with being penniless, so long as she had Felipe.

When she opened her eyes, something shifted inside of Valentina. The past two months, she'd been resigned to what had happened to her, told that she had no say in the matter due to her young age, bullied by her mother and now her husband. But there had to be a way to leave, to find her way back to Felipe, who'd promised to wait for her forever if he had to. There had to be a way to escape this horror of a marriage, but she couldn't conceive of a way to return to Felipe without ruining his family in the process.

A few weeks later, Valentina gripped the porcelain edge of the toilet seat as she vomited up the last of whatever had been left in her stomach from the previous night. Her knees ached on the cold tiles below, but every time she tried to rise, her stomach would lurch again and she'd find herself bent over the toilet.

It wasn't until she'd finally risen, splashing cold water on her face before staring at her reflection in the mirror, that she realised why she was so unwell. Valentina gasped, lifting her cotton nightdress off her body and standing in her undergarments. She stared at her stomach in the mirror, running her palm across it, and then looking at her breasts and touching them gently to see if they were sensitive. She'd always been slender, and her stomach was still small, but her breasts were bigger. And she knew. There was no denying what was wrong with her, and it certainly wasn't the *bife de chorizo* they'd had last night that had caused her nausea.

I'm pregnant.

Tears began to slide down Valentina's cheeks then as she reached for her nightgown, not bothering to slip it back on and instead walking half-naked back into her bedroom. The house was empty save for a maid or two; her husband had already left early for work, and she was too shocked to care about her state of undress.

The baby is his. I'm having a child with a man who isn't Felipe.

The thought continued to circle her mind as she got back into bed, pulling the covers high up to her chin, her fingers gripping tightly to the sheet as she stifled a cry. If she was pregnant, that meant she couldn't ever return to Felipe. What man would want a baby that wasn't his? And how would she ever leave now, anyway? Her husband was unkind and unsympathetic at the best of times—there was no way he'd ever agree to her leaving if he knew she was carrying his child. Valentina was under no illusion that he cared for her—he'd agreed to marry her quickly in exchange for money, and the longer they were together, the more money he would receive. If they had a child together?

I'll be stuck with him for the rest of my life.

Valentina closed her eyes and tried to picture her father,

desperately wishing she had him to turn to. But if she'd had him, then she would never have been in this predicament in the first place.

Treat the people who work for you with kindness and generosity, and they'll be there for you when you truly need them, mi chica.

Valentina sat bolt upright. With her father's words ringing in her mind, she knew what she had to do.

She jumped out of bed, dashing to her closet to find something suitable to wear. She couldn't have her husband find out where she'd been, so she would have to get their driver to take her somewhere else and then discreetly go the rest of the way on foot.

When she was finally dressed, with her hair carefully pinned back from her face, she went downstairs and had the maid call her a driver, under the illusion that she wanted to go into town to shop for her husband. It would mean she'd have to dash to get him a gift or two while she was there, but at least it wouldn't raise any suspicions among his staff.

You can do this, Valentina.

And do this she would. It was one thing for her to be trapped in a loveless marriage, but it would be something else entirely to bring a child into it.

———

By midmorning, Valentina was sitting in the reception area at the offices of her father's lawyer, trying to look as if she belonged there but at the same time finding it almost impossible not to keep watching the door. She was terrified that somehow her husband might find out and come looking for her, that he would march through the door and drag her back home by the hair.

'Valentina?'

The man she was hoping to meet stepped into the waiting area, taking off his glasses and rubbing his eyes as if he couldn't believe who was sitting there.

'I'm sorry to call unannounced, but—'

'No need to apologise, come this way,' he said, indicating that she should follow him. 'Maria, please move my next appointment and cancel my lunch meeting.'

'I don't want to cause—'

'Valentina, it's my pleasure to see you. Your father was one of my best clients for more than a decade, so let me assure you that seeing you today is not an inconvenience.'

He held open the door to his office for her and Valentina sat down, folding her hands in her lap.

'It is my understanding that my mother no longer uses you for my family's business affairs,' she said. 'After what happened with my father's will.'

The lawyer sat down across from her, his elbows braced on the solid wood desk. 'Unfortunately that is correct.'

'Lorenzo—if I may call you by your first name as my father did?'

'Of course you may.'

'Lorenzo, my father trusted you implicitly, and that's why I called on you today,' Valentina said. 'My father was an astute businessman, but he was also a very compassionate man who believed deeply in looking after those he loved. From the reading of his last will and testament, you will be aware that he not only intended for his estate to be left to me, but he also left generous sums and even gifts to many of those in his employ.'

He nodded, taking off his glasses and rubbing at his temple. 'Valentina, everything you say is true. In fact, I was there to draft his wishes and turn it into the document that became his will, so I know how passionately he felt about these things.'

'And yet despite that, I am seated before you, forced into a marriage I did not consent to, with no control over my father's estate or businesses, and in the knowledge that none of his wishes have been followed.'

'You're here to ask for my help?' Lorenzo asked.

She took a deep breath. 'I'm here to ask if you'll represent me. I would very much like for you to be my lawyer.'

If he was surprised, he didn't show it. 'I'm honoured that you'd even think to ask me.'

'Before you accept, though, I must tell you that I have no money from which to pay you right now, so I cannot offer you the kind of retainer that my father did, but what I will do is promise to pay you handsomely as soon as I secure my rightful inheritance.'

The lawyer sat back as a smile spread across his face.

'I have no doubt that you're as honourable as your father, Valentina, so the matter of payment isn't a problem. Basilio was a very special man.'

'But?'

'But I want to understand what you're asking of me,' he said. 'Challenging your mother in this way will divide your family and ruin any chance you might have at a reconciliation.'

'Let me make one thing clear,' Valentina said, a steely reserve settling over her that she'd never experienced before. 'As far as I'm concerned, I no longer have any family. My mother betrayed my father, and I will never forgive her for what she did to me, so maintaining a relationship with them isn't my concern.'

He nodded and reached for his pen, which he held poised above the notepad on his desk.

'Tell me what you would like me to do, Valentina, and I'll find a way to help you.'

'I want to honour my father's wishes, by ensuring that everything he detailed in his will is actioned. I want every word of his intentions followed.'

'I presume that includes inheriting what is rightfully yours?'

'Yes. I know that we might have to wait until I turn eighteen, but I want to remove my mother from the estate, and my stepbrother too, and divorce my husband. I don't care what you have to pay him, but I know that there is a price at which he would consent. Your job is to discover what that price is.'

'The divorce might be the hardest part, but I understand that you wouldn't want to remove your mother, only to have your husband step in to claim what was left to you.'

Valentina closed her eyes for a moment. 'There is one other thing that I need to tell you.'

When she opened them, he was staring back at her.

'I'm pregnant.'

He dropped his pen. 'Valentina—'

'Don't tell me that this changes things, because it doesn't. You are the only other person who knows that I'm expecting, and we're going to keep it that way,' she said. 'I need your help to leave Argentina until after the baby is born.'

'You want to leave Argentina?'

'Yes. And when I come back, it will be to claim what is mine.'

When Valentina returned to the lawyer's office five days later, she felt like a different woman. The bruise around her eye from her husband's last show of dominance was finally fading, and she was quietly confident that her plan was going to work. So long as the lawyer had done his part, she had every confidence that she would be leaving Argentina before the end of the month. And most important, before anyone else discovered that she was expecting. Her biggest worry was that one of the maids would hear her being sick in the mornings.

'Please go straight into his office,' Lorenzo's secretary said when she stepped through the door.

Valentina nodded to her, pleased that she didn't have to wait.

'Good morning,' she said, standing at the door a moment until the lawyer looked up.

When a smile lit the man's face, she breathed a sigh of relief.

'You have good news for me, don't you?'

'You can read me like a book,' he said, setting aside whatever papers he was working on to face her. 'It just so happens that I do.'

His secretary appeared then with a coffee pot but Valentina shook her head, not able to stomach it, sitting in silence until she'd gone and closed the door behind her. She didn't trust anyone other than Lorenzo.

'I have a proposition for you,' he said, as she folded her hands in her lap.

Valentina found herself leaning forward in her seat. 'Please, tell me.'

'I propose that we send you to London for the time being, well away from your mother and husband, until you turn eighteen.' He cleared his throat. 'And after you have had the baby, because that would certainly complicate matters if anyone were to find out.'

She nodded. It was only a couple of months until she was of age, but she understood that the baby complicated matters. 'Go on.'

'Once you're eighteen and the infant has been born, we will mount a claim to contest the will, and at the same time we will apply for an annulment of your marriage, rather than a divorce. Of course, we will have to offer your husband a significant sum of money to walk away from marriage, but everyone has a price, and if we are successful in challenging your mother in court, then you will be a young woman with enormous funds at your disposal.'

Valentina sat back in the chair. 'And how, exactly, do you suggest I hide my baby when I return?'

At that, the lawyer's cheeks turned a deep shade of pink, but she was impressed that he didn't break eye contact, however embarrassed the subject might make him.

'After some discreet research, I have found two options in London,' Lorenzo said. 'There is a woman running a place called Hope's House, only very recently opened and hardly known about yet, and you would be able to deliver your baby there and place the infant for adoption to an approved family. It seems to be a more progressive place, one that understands how these things happen without bringing judgement on the mother.'

Valentina's mouth went dry. 'Adoption?' She hadn't imagined the idea of actually giving her baby up. In truth, she hadn't thought what it would be like to have a child at all, or the logistics of hiding another human being as she fought her mother.

'I can't see any other way, I'm afraid,' he said. 'Although, of course, you would potentially be able to return for the child and come to an agreement with the adoptive parents after your annulment and inheritance. It would be difficult, but not impossible with the right guidance and of course funds.'

'So, I would have the baby, and then return immediately to Argentina?' Valentina asked. 'That would be seven months from now, give or take a few weeks. I'm afraid of what my mother could do during that time, the interests of my father's that she might dispose of. He was adamant that I not sell off any of the property and that I continue to run the olive oil business.'

Lorenzo stroked his chin and sat back, deep in concentration. 'Your father always believed that you would be more than capable of taking over his affairs, and although I wasn't convinced at the time, I can see that he was quite right.'

Valentina sat quietly, waiting for him to continue, flattered by his praise.

'There is little we can do to control what your mother does over the next seven months, but what we can do is agree to a plan. I have every confidence that you will win in a court of law, and I can assure you that I'll do my best to ensure success on your behalf.'

'You do understand that I can't pay you until—'

'Valentina, please don't concern yourself with my payment. You're your father's daughter, and I know that you will pay my account once you're reinstated as his rightful successor. Until that day, you're not to even think about it.'

She nodded. 'Thank you. In return, I can assure you that I will not look anywhere beyond your firm for advice and assistance on all legal matters, now or in the future.'

Lorenzo smiled. 'So, we are in agreement? You will leave for London just as soon as I can secure you passage on the next ship leaving from Buenos Aires. On the day of travel, you will make your way here, to my office, and I will have a car waiting to take you to the port.'

'Perhaps I could arrange to have some things sent here, a bag of essentials that I will need for the trip?'

'And I'm afraid I have to mention money, because you will need to sustain yourself for the seven months away from Argentina,' he said. 'I would offer to help you, but—'

'I have jewellery to sell,' Valentina said, opening her handbag and taking out a ruby necklace that her father had given her for her sixteenth birthday, along with a diamond tennis bracelet that he'd bought for her shortly before his death. She also had a handful of other rings and pieces of jewellery that held less sentimental value that she would part with, too.

Tears pricked her eyes as she placed them on the desk between them. 'Is it too much to ask you to sell these for me? I don't want to raise suspicion.'

'Of course,' he said, softly. 'And perhaps you could sell your engagement ring when you arrive in London.'

Valentina looked down at the large diamond on her finger. 'I will sell it with pleasure,' she said.

'I will give you a small loan, too,' he said. 'It's the least I can do.'

She took a deep breath and offered a shaky smile, knowing that her father would understand why she was selling the precious jewels he'd gifted her. She was doing this for him as much as for herself, to honour his memory in the only way she knew how.

'Thank you,' she said, reaching out and clasping Lorenzo's hands. 'I will never be able to repay you for your kindness.'

As she turned to walk away, Valentina was certain she saw tears in the old man's eyes.

I promise you, Papa, I will honour you. I will right every wrong. I won't stop until every last request in your will has been completed.

Valentina paused at the door, turning back to look at the lawyer who was still seated behind his desk, the jewellery she'd left still spread out in front of him. She reached into her pocket and felt the weight of the small wooden horse there, the one thing that she would never give up, and the one thing that reminded her every day of what her mother had taken from her.

'There's one more thing,' she said.

His eyebrows lifted in question.

'Once all this is done, I want you to have my mother escorted from the house. She may take her belongings, but I want her left penniless for what she's done to me.' Valentina placed a hand over her stomach. 'She will never be welcome on a Santiago property ever again.'

He looked as if he might question her, but there must have been something in her gaze that told Lorenzo it would be fruitless.

'And your stepbrother?'

She thought of the way he'd stood there as she'd cried and

begged her mother not to force her into marriage; the numerous times he could have put his foot down and allowed her to stay in the house, to follow the wishes of the man who'd taken him in and become a father to him. The night he'd come looking for her when she'd been hiding in the stables with Felipe.

'Turn them both out. I never want to set eyes on either of them ever again. Not after what they did to me.'

Valentina would be generous to her father's many employees—she would give them the money they were owed and spend the rest of her days honouring her father and showing the people around her how much she cared for them. But she would show no mercy when it came to her mother.

Even if it meant turning her out into the streets.

21

LONDON, 1939

Valentina straightened her shoulders and lifted her hand to knock again on the door of Hope's House. Inside she was a ball of nerves, but she tried her best to stand confidently as she waited for the door to open. There was a noise on the other side, but just when Valentina thought no one would ever answer, the door swung open.

'Sorry to keep you waiting,' said the dark-haired woman. She wore her hair pulled back into a soft bun, with some tendrils escaping around her face, and she was much, much younger than Valentina had expected. She also had a warmth about her that immediately put her at ease. 'You must be Valentina.'

She nodded. 'I am. And you are Hope?' Valentina half expected her to say that Hope was her mother, or that she just worked there. In her mind, the woman running a place like this would be no-nonsense and straight-faced; the complete opposite of the person standing in front of her.

'That's me. Now please, come in and let me help you with your bags.'

'I'm travelling light at the moment,' Valentina said, trying not to be embarrassed by her modest belongings. 'I had to leave Argentina in something of a hurry.'

'Well, I'm just pleased that your English is so good,' Hope said with a warm smile. 'I wasn't certain how well we'd be able to communicate, but I can see that we'll be just fine.'

'I learnt as a schoolgirl,' Valentina said, aware that she had a thick accent despite her ability to converse in the language. 'But being here in London has helped my language skills greatly. I've been here for a little while now.'

Hope indicated where she should leave her bags and led her into the kitchen, and Valentina was relieved that she didn't ask more about the time she'd already spent in England. 'Would you like tea? I've just made some sandwiches, and I'd very much like to catch my breath outside on the veranda. It's been a long day.'

Valentina stepped forward to help. 'Please, let me take these and meet you outside. I can find my way.'

Hope seemed grateful for the assistance. 'Through the living room there,' she said. 'We can make the most of the sunshine.'

Valentina took the plate of sandwiches, her stomach growling at the sight of them, and walked through the house and to the outdoor table as Hope had instructed. She sat down and admired the garden, which was a ramble of roses and other flowers all growing together. It was like organised chaos, and as different as it was to the landscape she was used to back home, Valentina liked it. She often dreamed of the property she'd left behind, of the hours she'd once spent riding across the seemingly endless fields with Felipe, or lying under the branches of low-hanging trees, even just staring from her bedroom window at the only view she'd ever known. The longer she spent away, the more she yearned for everything she'd lost, aching to go back to the country she loved.

Hope appeared within minutes, carrying two cups of tea

and a little jug of milk on a tray, pulling Valentina from her thoughts. 'I was surprised when I received correspondence from your lawyer,' Hope said. 'It's not often I have someone advocating for one of the young women who come to me, but he was very clear about seeking assurances before you came here. I was most impressed by how thorough he was, and how much he obviously cares about you.'

Valentina took one of the dainty sandwiches Hope offered to her.

'He's the only person who knows the truth about my situation, and I'm grateful that he was so understanding. I never saw myself in this position, and I would have been lost without him,' she said. 'Although I'm sure that's a common theme among the young women who come through your door.'

Hope's smile was kind, and she ate one of the sandwiches before speaking again. 'I helped a young mother give birth today, and she believed right up until she held that new baby in her arms that her lover would come for her. Sadly, most of the women in my care have been let down by a man—just not all of them can see it until they're faced with the reality of being alone and pregnant.'

Valentina swallowed her mouthful, noticing that Hope glanced at the wedding ring on her finger. Her throat felt suddenly dry. 'Is my being married a problem?'

'Not at all,' Hope said, sitting back and nursing her tea in her hands. It was clear she was tired, her eyes bracketed by lines that spoke of fatigue rather than age, but there was such a warmth about her that she kept putting Valentina at ease. 'I have little interest in the man who put you in this situation, and more interest in what I can do to help you and your baby. You'll receive no judgement from me about what you choose to do, or about why you chose to come here in the first place.'

They sat in a comfortable silence for some time as they both ate the sandwiches and sipped their tea, the afternoon sunshine bathing them in warmth. It gave time for Valentina to study Hope, and made her even more curious about how a young woman not significantly older than her had come to run such an establishment.

'Hope, if I asked you to care for my baby when I leave, to hold off from finding her adoptive parents, is that something you would be able to do?' Valentina asked. 'I intend on making a handsome donation to you once I return to Argentina, and—'

'What you're asking is not something I can do,' Hope said, gently, as if she were trying very hard not to hurt Valentina's feelings. 'If it were a matter of days or weeks, perhaps, but I care for women until they give birth, and for as long as it takes them to recover, and then I place each baby as soon as possible with their adoptive parents. I did respond to your lawyer telling him that I'm simply not set up to care for a child long term.'

Valentina took a moment to steady herself before speaking again, looking out into the garden. 'Do you have other mothers who don't want to give up their child? Is it something you've been asked before?'

'Many of the women who come here would rather stay with their child. But in the end, most don't have a choice. They do what they have to do, for both of their sakes, and to be honest it's why I started this place.' She paused. 'I haven't helped many mothers yet, it's only early days, but I want to be able to help as many women as I possibly can.'

'It's just, well, I can't take this baby back home with me immediately, but—'

'Valentina, may I give you some advice?'

Valentina nodded.

'Whatever your reason for being here, everything you do from this moment on is your choice,' Hope told her. 'I'll do everything I can to support you, and I will never part you from your baby if you don't want that, but you need to make the best decision for your child. We can talk through your options and figure out what's best for you, and don't forget that you still have time.'

Valentina swallowed. 'But what if I don't have a choice?' She'd been so careful with her money, making it stretch as far as possible, but she knew that the only way she could secure her future in Argentina would be to leave her child behind.

'We always have a choice, even when we feel that we don't.' Hope rose and disappeared for a moment, before coming back with a small wooden box. She passed it to Valentina, and Valentina ran her fingers over the smooth wood before opening it and looking inside. It was empty.

'What is this?' she asked, confused at what she'd been given.

'I had a handful of these made, for those mothers who want to leave something behind. Sometimes it makes the decision easier, knowing that you can prepare a memento or two for your child.'

Valentina stared down at the box. 'So I would put something precious inside, for my child to be given one day? If I chose to leave him or her behind?'

Hope reached for her hand and held it. 'That's right. It's your chance to leave something for your child, so they might have a connection to you or a clue, if they ever try to find you one day.'

She put her hand in her pocket and found the familiar shape of the tiny horse, the figurine that she'd kept against her body since the day Felipe had given it to her. It seemed almost meant to be that it was small enough to fit in the little box, as much as it would break her heart to part with it. Although she supposed she was going to break her heart the day she left her baby, anyway.

Besides, Valentina had already made her mind up—she was returning to Argentina to follow the plan she'd agreed upon with her lawyer—which meant that she would have to leave her baby in Hope's care. Without her inheritance, she would be faced with returning to her husband or being penniless in a foreign country, and she knew that her best chance of securing a future for her child one day was to return home. If Hope couldn't care for the baby in her absence, then she'd just have to cross her fingers and pray that when she returned to London, she'd be able to find a way to get her baby back.

Even if it meant leaving that child behind with only a tiny box of mementos, and the promise that one day, somehow, she would return.

'How long could you wait, Hope?' Valentina asked, needing to know the answer to her earlier question. 'If I asked you to wait before finding adoptive parents for my baby, is there *any* length of time you could give me? That we could agree upon?'

Hope seemed to study her, and Valentina watched as she took a big breath, as the answer was hard for her to give. 'In this hypothetical situation, you would be leaving the baby in my sole charge? It wouldn't be both of you staying?'

Valentina nodded.

'It would depend on how many other women were in my care, and what other responsibilities I had at the time,' Hope said. 'I have no family members or staff to assist me, so looking after a baby isn't something I could do for long. If I did, I wouldn't be able to help other women in need.'

'A few days then?' Valentina asked, as her hope began to fade. 'A week or two? I just need to know.'

'If you were confident that you could return within a week or two, then I would do my best,' Hope said. 'I've never had anyone ask me before, that's all, but I suppose there would always be someone staying here who could help. I can tell that it matters a great deal to you.'

'I would pay you handsomely on my return,' she said.

'Valentina, I don't do this for the money, but I appreciate the gesture. A donation towards costs is always welcome but not necessary, so I don't want you to ever think you're in my debt.'

Treat other people as you expect to be treated yourself. Show great generosity to those who are kind to you.

With her father's words echoing in her mind, Valentina reached out and touched Hope's hand.

'I won't think I'm in your debt, Hope, but if you assist me through childbirth and help me to keep my baby, I'll want to spend the rest of my life finding ways to repay you all the same. I've lost everything this past year, but I'm determined to change that, for the future of myself and my baby, and especially for those who go out of their way to help me.'

Hope's eyes met hers, and Valentina found herself wondering what she'd seen in her life, what had compelled her to open a house to help young pregnant women. Whatever her reason, Valentina was thankful she had, because she had no idea what she would have done if Hope hadn't opened her doors to her.

It had been either here or a convent in the countryside, and she doubted she would have lasted at the latter for more than a few days at best.

'Thank you, Hope, for welcoming me into your home,' Valentina said, at the same time as Hope nudged the plate of sandwiches towards her. 'I was forced from my own home, in Argentina, by my family, and yet you, a stranger, you've opened your home and your arms to me.'

Hope's eyes met hers. 'It's their loss, Valentina. One day they'll realise how foolish they were to treat you so poorly, and if they don't? Then they don't deserve to have you in their lives.'

Valentina couldn't have said it better herself, and she had to presume that Hope was speaking from experience to say it with such conviction.

22

PRESENT DAY

Rose couldn't have visualised a more perfect day. She'd lain in the grass and watched Benjamin work his horses, smiling and waving whenever he looked over at her, and now the man in question was striding towards her, no horse in sight. She propped herself up on her elbows to get a better look at him.

'I think you're missing something,' she said, dropping the book she'd been reading and holding up her hand to block the sun from her eyes. 'You don't have a horse.'

'I've finished for the day.'

She grinned. 'Does that mean I now have your undivided attention?'

He grinned straight back at her. 'I'm hot and sweaty, and I could really do with a shower, but if you want my attention now...'

Rose lay back in the grass as Benjamin lowered himself over her, propped up on his elbows as he dropped a sweet kiss to her lips. She couldn't resist, kissing him back, but when his damp hair touched her skin, she laughed and wriggled away.

'I've changed my mind! You do need a shower!'

He groaned and rolled to the side, catching her hand as they lay in the shade, staring up at the tree. Rose was relaxed in a way she'd never been before, her mind quiet where it was usually busy. The past couple of months since she'd arrived, she'd been almost scared of the quiet, determined to keep herself endlessly occupied rather than succumb to her own thoughts and worries, but it was as if she had nothing to fear in Argentina. It had been the reset she'd needed, and she knew she'd be forever grateful for the break it had given her from her life.

'Did watching me train tempt you to pick up a mallet?' Benjamin asked, turning to her and propping himself up on one elbow.

'A mallet?' she laughed. 'Most definitely not. But I think I could easily become a regular spectator. It's far more interesting than any other sport I've ever watched before.' Not that she'd ever really watched any sport previously, but she was fairly certain that gorgeous humans on gleaming ponies trumped everything else.

He sighed. 'Well, I suppose that's a start. And given you've never been around horses, perhaps my expectations were too high.'

She smiled back at him, rolling to her side and studying his face. His jaw was strong and angular, his cheeks covered in barely there stubble that she imagined he'd shaved the evening prior, after he'd finished riding for the day. And he had the darkest eyes she'd ever seen, that were somehow still soft enough to be inviting.

'I can see why you love it here so much,' she said. 'I still feel like an outsider, but I'm starting to feel a connection to the land. It's just so different to where I've always lived.'

'How so?' he asked, reaching out to stroke his fingers through her hair.

'Have you ever lived in a city?'

'I've stayed in the city, but I've never lived there, no.'

'But you've spent long enough there to understand that it is constantly living and breathing, with a noise that never ends? That this type of silence doesn't exist, where you can just escape from the world?'

'It sounds like the opposite of life here.'

She smiled. 'It is. Being here is the break from life that I needed. It was somehow what I was craving without even knowing it.'

Benjamin lay back down then, and she reached out her hand to touch his, intertwining her fingers over his as she breathed slowly and stared up at the green leaves waving above her, with glimpses of blue sky as the branches softly parted back and forth. Rose couldn't help but wonder what it would have been like for her mother if she'd spent her last months somewhere like this, in a part of the world that might have made her final weeks and days on earth so peaceful. If she'd passed away experiencing how beautiful the world truly was.

'Rose?' Benjamin asked, his voice barely a murmur. 'Are you okay?'

She realised then that her cheeks were damp, that he'd heard her crying. But instead of saying anything, she just squeezed her fingers around his and bless him, he didn't ask her again. That was the thing about a man who was used to spending his day with horses—he didn't seem to expect anything from her other than her quiet presence. He was easy to talk to, but he never filled the silences with unnecessary conversation.

Which was another reason she was falling so hard for Argentina.

'Do you want to lie here a while longer, or shall I go and take that shower so I can kiss you again?'

Rose laughed despite her tears. 'Let's just stay a little longer, if you don't mind. Just like this.'

'I don't mind a bit,' he replied, keeping hold of her hand, his fingers squeezing ever so gently against hers as if to remind her that he had hold of her.

And when she looked over at him, turning her head so that her cheek was against the grass, she saw that he'd closed his eyes, not in a hurry to go anywhere, and seemingly as content as could be lying on the ground beneath the tree and holding her hand for as long as she needed him.

'Benjamin?' Rose called a few hours later, curious as to where he'd got to with her glass of water. Rose padded barefoot through the house, shivering a little and wishing she'd slipped her robe on. He'd left her in bed, promising to return with water and something for them to eat, but it had been more than ten minutes and she was starting to think he'd either forgotten about her or left the house entirely.

She found him standing in the kitchen and went up behind him, slipping her arms around his bare torso and pressing her lips to his back. But he didn't move.

'Are you coming back to bed?' Rose whispered.

'Were you going to tell me?' he asked, his voice husky with anger as he turned, holding a piece of paper in one hand.

'Tell you what?' she asked, looking past him and seeing that he'd been looking at the letters and the most recent documentation she'd received from the lawyer. Heat rose inside of her as she realised what he was accusing her of. 'If I had something to hide, I wouldn't have left everything sprawled across the kitchen table for you to find.'

Anger flared inside her that he'd had the nerve to read her personal correspondence and then act as if she was the one in the wrong. She would have happily shown it all to him and had a conversation about it, but he seemed intent on accusing her of some terrible wrongdoing. When had she ever not been open with him about how she was feeling or her intentions?

'Were you ever going to stay here? Or did you just come to view your inheritance and find out how much it was worth?' he asked, his voice cold in a way she'd never heard him use before.

'Benjamin, please—'

'Just tell me, Rose. Were you even considering staying here? On keeping this place? Or were you just telling me what you thought I wanted to hear?'

She shook her head as she stared back at him. 'No, I was never intending on staying here forever,' she said, quietly, wrapping her arms around herself. 'My home is in London. I can't change the fact that Argentina isn't home for me or that I'm not Spanish. I've always told you that I was extending my trip rather than staying.'

'So you're going to sell this place to the highest bidder? Is that why you asked for this valuation?' Benjamin asked, holding up a piece of paper. 'You're going to walk away from your family's history, from everything that was created here?' He shook his head. 'I thought this was the start of something special, but you're just going to...' Benjamin didn't finish his sentence. He didn't have to.

She knew what else he wasn't saying—the unsaid words hung between them. *Walk away from me.* She would be walking away from him, too, not just the property. Rose felt tears welling up but refused to acknowledge them.

'You have valuations for all the horses on the property, on the land in Mendoza...'

'You really made sure to read all the paperwork in a short time,' Rose said, only half joking.

'So, it's true? You asked for all of this? These are the documents you've been waiting for?'

She felt as if she was going to explode, but she forced herself to at least try to sound calm. 'Benjamin, I don't know what I'm going to do. A few months ago, I couldn't have even shown you Argentina on a map, and I'd never even dreamed of coming here. And now, here I am with a property in my name and ancestors who I never knew existed. So please excuse me if I don't have a plan for what I'm going to do next, but what you're accusing me of is unfair.'

Rose glanced at his bare chest, his golden skin that only moments earlier she'd been running her fingertips across as he'd held her close, his mouth trailing across her body and making her question if she wasn't exactly where she was supposed to be. He'd emerged from her bathroom after his shower, following their afternoon outside, and she'd taken one look at his damp hair curling around his neck, water still glistening on his skin, and she'd known exactly what their evening was going to entail. They hadn't left her quarters since, until he'd come down to the kitchen under the guise of getting supplies.

'This property, the legacy of what has been created here, it needs a Santiago at the helm,' he said, and Rose could see the pain in his eyes. She'd unintentionally hurt him, but what he didn't realise was that he was hurting her, too. 'You can't just leave, Rose.'

'But I'm not a Santiago,' she whispered. 'I know you think I am, but I'm not, and I won't ever be.'

'It's not just a name, Rose,' he said, stepping forward and brushing his hand gently across her chest. 'It's in here. We are who our ancestors are, whether we want to be or not.'

'You're acting as if I've deceived you, as if I've done something terrible when all I did was accept the information that the lawyer had prepared for me,' she said. 'I want to believe that this could be my home, but it doesn't feel real. I'd always be a visitor here, Benjamin.'

He was shaking his head, as if he didn't believe her. Or maybe he didn't want to. 'You made me believe that you were falling in love with this place, with what you could have here, for what...'

She stared up at him, waiting for him to say the missing words, but instead his jaw hardened, his eyes cold as he looked at her. *For what we could have had.* Rose wished he'd said them, to tell her that what they'd had was real, that she hadn't imagined what had grown between them. That he hadn't been romancing her just to make her stay. But it seemed that he was intent on punishing her for something she hadn't done.

'I did fall in love, I have,' she whispered. 'But that doesn't change—'

'I think I should go,' he said, still standing there in front of her as if he was waiting for her to say something. But what could she say? He was right in the fact that she'd never truly seen herself staying there. In her dreams, if she'd dreamed of a life with him, then sure. But she had been dealt enough real life recently to know that lives weren't made of dreams. They were made up of reality, hard decisions and punches in the gut like cancer, and for her to think that she could have some magical, perfect new life here with Benjamin was nothing short of a fantasy.

'I don't know what to say to you,' Rose eventually said. 'I've enjoyed every moment of my time here with you, truly I have, and you've shown me the beauty of this place, of what it means to you and your family.' She paused, searching his eyes. 'For what it meant to *my* family.'

'But?'

Rose felt a catch in her throat. 'But I don't know if that's enough for me to uproot my entire life, everything I know, to move here and start over. Surely you can understand that? Put yourself in my position and truly ask yourself the question.' She took a breath. 'We barely know each other.' Her words stung, she could see that, and she immediately regretted them.

'I thought that was what we were doing, getting to know each other.'

Rose stepped towards him and reached up a hand, touching his face, gently pressing her palm to his skin, needing to touch him and know that what they had was real. But Benjamin pulled away, and her hand fell back to her side, leaving her cold.

'I'm sorry,' she said, not knowing what else she could say. 'The time I've had here with you, it's been nothing short of magical, but...' Rose swallowed. 'I really am sorry.'

He turned his gaze back to her, those eyes that had been so soft earlier now as cold as stone. 'So am I.'

'You can have the property,' Rose said. 'I don't need it, Benjamin. It was meant for you, not me. I'll book the next flight home and leave the keys on the table for you when I go.'

Benjamin gave her the saddest expression she'd ever seen. 'Rose, don't you see? If I was supposed to have this property, Valentina would have left it to me. But she didn't.' He seemed to search her face, as if waiting for her to understand. 'She left it to you. This property is supposed to be owned by a Santiago. By a Santiago *daughter*. That's not something you can just give away.'

His words hung over them, because she knew he was right. Her great-grandmother had fought to retain ownership of this property, and she couldn't be the one to give it away, not when she'd gone to such efforts to leave it to her biological family. It had meant something to her, and Rose couldn't ignore that.

'Then be the caretaker for now,' she said. 'For as long as you want to live here, it's yours. Whatever you say about her intentions, you can't deny that you belong here more than I do.'

'That's not what she wanted.'

Rose shook her head, her resolve hardening as she saw the way Benjamin was looking at her, trying to tell her how she should feel or what she should do. 'No, but it's what *I* want, and I need you to respect my decision.'

Benjamin paused a moment longer, as if expecting her to say something else, but she just waited for him to drop the paper he was holding, standing still as he finally walked past her and went upstairs to retrieve his things. And she hadn't moved when he came back down, fully clothed, coming up behind her and pressing a slow kiss to the back of her head, his lips lingering for one long, painful moment.

'For what it's worth, it might have only been a couple of months, but it was long enough for me to know how I felt about you,' he murmured. 'I'm only sorry you don't feel the same way.'

And then he walked out through the door and left her there, as tears streamed down her cheeks, wondering how she'd managed to end up so completely, utterly alone.

Rose had barely slept. She'd spent half the night either pacing or sitting at the kitchen table in the dark, replaying over and over in her mind what had happened between them, and then she'd tried to sleep before getting out of bed and packing up all her belongings. She'd found a flight out of Buenos Aires for New York later that day, and as much as she'd have liked to walk the property one last time or go and say goodbye to Benjamin's family, she had no intention of doing either. It would be easier to slip away without any fuss, without anyone seeing her or questioning why she was turning her back on what had been left for her. Or anyone trying to convince her to stay.

She'd also been waiting, hoping that Benjamin had come to see her, wishing she didn't have to leave like this; but no matter how hard she listened out for a knock at the door, none ever came.

Rose checked her watch for the hundredth time, then, seeing that she only had fifteen minutes until her taxi arrived, knew what she had to do. She took out her key ring and slid off the key to the front door of the house, placing it on the table, and then sat down with paper and pen. She'd been trying to compose the letter in her mind all morning, but in the end, she decided to keep it as short as possible.

Benjamin,

I'm sorry. I wish things could have been different.

She picked up the piece of paper and screwed it up into a tight ball, before starting again on a fresh piece.

Benjamin,

The house and grounds are yours for as long as you want to enjoy them. Please advise the family lawyer if your needs change.

Rose

Rose pushed the key onto the letter and stood, taking the screwed-up paper with her and throwing it into the rubbish. There was so much more she could have said, so much more in her heart that she might have said if he was standing in front of her, but he wasn't, and she wasn't about to go searching for him. Not after everything that had been said the night before.

She looked around one final time, before closing her eyes, the pain of it all almost too much to bear. First losing her mum, then coming here; trying to hold her head up, trying to protect her heart. And she'd failed at both.

'I'm sorry, Mum,' she whispered. 'I'm sorry, Valentina.'

She wished they could all have met, that she could have discovered Argentina and the Santiago estate with her mum when she was still alive; that she could have heard Valentina's story from her own mouth. That she could have started a new chapter of her life without feeling like she was just an imposter in someone else's. Or feeling like a failure.

But none of that was meant to be.

Rose heard the sound of the taxi pulling up outside, the tyres crunching over the gravel, and she wiped her tears away and picked up her bags, rolling her suitcase beside her and opening the door. The hardest part was shutting it behind her, though, and she found that she did it without looking back into the house, not wanting to admit that she might never set foot in there again.

She smiled at the driver when he got out of the car, thanking him for helping her with her case as she followed with her bags. Rose had taken some things with her that had belonged to Valentina, a few photos and a beautiful scarf that she'd found over the back of a chair, feeling a connection to it when Clara had mentioned that it had been one of Valentina's favourites.

'That's all?' the driver asked.

Rose nodded, but as she opened her handbag to slide her phone inside, she saw the little box she'd carried with her since she'd left London. The wooden box that Valentina had left for her daughter all those years ago.

'Can you give me one moment?' she asked, not waiting for a response before running back to the house and opening the door.

Rose took the box out of her bag and removed the horse figurine, staring down at it before placing it on the letter, beside the key. It had never belonged to her, and if it belonged to anyone, it was to Benjamin and his family.

She didn't give herself time to overthink it, but she did turn around and look back at the house one last time before getting into the taxi. She committed the architecture to memory, and as she did so, she gave herself permission to glance at the stables, too.

Benjamin was standing there, at the entrance, facing her. But as she stood and stared back at him, he remained immobile, and so she turned and got into the taxi, wishing she'd been braver.

Because if she had been, she would have run into his arms for one final embrace, and to tell him that even though it was over, she loved him. That despite the fact that they might not see each other again, she would never forget the time they'd spent together.

And that she was sorry. So painfully, horribly sorry for the way things had ended between them.

But instead, she let the taxi drive her away from the property that should have been her destiny, and from the man she wished she could have loved enough to stay.

23

Valentina felt as if her heart was being torn in half. Her daughter had come into the world with a cry as fierce as a lion, her little fist thrust into the air defiantly as her eyes had slowly come to focus on her mother. And now, ten days later, Valentina already couldn't imagine a moment without her daughter by her side, tucked into her arms. She fed vigorously as if the world depended upon it, slept fitfully, and spent most of her waking hours gazing at her mother, as Valentina did in return. She wanted to memorise every inch of her face, to never forget the softness of her head and the sweet smell of her breath, the thrust of her little fist in the air or the warmth of her tiny body tucked against hers.

Which was why five days had turned into seven, and seven had turned into fourteen. It was proving impossible to leave her beautiful daughter behind, but thankfully Hope had never questioned her, instead letting her spend every precious moment with her daughter.

'Valentina,' Hope said, knocking softly against the wood as she stood in the open doorway. 'Could we talk for a moment?'

Valentina immediately moved over on the bed so Hope

could come and sit beside her. In the time that she'd lived at Hope's House, she'd come to see what a compassionate, loving woman Hope was, and she knew that she'd miss her for a long time to come once she did finally leave. Their ages might not be so far apart, but Hope had felt like the big sister she'd wished she'd always had—always seeming to know the right thing to say.

'I don't know how I'm going to leave her,' Valentina whispered.

'You're certain there's not a way that you could take her with you?' Hope asked, gently. 'I've never said this to any of my other mothers before, but is there any way you could keep her hidden in Argentina until you're ready? Do you have any relatives you could call on while you sort through your family's affairs?'

Valentina forced her gaze from her daughter's face. 'I've gone over this countless times in my mind, trying to figure out a way to keep her with me, but if I don't succeed at keeping her concealed, then there's no way my marriage could be annulled. We would be forced to return to my husband, both of us, and the only way I'd ever be able to divorce him would be if I left her with him. And I can't do that. I *won't* do that.'

Hope nodded. 'I understand, I promise I do. I was only trying to think of a different way for you, if that's what you wanted.'

Valentina thought of the last correspondence she'd had from her lawyer, and of her dwindling funds. Without his help, she wouldn't have even been able to pay her passage back to Buenos Aires to fight her mother. There was no way she could take her daughter with her, as much as she wished she could. And the ongoing war in Europe had made everything difficult, particularly travel.

'I don't know if it will take weeks, months or even years to fight my family and receive my annulment,' she said. 'I have to actually make it home, we have to go through the courts, and—'

'Valentina, you know what's best for you and your baby,' Hope said. 'I was only asking because your situation is so different to many of the other young women I help. I keep thinking about you asking me to keep her, that first day we met.'

'She has to be a secret,' Valentina murmured, her eyes fixed on her daughter again. 'She's the most precious thing in my life, but no one can know about her. No one can discover that I've had a baby.' It wasn't just her husband, it was the judges she would have to stand in front of, too. She had to plead her case as her father's only child, an innocent young woman who'd been forced into a marriage that hadn't been consummated, and who was ready to step into her father's shoes. For a price, her husband would go along with it, of that she was almost certain, but not if he knew they had a child.

'I want you to search for the best family for her,' Valentina said. 'If you find that family, then you're to place her with them, and I will leave the box behind for her to discover when she's older. It was selfish of me asking if you could look after her until I return, when I don't have any idea when I'd be able to come for her.'

'I will wait, for as long as I can,' Hope said. 'But I under-stand what you're telling me. If the perfect family comes along...'

Hope's eyes met hers, and Valentina couldn't help but see they were filled with tears. She reached out and Hope took her hand, holding it tightly.

'I don't presume this ever gets any easier for you, does it?' Valentina asked.

'Some of the girls want to have their baby and get out of here as quickly as possible, almost as if they want to forget the entire ordeal and pretend it never happened,' Hope said. 'But sometimes, *most* times, the pain of separation is almost too much for the mother to bear. I have to tell myself each time that my job is to take some of that pain, to let them know that everything will be all right. Because it will be. No matter how bad the pain is, each day will get a little easier, until the loss becomes a simmer inside of you that somehow you learn to live with.'

Tears began to fill Valentina's eyes. It sounded to her as if Hope knew her pain, as if she'd experienced something similar herself, which made her curious all over again. But Hope had never volunteered any information on why she'd started her house, and Valentina didn't want to ask her.

'I keep telling myself that I'm doing this for her, but in truth, I'm doing it for me. We could stay together, we could run away and never be found—'

'But what sort of life would you have together?' Hope said softly. 'There is no shame in acknowledging that you can't give her the life she deserves, the life you want her to have.'

'Exactly,' Valentina said. 'She deserves better.'

They sat in silence for a long moment, with Hope reaching out to stroke the top of the baby's head as Valentina watched on.

'Only the very best family for her,' Valentina whispered, as her tears fell onto the baby's blanket. 'I want to watch her from afar and know that she's better with them than she would have been with me. I want her to have a loving mother and father, parents who will cherish her.'

'I promise, she will not leave this house with anyone less than wonderful. You can trust me, Valentina, I promise you can. I promised the very first young woman I helped not so long ago, a French mother named Evelina, the same thing, and I can say with my hand on my heart that I did. Just as I will do for you.'

And Valentina believed her, because Hope was one of the few people in her life who had treated her with true respect and kindness, and she knew unreservedly that she could trust her with her precious daughter. There was no one else in this world she would trust with this responsibility—somehow a woman she'd barely known a few months seemed to be more trust-worthy than anyone from her former life.

Except for you, Papa. Because you would have let me marry Felipe, and then I would never have been faced with having to give up my own child in the first place.

Valentina tried so hard not to cry, not wanting her daughter to have her mother's tears landing on her soft cheeks as they said their final goodbye, but it was impossible not to. She'd walked her around the garden and marvelled at her dewy, newborn skin; whispered to her as the sun rose and she'd held her to her breast for the final time; nuzzling her soft, downy head as she'd rocked her to sleep in her arms. And now, as the hour of her leaving approached, Valentina felt an internal pull that threat-ened to upend all of her careful plans.

I can't do this. I can't leave her.

'Valentina?' Hope's voice pulled her from her thoughts as she entered the room.

'I can't do it,' she whispered. 'What kind of mother am I if I leave her?'

Hope's hand fell across her shoulders as she stared into Valentina's eyes. 'You would be the kind of mother who's putting her child first,' she said. 'Not everyone is brave enough to do what you're doing. If you truly believe that you cannot provide for your baby, if you won't be able to prosper together, then you can know in your heart that you're doing the right thing.'

'If it's right, then why does it feel so wrong?'

'Because the love a mother feels for a child, the moment they're born, is often like nothing else we've ever experienced before. It's not immediate for every mother, but you knew your time with your daughter was limited from the moment she was born, and that gave you an urgency to have the precious moments you did with her.'

'Have you had anyone suitable contact you about...?' Valentina found that she couldn't even say the words.

'I have a small list of couples who are desperate for a child of their own. Many have tried for years to have a family,' Hope said. 'But I wanted to wait until you'd left, until I knew you weren't going to change your mind. Or in case you wanted to meet them first.'

Valentina shook her head and looked up at the light, staring at it as she tried to stop the tears that kept threatening to spill all over again.

'When I pass her to you for the last time, I'm going to walk away and not look back,' Valentina said, swallowing her emotion down. 'It's not because I don't love her, or because my heart isn't breaking, because I do and it is, but if I look back I won't be able to keep going.'

Hope squeezed her shoulder. 'I understand. More than you could ever imagine, Valentina, I understand.'

Valentina leaned down and kissed her daughter's forehead, whispering her lips back and forth.

'May I ask you a personal question?' Hope asked, quietly.

Valentina smiled at her baby as her tiny fingers caught her mother's. 'Of course.'

'How old are you? I feel that you're one of the youngest mothers to come through my doors, although you have the strength and demeanour of someone much older.'

'I'm eighteen,' she said. 'Although I feel like I've lived a lifetime already.' *My father died before my eighteenth birthday. I've lived a year now without him in my life.*

'Valentina, no one your age should be faced with having a baby alone,' she said. 'Whenever you start to doubt yourself, remember that it wasn't so long ago that you were a child yourself.'

'But I didn't have her alone, I had you,' she said, as Hope leaned in and put an arm around her. 'I'll be forever grateful that I *wasn't* alone.'

'Even so, what you've been through would be unimaginable to so many young women. You should be having fun and going to dances, not hiding from a husband in a foreign country and giving birth alone.'

'The thing is, I fell in love when I was only fourteen, maybe even earlier. I knew for years whom I wanted to marry, the man I was destined to be with, and he would never have let me come here alone. Felipe would have wrapped me in his arms and never let me go.'

'And you're hoping to reunite with this man? This Felipe?'

'I can't imagine living my life without him, any more than I can conceive of living without my daughter,' she said. 'Right now, it's the only thing about my life that I know for sure, that I'll be returning to him once this nightmare with my family is over.'

'Then make it happen,' Hope said. 'We only get one life, Valentina, and you deserve for it to be the very best. Don't stop until you have everything you want. If Felipe is half the man you say he is, fight as hard as you can to get back to him.'

When Hope let go of her, Valentina glanced at her bags, packed and waiting near the door. *It's time.* She wasn't ready, but then she doubted if she would ever be ready. The car was waiting, and if she didn't leave soon she'd miss her passage back to Buenos Aires. She was lucky she was even able to get home with the war continuing to rage on, and she only hoped she wouldn't be turned back because of it.

And so she leaned over and kissed Hope's cheek. 'Thank you,' she whispered. Before holding her daughter one last time, feathering kisses over her face, her lips and then her fingers as she whispered to her, 'One day it will be different. One day we'll be together again, and it will be the two of us against the world. I'll never stop searching for you, my love. I promise.'

She had no more words, and she knew she was only making it harder on herself saying goodbye, so she passed her to Hope, looking into the other woman's eyes, and then turning around.

Valentina's cries came from deep inside her chest, each breath an almost impossible pull of her lungs as she stood, her eyes shut, her back to the daughter she so desperately wanted to take with her, until she forced herself to put one foot in front of the other and walk out of the door to the waiting car.

Goodbye, my love, she said silently in her mind.

And then as tears blurred her vision: *I hope one day you'll be able to forgive me for what I've done.*

24

PRESENT DAY

Rose burst into tears the moment Jessica opened the door, dropping her luggage to the ground as her friend enveloped her in a big hug, her arms tight around her.

'I'm so sorry it didn't work out,' Jessica whispered. 'But you're here now, and that's what matters.'

Rose swallowed and took a deep breath. She'd been determined not to become emotional, but seeing Jessica had brought everything back in a wave of sadness that suddenly seemed impossible to fight. 'The girls are asleep?' she asked, as she quickly wiped under her eyes. She didn't need her goddaughters to see her in such a state.

'They're asleep, and Ryan's watching TV in the bedroom, so it's just us,' Jessica said, taking her luggage into the house. 'You've got nothing to worry about.'

Rose followed her, shutting the door behind her. She looked around, smiling at the familiarity of Jessica's home. It had been a long time since she'd visited, but she saw it in the background of all their many calls, and she strangely felt as if she'd arrived home, in the way she guessed other people felt when they came back to a family home after a long absence. It was warm and inviting, with white walls and furniture that looked beautiful but not precious, as if the girls could build a pillow fort in the middle of the room and it wouldn't matter. The only hint that Jessica and Ryan had spent a small fortune in furnishing their interior came from the exquisite artworks displayed on some of the walls—they'd collected art since before they were married.

'I'm sorry for just turning up like this.'

'I invited you, remember? The girls are going to be in heaven when they wake up and find you in the guest room. You've just made their weekend, and mine, too.'

Rose sat down at the kitchen table, running her hands across the rough edge of the wood and realising how much it reminded her of the big kitchen table at the house in Argentina. She distracted herself by reaching for a child's painting, smiling at the colourful splodges and wondering what they were supposed to be, imagining what it would be like to have her own children and be surrounded by the kind of colourful mess that was such an integral part of her best friend's life now.

'A dinosaur, in case you weren't sure,' Jess said with a grin. 'Now, hot chocolate or wine?'

'Hot chocolate,' Rose replied, letting go of the paper and watching as Jessica took two large white mugs down from the cupboard and started to scoop hot chocolate mix into them.

'Thank goodness. I was hoping you weren't going to say wine.'

When Jessica brought the steaming mugs to the table, she gratefully wrapped her fingers around the warm ceramic and inhaled the sweet smell of chocolate.

'Rose, what happened?' Jessica asked, holding up her own mug and blowing on it.

Rose took a sip, closing her eyes and seeing Benjamin standing outside the stables, the way he watched her as she loaded her bags into the taxi. He'd just blinked back at her, not even holding up a hand in a wave, their eyes meeting silently with so much left unsaid between them. Walking away from him and the property in Argentina had been one of the hardest things she'd ever done.

'It sounded like you were having such a great time there, and Benjamin sounded, well, he sounded like just what you needed right now.'

'We just, I don't know.' Rose sighed. 'In the end, I felt like I was playing make-believe, like I was living someone else's life.' She glanced at the dinosaur picture again, feeling a tug in her heart that she couldn't explain. 'None of it was real, it was a fantasy or a holiday romance or whatever you want to call it, but it was never meant to be.'

'You've been through more than most people could even imagine this past year, let alone cope with, but don't tell yourself that what you had with Benjamin wasn't real, because it was.'

She looked up at Jessica. 'Then why do I feel like I just made a fool of myself? I never belonged in Argentina, but there was this little part of me that wanted to believe it was my new home, that it was the place I was supposed to end up. That after so much tragedy, that was supposed to be my happy ever after.'

'Maybe it was, maybe it wasn't,' Jessica said, sitting back in her chair and nursing her hot chocolate. 'But don't tell yourself that it was make-believe, because it wasn't. Whatever you had with Benjamin was real for the time you were there. How did you leave things?'

Rose took a moment to gather her thoughts. She knew that Jessica was right, but it didn't stop the way she was feeling. It was as if her life was one tragedy after another.

'I left him the key to the house and told him that I wouldn't sell the property for as long as he or his family had a connection to it,' she said. 'We went from living in a little bubble to everything just ending before I even knew what was happening.'

Jessica's eyes softened. 'You didn't say goodbye?'

'We had a big argument the night before. I told him I was leaving before he walked out the door, and then I got in a taxi and jumped on a plane the next day.'

Jessica was silent.

'I was never going to live there, Jess. That's what I mean about playing make-believe. I mean, was I supposed to uproot my entire life for another country just because I inherited a property and met a man? He was probably just being nice to me because he didn't want me to sell it from under him.'

'Don't do that,' Jessica said. 'Don't start pretending like he didn't like you or that it wasn't real. No matter whether you see him again or not, don't taint the memories you have. And it sounds to me like you left without even giving him a chance.' She frowned. 'Would you have stayed if he wanted you to? If he'd asked you not to get on the plane?'

'Maybe. No. Yes. I don't know!' Rose wiped at her eyes as fresh tears formed. 'I don't know what I want. I'm even more confused about what to do with my life than when...' Her voice trailed away.

'Than when your mum passed away?' Jessica asked, gently.

Rose nodded, not trusting her voice. 'Everything seems so hard,' she whispered. 'I was just starting to feel like myself again, and now...' She didn't even know what she was trying to say. 'Everything is a mess. I don't know what I want or what to do.'

'So, tell me about Benjamin. Was he just a fling to you, or did you fall in love with him? How did things fall apart so spectacularly when you'd been having so much fun together?'

'At the time he felt like the best thing that had ever happened to me,' she admitted. 'But when it came to it, he didn't even ask me not to go, he just left.'

Jessica's eyes never left hers. 'Meaning?'

'Meaning that I wanted him to stop me from walking away and say something that made it impossible to leave, to make me believe that we were more than just a holiday romance,' she said. 'I wanted him to tell me that home was wherever he was, or something, to stop me from leaving. I just wanted him to want me.'

Jessica sighed, and when Rose looked at her she could see that her friend was biting down hard on her bottom lip to stop from laughing.

'Jess!' she cried. 'I'm pouring my heart out to you, and you're laughing?'

'I'm sorry, it's just that you're expecting too much,' she said. 'You're talking about a man who works with horses all day and has probably never said anything so ridiculously romantic to anyone in his life before. Men don't beg women to stay, not in real life, and when I told you to start looking for signs, I didn't mean anything quite that dramatic.'

'I bet Ryan would beg you to stay.'

Jessica snorted. 'Of course he would, because he'd be terri-fied of being left alone with the girls.' She smiled. 'But seriously, Rose, it sounds very much like this man showed you how much he cared for you, in his own way, while you were there, and instead of seeing that, or just understanding that you'd hit a bump in the road, you wanted him to deliver lines like he's in a romantic comedy.'

Rose looked up at her. Why was Jess always right? Now that she'd said it out loud, she could hear how ridiculous she sounded.

'As far as I can tell, you told him that Argentina wasn't your home, you left him the key and then you were gone. *You* didn't give him a choice.'

She nodded. 'That's a very simplified version, but in a nutshell, yes.'

'And despite pushing him away and telling him that you had no intention of relocating to Argentina, you're waiting for him to make some big romantic gesture?'

Rose sighed. 'You're right. I know you're right. I just...'

'Wanted to know that your feelings were valid?' Jessica asked, gently.

'That he was prepared to fight for me,' Rose said. 'If I'm honest, that's what I wanted. I wanted him to demand that I stay, to tell me not to leave. I wanted him to give me a reason to uproot my life, to believe that what we had was more than a holiday fling.'

'And he probably wanted nothing more than for you to *want* to stay,' Jessica said. 'It sounds to me as if he let you go because that's what he thought you wanted, because you told him that your life was somewhere else. He needed to believe that you could see yourself making a life in Argentina.'

'You truly think so?' Rose asked.

'Think so?' Jessica asked. 'I know so!'

Rose finished her hot chocolate, staring into the bottom of the mug and trying to figure out if she felt better or worse for having poured her heart out.

'Come on, let's go to bed. Everything always feels better in the morning.'

When Jessica rose and leaned over to take her mug, Rose placed her hand over hers. 'Thank you.'

'You're very welcome,' Jessica said. 'That's what I'm here for.'

'You're right about everything always feeling better in the morning. I just need a good night's sleep.'

'Rose?'

She turned back.

'Did you solve the mystery of your great-grandmother in the end? You never did tell me if you'd figured everything out.'

'I feel like I discovered the woman she was, but I still have as many questions as I have answers. She was a pretty special woman from what I could gather, though, and I feel like one day more of her story will unravel, or at least I hope so.'

Rose picked up her suitcase in one hand and her bag in the other, and she followed after Jessica, who was turning off the lights as she went. At the door to the guest room, she said good-night and closed the door behind her, finding her pyjamas and quickly changing, before slipping back out into the hallway to the bathroom so she could clean her teeth.

The bathroom was as stylish as the rest of the house, with white subway tiles on the walls and black taps, but it was the brightly coloured bath toys scattered in the big oval tub that made Rose smile, and the Barbie toothbrushes displayed on the edge of the sink.

It was what scared her most about going back to London, to the quiet of her flat. This house was so clearly loved and lived-in; whereas hers was as empty as when she'd left it. Not to mention that she'd have to face all her mother's things.

'Rosie?'

The little voice took her by surprise, and Rose turned and found Jessica's daughter, Serena, standing in the doorway, her blonde hair a tousled mess around her head, her eyes squinting as she rubbed them with her fist.

'Hey, beautiful girl,' she whispered, bending down to hug her. 'I was supposed to be your surprise for the morning.'

Serena's little arms were tight around her, and Rose kissed the top of her head, inhaling the coconut smell of her shampoo.

'Can you come back to bed with me? I had a scary dream.'

Rose smiled. She'd never been so happy to be asked to do something in her entire life.

'Of course, sweetheart. Snuggles with you are exactly what I need tonight.'

———

Rose woke in the morning to a little face squished into hers, and warm breath telling her that someone was already awake and trying to compel her to wake up, too.

'Grrr,' she pretend-growled. 'It's still sleep time.'

'It's six o'clock, Rosie!' Serena said, sounding as if she'd never been so wide awake. 'Maisy, come look who I found!'

But it was Jessica who came running into the bedroom first. 'Oh no, she already woke you up? I'm so sorry.'

'Let's just say she found me in the night,' Rose said, hauling herself up. 'But it was nice. She cuddled me like I was her soft toy and put me straight to sleep. I don't think I would have slept a wink without her.'

'Morning, Rose,' Ryan called out from the hallway, and she saw that he was in his robe and carrying Maisy on his hip.

'Geez, this is what time people with kids get up? I don't know how you do it.'

Jessica groaned. 'This is why I don't drink anymore. The hangovers just aren't worth it.'

They both laughed, and Rose bent down to scoop Maisy up when she ran towards her, launching into her arms.

'You guys go back to bed,' she said. 'Enjoy a Saturday lie-in and I'll take the girls.'

Jessica didn't look convinced. 'You're sure? They can be a handful.'

'I'm sure. What do you say, girls? We leave Mummy and Daddy for a bit, and we can make chocolate-chip pancakes and then walk down to the park. Are there any good swings there?'

The girls began chatting animatedly about all the things they could do, and Ryan mouthed 'thank you' and disappeared back into the main bedroom, clearly not needing to be convinced. Jessica still looked torn, though, as if the offer were too good to be true.

'I promise I'll look after them,' Rose said. 'Just go and relax.'

'That's not what I'm worried about,' she said. 'They—'

'Are a handful. I know, you've warned me already.' Rose

laughed. 'But don't worry. I love their sticky little fingers and belly laughs, it's what I need right now. In fact, I couldn't think of a better way to spend a Saturday morning, honestly.'

Jessica slowly began to nod. 'Okay, well, if you're sure...'

'She's sure!' Ryan called out from the bedroom.

The girls ran to their mum and Jessica kissed them and made them promise to be on their best behaviour as they ran off down the hallway to the kitchen.

'Have you heard from him?' Jessica asked in a low voice.

Rose shook her head.

'You could always call or text him, you know, and tell him how you feel.'

Rose nodded and touched Jessica's shoulder on the way past, before calling out to the girls.

'Chocolate-chip pancakes, here I come!'

Rose sat in bed that night, her phone resting in the palm of her hand as she stared down at his name. *Just text him and tell him how you feel*. Jessica had said the words as if they were so easy, and yet Rose had been holding her phone for at least ten minutes trying to decide what to type.

She lifted her thumb, hovering over the keys for a moment before finally typing.

I miss you.

Rose pressed send and stared at the message she'd just sent. She shut her eyes for a beat and when she opened them, she saw three little bubbles on the screen. *He's typing back*. But as quickly as the bubbles had appeared, they disappeared, leaving her staring at her own message again. It happened twice more as she sat there, until they finally disappeared and never reappeared again.

It's over. She put her phone on the bedside table and snuggled down under the covers, thankful for Jessica's ludicrously comfy bed. Tomorrow she would book her flight back to London, and then she would enjoy every day with the girls and Jessica, exploring New York and being part of their lives. Then it was time to return to reality, and see if her old firm would have her back.

When Rose awoke, she stretched and blinked at the light streaming through the white linen curtains. She'd forgotten to close them fully the night before, and as much as she would have preferred to pull the covers over her head and pretend she wasn't awake, she was. The house was quiet, and she reached for her phone, deciding to lie quietly in bed and read the news until the girls were up.

Her phone showed a new message and she clicked on it, at the same time as propping her pillows up behind her. When she sank back into them, she looked at the screen again.

The text was from Benjamin.

I miss you, too.

Followed by: *I wish you were still here.*

Rose felt as if her heart had stopped beating as she reread his messages. He'd replied hours after she'd sent hers, and the second message had only been sent a few hours ago. And she knew then that if she'd been waiting for a sign or some big romantic gesture, then this was it.

She'd been so scared that what they had wasn't real, that he didn't care enough to stop her from leaving, when in reality they'd had a fight. An argument that could have been resolved by an honest discussion about how she was feeling. He'd been hurt and so had she, but she could see now that they'd both overreacted.

Rose typed back before she lost her nerve.

I wish I was still there, too.

She didn't have to wait for a reply this time.

Then come home.

Home. The word terrified Rose. Because she no longer knew where home was, and the more she'd had time to think about it, the more she realised that home had been wherever her mum was, wherever her family were, and that she no longer had anyone to go back to. *Maybe Argentina could be home.*

Rose decided to stop overthinking everything as a pool of excitement spread across her belly, and she opened a new browser on her phone and looked up flights, finding one departing New York for Buenos Aires in just over four hours. With traffic and security at the airport it might be a stretch, but Rose knew that if she didn't go now, she might lose her nerve completely.

She jumped out of bed, plugged her phone in to charge and quickly packed her things, tying her hair into a high topknot and pulling on sweatpants and a comfy jumper. She could get changed into something nicer later—right now, she had a plane to catch.

Rose checked she had everything, put her phone in her bag and opened the door, looking back at the elegant room she'd been staying in and knowing how lucky she'd been to have Jessica's house as her refuge when she'd needed it. *Maybe I have more than one home now. Maybe I don't have to choose.*

'Where are you sneaking off to?'

Jessica's voice took her by surprise, and Rose found her standing in the hallway with a coffee in hand.

'What are you doing up so early?' she asked.

'Catching up on emails before the girls wake up.' Jessica looked her up and down. 'You're leaving?'

'He texted me back,' Rose said.

Jessica's face broke into a smile and she held out her cup so Rose could have a slurp of her coffee.

'Then what are you waiting for. Go!'

Rose hesitated, taking another sip of coffee before passing it back to her. 'I'm not being crazy and impulsive?'

'You most certainly are. And given that you've never been either of those things in your life before, I think that's the universe telling you this is exactly what you should be doing.'

Rose was so nervous she felt she might actually be sick, but Jessica was right. She was going back to Argentina, and she'd never felt so alive and excited in her life before.

'Tell the girls I love them and I'll see them again soon.'

'You know I will. I love you, Rose.'

Rose threw her arms around her friend, coming dangerously close to sloshing coffee all over her. 'I love you, too.'

25

ARGENTINA, 1940

'Valentina, I'm sorry to be the bearer of bad news, but we always knew this could happen.'

Valentina sat stiff-backed as she faced the lawyer, trying her very hardest to maintain her composure and not crumble. Her breasts were still aching, her body craving the touch of the baby she'd left behind, and her heart felt as if it had splintered beyond repair, and yet she sat in the lawyer's office in the last of her best clothes, trying to pretend as if her world wasn't falling apart for the second time.

'Just tell me,' she said, forcing the words out as her throat felt like it was closing over. 'I want to know everything that has happened in my absence.'

He nodded. 'Very well. But let me assure you that once you're in control, once—'

'Tell me the bad news.'

'The company has been sold.'

Valentina's eyes widened as she gasped. 'Sold?'

'Your mother appointed your brother director of the company, and it was sold four months ago. Unfortunately, from what I understand, there would be no way to reverse the sale—

unless you could convince the new owner to sell it back to you, of course. Which I have to point out would need to be at a premium, most likely a greatly inflated amount over what they paid to secure it.'

'Tell me the rest,' she said, unable to contain her sigh. It was as if everything had collapsed in the short time she was gone. 'I can tell there's more.'

'Your family home is up for sale, as is the property in Mendoza.'

'So, she's trying to sell everything? To erase every memory of my father,' Valentina said bitterly.

'Publicly, she's the image of the grieving widow,' he said. 'I won't paint the picture for you, I'm certain you can do that yourself, but she certainly knows how to act.'

Valentina looked out of the window for a long moment, before taking a deep breath. She'd given up so much to come back to Argentina, and she wasn't going to back down now.

'Lorenzo, I returned home for a fight, and I intend on having one,' she said. 'Are you still confident that my father's last will and testament would be upheld in a court of law, now that I am an adult, when we contest it?'

'I am.'

'Then please go ahead with the annulment proceedings, so we can have that in place, and file whatever court documents are required on the matter of my inheritance. I want to start this fight tomorrow.'

'Your instructions are clear, Valentina, and I will proceed immediately,' he said, before adding more softly, 'and I have a small apartment near my offices arranged for you. It's very modest, but—'

'It will be perfect, thank you.'

'I have to warn you, this could stretch on for months, and if your husband isn't agreeable—'

'Offer him enough money that he would agree to sell his

own mother,' she said. 'So long as he's erased from my life, I don't care how much it costs to extricate myself from him.'

'Very well, but I will have to make it clear that any payment will need to be made after you challenge the contents of the will.'

'All he'll hear is the amount you're offering—he won't mind if he has to wait for it, I'm certain. Just, please, make it happen.'

He went on to show Valentina paperwork and have her sign documents, and by the time his secretary took her to the apartment he'd found for her, she was so exhausted she could barely stand. But in bed, curled into a ball as she prayed for sleep, all Valentina could think about was the beautiful little baby who should be cradled in her arms, which kept her from sleeping at all.

Te amo, cariño. *I miss you so much.*

And she also thought of Felipe, and what she wouldn't give to go and find him, to tell him that she was back, that they could finally be together. But she'd waited this long, and she knew that once this was all over, they'd have a lifetime together. She just had to be patient and wait.

———

Valentina had expected to feel differently when her lawyer personally called by to tell her about the annulment. It had just been granted, thanks to her husband agreeing to sign the petition, in exchange for the deeds to the Mendoza property and almost ten million pesos in cash, and she'd reluctantly given her consent. The money she was ambivalent about, but giving up the property had hurt, and made her feel as if she were betraying her papa. It was close to adjoining the land where her father had grown his best olives, land that he'd purchased when he'd first moved to Argentina, and she knew how much he'd have hated to see it let go. But with the business already sold, and the large piece of land with it, she could see no point in refusing to part with it.

Agreeing to this brings me one step closer to going home, and to returning for my daughter. Papa would have understood, and he'd have wanted me to do anything to regain control of what he left.

Only the day before she'd received a letter from Hope, telling her that her daughter was thriving, despite being unsettled the first two nights without her mother to hold her. It had given her the strength she needed to push on, knowing that she had to continue what she'd started. And so she'd signed on the dotted line, agreeing to give her husband what her lawyer had negotiated within six months of the date of annulment—something she could only do if she successfully challenged her mother. If she didn't win in her court case, then she wouldn't be able to fulfil the agreement with her husband.

And today was the day she would stand in front of the judge who would be deciding her fate.

Valentina dressed carefully in a demure black jacket, blouse and skirt—the same outfit she'd worn to her father's funeral a year earlier, and the only good clothes she'd taken when she'd fled her marital home. It was also all she had that was appropriate, and it somehow felt like exactly what she was supposed to wear.

There was a knock at the door then, and Valentina looked at herself in the mirror. She held her head high, considered her appearance, and realised how much more mature she looked. Her face had lost some of its fullness, and the eyes staring back at her seemed older. It didn't surprise her though, after everything that had happened, but she did have to remind herself just how young she still was.

'I'm ready,' she said, when she finally opened the door.

The lawyer looked her up and down, seeming happy with her appearance.

'You're feeling prepared?' he asked.

'I am. I'm ready for this to be over so that I can move on with my life.'

He gestured for her to go ahead, and they walked downstairs and to the waiting car. It was only a short drive, and when they arrived at the court, she was surprised to see a crowd outside.

'Is there something happening here today?' she asked. 'It looks like these people have gathered for a protest.'

She looked back at Lorenzo when he didn't answer her, surprised to see him smiling.

'Valentina, all these people worked for your father. They're here for you.'

'For me?' she asked, incredulously.

'I made a few calls, and it turns out your father was even more loved than perhaps we realised, and all of these employees knew that it was you whom he intended to take over the business one day.'

She stared back out at the crowd as the car pulled up at the kerb.

'It may have helped that I told them just how much your father generously bequeathed them in his will,' Lorenzo said with a chuckle. 'And that you intended on reinstating that wish. But I think we can divulge information on a need-to-know basis.'

If Valentina could have, she would have thrown her arms around the man beside her, but before she knew it the door was being opened for her and she was stepping out onto the pavement. The crowd saw her immediately, and all of the men took off their hats as she approached, holding them to their chests and calling out greetings to her.

'Thank you all for coming,' she said, raising her voice even as it began to wobble. 'I know you all meant so much to my father, Basilio, and I only wish he could have seen how many of you came today to support me.'

Each man greeted her as she passed, and Valentina was pleased for the distraction as she entered the courtroom and saw her mother already seated, straight-backed and looking as elegant as ever. She was clutching a handkerchief to her breast, as if she might burst into tears at any moment, and Valentina knew then that she was about to see a performance like no other.

'Keep walking and don't make eye contact with her,' her lawyer said. 'If she addresses you, nod your head and say hello in return. Remember, we want you to seem like the better person at all times, no matter what performance she delivers.'

Valentina felt an anger she'd never known before flaring inside her, but she forced it down, knowing this was not the time or place. She would have her chance to show her mother how much she'd hurt her, but it wasn't now. Now, she was to be the perfect daughter.

And when the judge entered and they all stood, she realised that her mother wasn't the only one capable of a performance. If all those people were anything to go by, she was doing what was right, honouring her father, and she didn't intend on leaving the courtroom without what she'd come for.

———

An hour later, Valentina had her chance to speak, and she turned her back slightly so that she couldn't see her mother as she did so. Her only distraction was the arrival of a very familiar face—José—and it warmed her heart to see the man who'd meant so much to her father there in the room to show his support. Although she couldn't help but search the other faces for Felipe, hoping that he might have slipped through the door with his father, but if he was there, she couldn't see him.

'The contents of your father's will are being challenged here today, Mrs Ruiz, and we've already heard petitions about whether he was or was not of sound mind at the time of writing his last will and testament,' the judge said.

'Excuse me, your honour, but it's Miss Santiago,' she said, saying what they'd rehearsed countless times in her lawyer's office.

The lawyer looked down his glasses at her.

'Your honour, my daughter is lying! She's a married woman!'

Valentina stood patiently as her mother was sanctioned by the judge, before being asked, 'Could you please advise the court of your marital status? I was expecting your husband to be here challenging the contents of the will with you.'

'I recently received an annulment,' she said. 'My lawyer has the documents here to show you. Unfortunately, the marriage was arranged by my mother as part of her plan to ensure my father's wishes were not adhered to, hence the annulment.'

Valentina stood patiently as her lawyer presented the document, breathing a sigh of relief when the judge addressed her again.

'Apologies, Miss Santiago. I would very much like to hear what you have to say about your father's wishes, and why you would like me to uphold his original will.'

'My father was a man of honour before anything else. His word was as good as a signed contract, and he spent his life ensuring that those around him were taken care of and provided for. I think the fact that so many of his former employees have gathered outside today, taking an unpaid day off work, is testament to how much they cared for him.'

The judge nodded. 'Please go on.'

'My entire life, my father was preparing me to take over his company. He told me many times what he expected of me, what I was to do with the business and his property, and I assured him that I would follow his wishes. But when he died, unexpectedly and of sound mind, I was only a minor and could not challenge my mother.'

The lawyer looked down at his papers. 'But you are now of age?'

'I am. And I want my father's wishes to be followed. I want to gift his employees the money he earmarked for them in his will, I want to buy back the business that my mother sold without my consent and without the best interests of our family in mind, and I want to ensure that our family estate is retained and preserved for generations to come.' She paused, taking a breath and remembering to smile. 'I am my father's daughter, and I will spend the rest of my life honouring his memory and fighting to uphold his wishes.'

'I would like to ask if there is any chance this could have been settled out of court?' the judge asked. 'Given that this is a family matter.'

Valentina closed her eyes, letting her shoulders fall. 'Your honour, I haven't set foot in my family home for almost a year. I've been effectively exiled from the home that was left to me, but that has instead been given to my brother, who had no biological connection to my father, and whom he never intended on leaving anything.'

Her mother called out then, but Valentina ignored her, continuing to answer the judge's questions, before being taken back to her seat and watching as Felipe's father was called. She only wished that Felipe was there too—what she would have given to have him holding her hand, or smiling across the room at her, telling her that she was doing the right thing.

By the end of the day, she'd know whether she was going home or not, and it was enough to break her heart. But she had to believe that the truth would prevail. Because if it didn't, she'd be left with nothing.

26

PRESENT DAY

When Rose stepped out of the taxi this time, Benjamin was sitting on the porch, one leg stretched out as he leaned against the front door. He wasn't alone, either. The cat she'd befriended was lying in a pool of sunlight beside him, and when they saw her, she wasn't sure who was happiest to see her.

The cat leapt up and bounded down the steps, immediately wrapping himself around her legs, whereas Benjamin stood more slowly, his eyes never leaving hers as a slow smile lit his face. Rose thanked the taxi driver without turning, hearing him place the bags behind her, but she stayed where she was standing as Benjamin covered the distance between them.

'I'm so glad you're here,' he said, pulling her into his embrace.

Rose held him, too, her arms looping around his waist as she pressed her cheek to his chest, listening to the steady beat of his heart.

'I didn't think I was ever going to see you again,' he murmured into her hair, before loosening his hold on her.

'I didn't think I was ever coming back,' she replied, smiling up at him as he caught her eyes in his gaze.

'I'm sorry,' he said.

'I'm sorry, too,' she whispered as tears stung her eyes. 'I'm hoping we can both forget the way we ended things. I said things I didn't mean, and I'm sorry for that.'

'So, we can skip the apologies and head straight to making up?' he asked, looking hopeful. 'Because I think we can both agree that we didn't handle things very well before you left.'

'We most definitely can,' she said, as a loud meow captured her attention.

Rose stepped away from Benjamin and bent down, carefully scooping the cat up and smiling down at him. 'He's never let me pick him up before. It's almost as if he missed me.'

She gently lowered her head and the cat pressed into her, purring loudly.

'That damn cat used to live in the stables, and I swear he's laughing at me because I kicked him out months ago,' Benjamin said. 'Then he found his way to the house. And to you.'

Rose put the cat back down and looped her arms around his neck again. 'He found his way to me, and somehow, I found my way to you. I think we're a package deal.'

He laughed, but his smile faded a little when he spoke. 'Rose, I'm sorry if I tried to make you feel as if you had to stay,' he said as he stared down at her. 'Whether this will ever feel like home to you or not, whatever your decision is, it's your decision to make. I should never have acted the way I did, it was out of line.'

'Coming back to this place, to you,' she took a breath. 'I don't know how to describe it, but the idea of not returning absolutely broke my heart. I felt lost when I left.'

'How about you stay for now, and see what happens?' Benjamin asked, holding out his hand. 'No pressure. We can just enjoy being together and take it one day at a time, although I can't promise that I won't try to show you every reason that I love Argentina.'

Rose took his hand, smiling up at him as he linked his fingers with hers and then pulled her closer so that she was standing directly in front of him. 'I like the sound of that.'

Benjamin's other hand gently cupped her chin, tilting her face to his, and she parted her lips as he lowered his mouth over hers. Rose shut her eyes, her lips softly meeting his for a kiss that she knew she'd remember for the rest of her life.

'We can take this as slow as you want, just don't leave like that again,' he said, pressing his forehead to hers.

'I promise.'

The cat meowed at their feet again and made them both laugh.

'I think he's trying to tell us he agrees,' she said.

'I think he's trying to tell you he doesn't ever want you to leave again,' Benjamin said, kissing her forehead before straightening, still holding her hand.

'What happened to no pressure?'

He shrugged. 'I can't control how the cat feels, but I'm fairly sure he begged you to stay.'

Rose found herself being led up the steps to the house then, keeping hold of Benjamin's fingers as he opened the door.

'How about a home-cooked meal out by the pool, and while I cook you can tell me all about what you've been doing these past few days.'

She smiled up at him as they stepped inside. 'You know, I think I'm ready to tell you about my mum, if that's okay?'

Benjamin lifted her hand and kissed it. 'It just so happens I love the sound of that. I wish I could have met her.'

She squeezed his hand. 'I wish you could have met her, too.' *Because I know she would have loved you.*

27

SANTIAGO FAMILY ESTATE, ARGENTINA,
1940

'You can't do this!' Valentina's mother begged. 'I'm your mother. Where will I go?'

Valentina stared at her mother in the same way her mother had stared at her on her wedding day, as she'd begged not to be forced into marriage. 'Mother, you have a stipend that is more than enough to provide the essentials for the rest of your life.'

'Valentina, I'm sorry, please, I—'

'You've had days to gather your things, and after everything I've been through, I care little about how sorry you are.' *You have no idea what I went through, what I endured because of you.*

'And what of Bruno? What is he supposed to do?'

'He can get a job like any other young man of his age,' she said. 'Now go, before I have you escorted from the grounds.'

'Valentina—'

'If you enter the property again, you will be charged with trespassing. Now please, save yourself further embarrassment and leave.'

Valentina looked over at the stables and saw that Felipe's father was standing, watching the commotion. It had been her greatest pleasure telling her lawyer to transfer the deeds of Felipe's family's home to them, and today she intended on telling him that he could choose whichever polo ponies he wanted for his own, as per her father's wishes. But before she did that, there was someone else she couldn't wait to see.

Felipe.

It had taken all her self-control not to reach out to him, but since the court ruling she'd had a whirlwind five days in the city making arrangements and signing paperwork, as well as managing to buy back a small stake in her father's olive oil company, but as soon as her mother left, she intended on finding him.

And as much as it hurt to see her mother yell and spit at her before getting into the car, her stepbrother lifting his middle finger and swearing at her, Valentina refused to change her mind. She had her whole life ahead of her now, and she intended on living every day to the fullest.

'Valentina!' José called, waving to her.

'I'll come and see you soon,' she called back, waving to him as she ran across the driveway. 'Have you seen Felipe?'

'That's what I need to talk to you about.'

'I promise I'll be back soon!'

'Valentina,' he called after her, but she kept running, hoping he'd forgive her for her rudeness, because there was only one thing she wanted to do and that was throw herself into Felipe's arms. She'd dreamed of this for months, imagining what it would be like to see him again, and the following week she would be flying in a plane to London to reunite with her daughter. Everything was falling into place. Finally, the life she'd dreamed of was going to become a reality.

'Felipe!' Valentina called as she neared their house, not caring who might hear her. 'Felipe! I'm home!'

She was breathless when she knocked on the door, standing back and trying to calm her racing heart, but when she heard footsteps and then the creak of the door opening, it almost exploded from her chest in anticipation.

Until a woman she'd never seen before answered it.

'May I help you?'

Valentina's heart stopped racing and she struggled not to stutter when she spoke, her words catching in her throat. 'I'm sorry, I was looking for Felipe.'

The woman was pretty, with wide dark eyes and long hair that tumbled over her shoulder, and Valentina couldn't help but notice her rounded stomach. She appeared to be perhaps five or six months pregnant, and Valentina was certain she'd never met her. In fact, she was so confused that she took a step back to ensure she hadn't raced up to the wrong house in her excitement.

'Who is it, my love?'

Valentina would have known his voice anywhere. And when she saw Felipe come up behind the woman, his hand falling over her shoulder in the familiar way of a lover, she felt as if she might be sick. Bile rose in her throat and her head started to pound.

'Valentina?' When he said her name, another piece of her heart broke.

She tried to smile, despite her pain, but couldn't. 'Felipe,' she said, weakly. 'I've just returned, and I, I...' Valentina could no longer find the words.

'*You're* Valentina Santiago?' the woman asked.

Valentina balled her fists and dug her fingernails into her palms, trying not to cry. 'I am.'

The woman's eyes widened and she stepped forward to kiss Valentina's cheeks, taking her by surprise. 'Thank you for the gift you've given Felipe's family. They must have meant so much to your father for him to be so generous, and you, too. We will never forget it.'

'You're very welcome, and I'm sorry for calling unannounced like this, I—'

'Would you like to come inside for coffee?' the woman asked, as Valentina's eyes were drawn to the way she placed her palm over her stomach and gently rubbed it. She found it almost impossible to look away.

'Thank you, but no. I shouldn't have come, I just—' Valentina was lost for words again. *I came to tell your husband how much I love him, that we were finally free to be together. I came to be with him. I came to tell him he didn't have to wait any longer.*

'Valentina, please, wait,' Felipe said as she took a step back, and she heard how gravelly his voice sounded, almost as if he was pleading with her.

But Valentina shook her head, glancing at the woman's rounded belly once more, taking in the simple gold band on Felipe's finger. Valentina turned and lifted her skirt, running back the way she'd come, even as Felipe called behind her. But she couldn't stop, not now that she'd seen his wife.

His pregnant wife.

But as much as it hurt, she could hardly blame him. She'd been gone for over a year and he would have had no reason to believe that she wouldn't be married, that they could be together, but the sting of what very much felt like betrayal was almost impossible to bear, nonetheless.

'You're certain that I can't travel to London?' she asked.

'Valentina, the fighting has only intensified, and the risk of travelling along with it,' Lorenzo said, rubbing at his temple in the way she'd noticed he only did over problems he couldn't easily solve. 'I wish I had different news for you, but I think it's

too dangerous for you to travel right now. I recommend that you
wait until the war is over.'

'How long could that be?'

He shrugged. 'Truly, I don't know, but I doubt war could
rage in Europe for much longer, which makes even more sense
for you to wait it out.'

Valentina digested the news, her shoulders falling in disap-
pointment as she collapsed back into the chair. 'So I'm supposed
to just sit here until it's over?' she asked, hearing the way her
voice was rising and not able to stop it. 'If I go now, I might get
there in time to bring her home with me, but if I have to wait...'

Her lawyer didn't answer, but he didn't look away either,
his eyes fixed on hers, telling her that what she was saying
wasn't wrong.

'I understand, Valentina, I do. But you expect me to give
you advice, and that's what I'm doing.'

She nodded. He was only doing his job, she understood
that, but it didn't mean she liked what he had to say.

'A letter arrived for you today, though,' he said, before
clearing his throat. 'From

London.'

'A letter?' She was about to ask who it was from when he
reached into his top drawer and took it out, passing it to her.

'I'm going to leave you to read it, and I'll have my secretary
bring in paper and a pen, in case you'd like to reply,' he said.
'I've made enquiries into the postal service, and although it
might be slow, any replies will still reach their intended
recipient.'

Valentina felt the weight of the envelope in her hand, her
pulse racing as she turned it over and saw the return address. It
was from Hope. But she didn't move until she was alone,
reaching over then for a letter opener from the other side of the
desk.

The letter inside was only one page long, and she sat back in her chair to read it, forcing her eyes to read slowly instead of jumping ahead and skimming over the words.

Dearest Valentina,

It is with a heavy yet hopeful heart that I write to tell you that your beautiful daughter has been adopted. I kept her with me for much longer than I intended, four weeks in the end, but you told me that if the perfect family came along that I was to proceed with the adoption, which is what I did.

Your darling little girl stole the hearts of a lovely couple in their thirties, who'd struggled for many years to conceive. He is a doctor, and she was a music teacher who now teaches piano from home. I personally visited their home and met with them twice before agreeing to the adoption, and I can assure you that they will give her a stable home and a lovely life—all the things we spoke of when we discussed adoption.

I wanted to write to you immediately, although with the situation in Europe so volatile, I fear that by the time this reaches you the outlook might be even worse. My greatest fear was that you would arrive soon after the adoption was confirmed, hoping to be reunited with your daughter, and I certainly hope you receive this before travelling back here. I'm not even certain travel is a possibility, but I wanted to let you know all the same.

My intention is that the memory box you left behind will be given to your daughter soon after she turns twenty-one. I know how important it was to you, for your child to have a connection to you, and I made sure to tell her parents that you might want to contact them in the near future. They weren't overjoyed, but of course they did understand.

I hope that you will forgive me the decision I made, and

*trust that I did what was best in the moment for your beautiful
girl.*

With all my love and best wishes,

Hope

Valentina pressed her fist to her mouth as she stifled a cry.
She was too late. Even if the war hadn't made travel impossible,
she wouldn't have made it in time. Her daughter was gone.

There was a soft knock at the door then, and she dabbed at
her eyes with her knuckles before clearing her throat.

'Come in.'

'Mr Gonzalez asked me to give this to you.'

Valentina took the pen and paper offered to her, but as she
stared down at the blank page, she couldn't find the words she
needed. What did she say to the woman who'd helped her so
graciously through one of her darkest moments? To the woman
who'd found a home for her daughter, rightly or wrongly, with
her best interests at heart?

She was tempted to discard the paper and instruct her
lawyer to take over communications, but Valentina owed Hope
more than that. And so she reluctantly lifted the pen and leaned
forward, the inky nib hovering over the paper.

Dear Hope,

My heart is broken.

She picked up the piece of paper and crushed it into a tight
ball in her palm, before taking a deep breath and starting again.

Dearest Hope,

Thank you for your heartfelt letter. I intended on travelling back to London immediately, now that my family's affairs have been taken care of, but the war has changed everything. My greatest wish was to be reunited with my daughter, but I trust in you and your decision. I know how hard it must have been for you, and I want you to know how much I appreciate everything you've done.

Please pass on my best wishes to her new parents, and tell them that I am here if they ever need anything, or if their circumstances change. If for any reason they could no longer care for her... you know the rest.

As promised, I intend on making a substantial donation to ensure the continued success of Hope's House. I will never forget the care and kindness you showed me when I needed someone the most, and my lawyer will ensure the money is transferred to you as soon as possible.

With love and my best wishes,

Valentina Santiago

She folded the letter in half and placed it in the envelope, carefully copying out the address before leaving it on the desk and wiping her tears.

Valentina took a moment to gather herself, then she stood and turned to the door. Her lawyer stood there—the man who'd helped her when she had nothing, who'd fought for her because of the respect he'd had for her father.

She would have liked to hug him, but instead she held out her hand, seeing the look on his face. He knew she was hurt, she could tell from his pained expression as he stepped towards her and took her one hand in both of his. But before he could say anything, she spoke.

'Thank you, Lorenzo, for everything you've done for me,'

she said, smiling through her tears. 'The care and compassion you showed me when I turned up unannounced in your office shows your true nature, and I will never forget your good deed. Your firm has my business for as long as I am alive.'

'Thank you,' he said, still holding her hand tightly in his. 'Your father always told me how special his daughter was, and I see that, too. You're a remarkable woman, Valentina.'

She wished he knew how much his words meant to her.

'I've left a letter on your desk to be mailed, and I intend on composing another letter that I'd like you to hold for me. It's to be sent to my daughter when I'm no longer here, when she inherits the Santiago estate.'

He nodded, and she appreciated that he didn't ask questions.

'I would also like an appropriate amount of funds to be transferred to Hope Berenson, and I'd like your firm to keep abreast of her situation. I don't want to see her doors close due to lack of funds, so please ensure that doesn't happen. You may make ongoing donations as required.'

'I understand,' he said, as he slowly let go of her hand.

'My daughter...' Valentina paused, steadying herself and forcing her emotions down. 'My daughter has been adopted by a family in London. In the first instance, I would like you to offer them money to return her to me. If they are the family Hope suggests they are, I foresee that they will refuse, and if that happens I'd like an investigator to stay informed of her whereabouts and the family's situation. I would like for you to make donations to her school and any clubs she may be part of as she grows up, anonymously of course, and when I pass away, everything will be left to her or to her children.'

'Valentina, if I may, you're only a young woman. You might change your mind about whom you'd like to leave your estate to, especially when you marry and start a family.'

She touched his shoulder, knowing that he had her best

interests at heart, but also how hard it would be for him to ever comprehend what she'd been through, and how that would affect the decisions she made for the rest of her life.

'I don't intend on marrying ever again, or having any more children, but I will keep your advice in mind,' she said.

'You're going to have a wonderful life, Valentina,' he said. 'I've never met a young woman quite like you.'

'Thank you,' she said, as she walked out of his office, through the reception area and into the sunshine.

It felt like a lifetime ago that she'd made her way to this office, pregnant and afraid. It was as if she'd been a girl then, and now she was a woman, with a fractured heart that she doubted would ever heal from the wounds it had sustained. She'd lost her father and mother, but she'd gained an understanding of the world and now knew how much pain one person could endure yet somehow still survive.

But she was alive, and she had her freedom. She would forever yearn for her daughter and mourn the loss of Felipe from her life, but she wouldn't let that stop her from living. With the estate her father had left behind, she had the ability to help others, to live a full life despite what she'd lost. And in his memory, that was what she intended on doing.

For my daughter, for my father, I have to live. For now, she could mourn the loss of everything she'd loved, for everything she'd wanted but could no longer have, with the memory of her daughter tucked in her arms; but tomorrow she would force herself to start living.

28

PRESENT DAY

Rose couldn't remember feeling so content. She guessed the last time would have been before her mother's cancer diagnosis, but ever since then she'd moved through life with urgency, almost as if she needed to fill every moment, to commit every second with her mum to memory, not knowing how much longer they had together.

But now, with Benjamin, it was almost as if she'd finally caught her breath and could just be. He reached over and strummed his fingers against her arm, and she lifted her wine glass to take a sip. He'd made her a spaghetti dinner and opened a bottle of red wine, and she was still enjoying the last of her glass as they sat on the sofa, their bowls empty on the table.

'You look lost in thought,' he said.

'I am. I just, I don't know, but this time, coming back here, I actually feel like I'm at home. It's a strange feeling that I can't quite describe.'

'You've lived in the same place all your life?'

'When I was very young, we lived with my father, but as far as I can remember, we lived in my grandmother's place, and we stayed there after she passed away, too.'

'My family are the same, we haven't moved far. I like having that connection to my past though.'

She watched as his fingers kept gracing her skin.

'How long ago did your great-grandfather pass away, Benjamin?'

'When he was ninety, so more than ten years ago now.'

'Do you think he and Valentina remained friends? Were they part of each other's lives?'

Benjamin didn't answer straightaway, but when he did, she could sense his hesitation. 'Rose, there's something I never told you, when you asked me about your great-grandmother.'

She settled back on the sofa to listen, still nursing her glass of wine and with her feet tucked up beneath her. She had a feeling this was something she wanted to hear from the awkward way he was looking at her.

'When I was just a boy of maybe six or seven, I saw my great-grandfather, Felipe, kiss Valentina. It was only once, and I never mentioned it to anyone because I didn't really understand what I was seeing, but I've never forgotten the way they looked at each other.'

Rose felt her eyebrows shoot up in surprise. 'And you're sure it was them?'

'I'd been down at the stables with my father. Valentina was very generously his patron for many years, so we were often there, and I'd always been curious about her. I remember walking the long way home so I could go past her house, and I saw them sitting on the veranda, and I've never forgotten the way my great-grandfather looked at her before he kissed her.'

'Did they see you?'

He shook his head. 'No, I hid so they couldn't see me, and I never told anyone about what I saw until just a few days ago.'

'You've told someone other than me?'

'I mentioned it to my dad just last week, and he suggested we visit Valentina's previous lawyer. He thinks he might have the answers you're searching for,' Benjamin said. 'I feel like maybe my dad knew they were linked romantically at some point, but if he knows he's not saying anything.'

'Do you think it might finally solve the mystery about how my grandmother ended up being adopted from Hope's House?'

'Perhaps. But regardless, I wanted you to know. It didn't seem right to keep it secret from you.'

'Thank you,' Rose said, sighing as she tried to piece everything together. 'You know, your great-grandfather has come up more than once, but whatever happened between them doesn't explain the questions I have.'

'Would you be annoyed if I told you I'd left a message to see if we can see him tomorrow?'

'The lawyer?'

'Valentina's original lawyer died some years ago, but his son took over the practice. I believe the lawyer you've been dealing with is his grandson.'

'But Luis told me he didn't know anything, that there were no records.'

'Maybe he doesn't, but I still think we should try to visit his father at his house tomorrow afternoon. Perhaps it's a dead end, but the very least we can do is try to see what he knows.'

'Thank you,' she said. 'You don't need to do any of this, but it means a lot to me that you're helping.'

'It's my way of saying that I'm sorry,' he said.

'Sorry? For what?'

'For everything that happened before you left,' he said, taking her hand and pressing it to his lips. 'For not telling you how much you meant to me before I let you walk away.'

Rose watched as his mouth hovered over her knuckles. 'You're already forgiven, but feel free to keep trying to make it up to me.'

Benjamin laughed and jumped to his feet, scooping her up

into his arms as she fought against him, protesting but at the same time hoping he never took his hands from her body.

The next day, she sat with Benjamin in front of the old lawyer, at his home near the city. He'd been reluctant to take an appointment with her, but when Rose had pointed out what a long history her family had of using his family's law firm, not to mention that her intention was to continue that relationship, he'd finally relented. And now she was at last hoping to piece together the rest of Valentina's life.

'I wasn't sure if there'd be any resemblance, but when I think back to what Valentina looked like as a young woman...'

Rose smiled politely. She was fairly certain he was trying to flatter her, but the only thing she was interested in was whether he could help her solve the final piece of the puzzle when it came to her family's secrets.

'I was told that your son, Luis, Valentina's most recent lawyer, didn't know about my great-grandmother's personal life,' she said, 'but I have an inkling that you might know more about how she came to place her baby for adoption all those years ago.'

He gave her a stern kind of look, as if she were asking something that she shouldn't, but when Benjamin cleared his throat beside her, as if to encourage the man to speak, he finally sighed and uncrossed his arms.

'Look, I only know what my father shared with me, and it wasn't a lot,' he said. 'He represented Basilio Santiago before his death, and then Valentina when she came to him as a young girl in need of assistance. She became his most important client, just as Basilio had once been, and he remained her lawyer until the day he retired. Even then, he kept working for her for some time, until eventually she became my client.' He paused. 'She was very loyal, and due to the relationship she had with my father, she never withdrew her business from our firm.'

'When you say that your father assisted her,' Rose said, 'what exactly do you mean? Did he help her with the adoption?'

'He never spoke about the adoption, and neither did she, not in all the years I worked for her. But I was tasked with compiling a report each year about her biological daughter. It was a closely held secret that I never disclosed, and she had me anonymously donate money to her daughter's school, or to any sports clubs or such that she attended. It was her way of helping from afar, I suppose.'

'And she never asked you to approach her daughter?' Rose asked. 'My grandmother?'

He shook his head. 'No. She didn't want to interfere in her life. I was under the impression that it broke her heart to remain hidden, but that she felt it was for the best. You have to believe me when I say that's all I knew.'

Rose stood then, feeling as if she'd heard enough. 'Thank you for your time. I appreciate everything you've shared with me.'

'Rose,' the old man said, rising as she did.

Benjamin stood protectively by her side, his hand touching gently against her back.

'She was very proud when you graduated from the University of Cambridge.'

Rose felt her jaw hang open. 'She knew about me?'

'She was there,' he said. 'She told me it was likely the last time she'd be able to travel, and she sat among the audience to cheer you on.'

'You're certain she was there on the day I graduated?' she asked.

'Valentina might not have been physically present in her daughter's life, but it wasn't because she didn't love her. She insisted on knowing everything about you, about your mother, and of course about your grandmother. It was her way of being part of your lives without feeling as if she was intruding.'

'Thank you,' Rose said, her hand shaking until Benjamin closed his palm around hers to steady it. 'I hope you know how much this means to me. It's as if everything has finally come together.'

'There's one last thing, though,' Benjamin said. 'Who was the father of her child? It is the one thing that we haven't come close to finding out.'

'Valentina never mentioned the father, and I never saw a birth certificate,' he said. 'But she was married for a brief time, almost a year, in fact. The marriage was annulled after her husband was offered a significant amount of money to walk away, and the implication was that he was the father. No one in Argentina, other than my father, even knew that she'd given birth. It was a closely guarded secret that I only became aware of when I took over as her lawyer. It's fair to say that she would never have been able to leave the marriage if her husband had found out, and certainly there couldn't have been an annulment. She was an heiress worth a small fortune, and a child would have meant she couldn't so easily extract herself, even with a divorce. He would never have consented.'

'This is all a lot to process, but thank you again. For everything you've shared.'

'You're very welcome,' he said. 'If I remember anything else, or you have any other questions, you know where to find me.'

'I do,' Rose said.

Rose and Benjamin said their goodbyes and left, walking silently through the building and to his car. It wasn't until they were seated with the engine running that they spoke.

'I can't believe that she knew who I was. That she was there at my graduation,' Rose said. 'It's almost as if she was part of my life without me even knowing.'

'You would have loved her, Rose. I'm so sorry you never got to meet her.'

'I just feel so sorry for her,' she said, leaning back into her seat and turning slightly to face Benjamin. 'She must have been so lonely.'

'Perhaps, but she never showed it. She lived a full life, surrounded by people and giving generously to the things she cared about. She was a remarkable woman.'

'Do you believe that she loved your great-grandfather?'

He nodded. 'I believe they were in love, but weren't allowed to be together. Perhaps her pregnancy put an end to things, or their young age, or her marriage. I suppose we'll never know. But I do believe that if times had been different, they would have been together.'

Rose stared out of the window and tried to picture her great-grandmother as a young woman, thinking of the photos she'd found of her in her younger years. Did she walk these streets, pregnant and alone, trying to figure out what to do? Was she heartbroken when she left her baby behind in London, or relieved? They were questions Rose would never know the answers to, even though she knew she'd most likely turn them over and over in her mind for years to come.

'Benjamin, I know nothing about horses, but I want to honour Valentina's memory and ensure that she has a legacy that outlasts all of us,' Rose said. 'Would you help me with this? I'll need someone by my side to guide me, but I very much want to remain a patron of the game of polo, and to expand our ability to care for retired ponies.'

'It would be my honour,' Benjamin said.

She beamed at him, so grateful to have him with her.

'But first, there's something I'd like to do,' he said.

She waited, watching the smile that spread across his lips.

'Can I please take you to lunch? I think it's time I took you on a proper date.'

His stomach grumbled and they both laughed.

'Are you sure? Or are you just very, very hungry and can't wait for home?'

Benjamin grimaced and Rose leaned over to kiss him. 'I don't care why, but yes, Benjamin, you can take me for lunch. Nothing would make me happier.'

'Well, good, because I'm starving.'

She tried to play-hit him but he ducked out of the way and pulled the car out into the traffic. And as Rose settled back into the seat, watching as Buenos Aires became a blur of streets and cars, in that moment she knew she was home.

Perhaps Benjamin was right all along. Maybe Argentina is in my blood. It had just taken coming back to realise just how much she'd missed it, and how much she felt that she belonged.

29

ARGENTINA, 1940

Valentina stopped when she saw Felipe ahead of her. She'd tried so hard since she'd last seen him not to cross paths with him, to avoid the feeling of their eyes meeting or having to make small talk when her heart was still healing. But today, it was inevitable.

'I was hoping to see you,' he said.

And I was hoping not to see you. 'Felipe,' she said, leaning into the open doorway of the stable building.

'You look well,' he said, and she could tell by the hesitation in his voice that he was as nervous about seeing her as she was him.

'Thank you.'

'Are you riding?' he asked.

Valentina shook her head. 'No. I haven't ridden since...' Her voice trailed off and she found that she didn't want to finish her sentence. 'It's not the same, riding alone.'

Felipe stared at her, and she wondered if he felt the same, gnawing pain inside as she did from standing so close and yet so far from him.

'Valentina, I need you to know—'

'Please, stop,' she said, holding up her hand. 'You don't need to say anything.'

But Felipe didn't stop. He came closer, taking her hand in his and not letting her pull away when she half-heartedly tried.

'Valentina, please let me say this. I promise that I won't come looking for you again, but I need to tell you this.'

She looked down at her hand in his, closing her eyes for a beat, before finally looking up at him.

'If I'd known there was even a chance of you coming back, if I'd thought there was a possibility of us being together again, I would have waited for you,' he said, tears shining from his eyes as he spoke. 'You will always be the love of my life, Valentina. I need you to know that I will never love anyone in the way I loved you. But I thought you were lost to me.'

Valentina had been so careful not to see Felipe, because she didn't trust herself around him. And now that he was so close, she couldn't help but lift a hand to touch his cheek, her palm resting softly against his skin.

'Will you ever be able to forgive me?' he whispered.

She smiled. How could she not smile when she was looking into the eyes of the man she loved? 'There are people in my life whom I will never forgive, Felipe, but you are not one of them,' she said, surprised at how strong her voice sounded when inside she was breaking. 'But if you need to hear me say it, then I forgive you.'

'I don't know what to do,' he said. 'I—'

'You don't need to do anything,' she said. 'You're married, you're about to be a father. You have your whole life ahead of you.' Valentina took a breath. 'With your wife.'

She could see the pain etched on his face, the haunted way he stared at her as if he couldn't live with himself; and she only recognised it because she felt the same.

'I wish things could have been different.'

Valentina sighed, knowing she was only going to be able to

hold her tears for so long. 'So do I. We would have had a beautiful life together.' *But it wasn't to be.*

'One day, far in the future, if we ever find ourselves alone, if—'

'Yes,' she whispered, not letting him finish. 'I will always be here. Even if we're eighty, if we ever have the opportunity to be together, the answer will always be yes.'

Felipe kept his hold on her hand, looking down at their skin touching before letting go of her and placing both his palms to her face. He hesitated, as if waiting for her to pull away, but Valentina was powerless to move. When he kissed her, she let him. It was a slow, warm kiss—a goodbye kiss—and she hoped that his wife would forgive him if she ever found out.

'I'm going to miss you forever,' he murmured.

'I'm going to miss you forever, too,' she whispered back.

Felipe hovered, his face barely an inch from hers, his breath mixing with hers, until he finally stepped away.

'Would you like to go for a ride together, one last time?'

She was going to say no, to walk away from him and tend to her broken heart alone, but when she saw the way he was looking at her, she couldn't help it.

'Yes.'

One last ride. One last moment in time together before he spent the rest of his life with another woman, another woman to whom Valentina would show the utmost respect. Her marriage might have been a sham, but Felipe's wasn't, and she would not be responsible for breaking up a family, or another woman's heart.

The ride was as beautiful as it was lonely. Valentina couldn't understand how she could be so close to the man she loved, and yet somehow feel so alone.

They started at a walk and then cantered, and she was grateful for the wind whipping against her cheeks and the sun beating down on her arms as her horse stretched and pulled beneath her. But when they finally slowed, she saw that they'd come to the one place she'd never imagined coming back to— their tree at the farthest reaches of the estate.

She asked her horse to halt and stared at Felipe, who appeared equally as breathless as her.

'I didn't intend on bringing you here.'

Valentina nodded. 'Old habits, or maybe our horses chose for us.'

Neither of them made an attempt to dismount, and she was grateful to stay at a distance from him so that she wasn't tempted to touch him again.

'Felipe, I have a daughter,' she suddenly said, the words falling from her mouth before she had time to think through what she was telling him.

His eyes widened. 'A daughter?'

'When I left my husband, when I disappeared, the reason I had to leave was because I was pregnant.'

His eyes never left hers. 'You knew he would never agree to end your marriage if he found out.'

Valentina swallowed. She could have left it there, but she needed him to know. 'And I knew I would never find my way back to you if I had to stay married.'

'I'm sorry,' Felipe said. 'I'm so sorry for what I did.'

'I know you are,' she replied, forcing a small smile. 'But it also wasn't just that. It was about honouring my father, righting the wrongs that had happened after his passing. I had to make everything right.'

They sat a while longer, neither of them talking as they both stared out across the property, as the sun continued to rise higher in the sky. It was moments like these that Valentina knew she'd miss more than anything else—being in Felipe's quiet company, trusting the person she loved with all her heart.

'Where is she now? Your daughter?' he asked.

'In London,' Valentina replied, glancing over at him and seeing the hard set of his jaw as he continued to look into the distance. 'That's where I went, when I left. I had her at a special home where I was very well cared for, and a family adopted her after I left.'

'If you'd known about me, that I was married, would you still have left her?' Felipe asked.

'Yes,' Valentina said, immediately. 'I left her to escape my marriage, to avenge my father, and to allow her to have a life that I didn't believe I would be able to provide for her.' *A life that I could provide now, if I could find a way to get her back. If I truly believed she would be better with me than the family who adopted her.*

Felipe turned his horse around then and met her gaze.

'Valentina Santiago, I've loved you since you were a girl and I was a boy, and I will love you until my dying breath,' he said. 'I just wish I knew how to live without you.'

'Live knowing that your love is returned, and that it's okay to be in love with your wife and still love me. Just as I will always be a mother even though I will never hold my child in my arms again.'

She watched as Felipe's tears left his cheeks damp, at the same time as a steely resolve settled over her. She'd fought, and won. She'd loved, and lost. But she was still here, on the land that had meant everything to her father, with her entire future ahead of her.

'Goodbye, Felipe,' she said, turning away from him and nudging her heels against her horse's sides.

But unlike when she said her final farewell to her daughter, this time she did look back. Valentina turned in the saddle and glanced at the man she loved one last time, before urging her horse into a canter and racing back to the stables.

She doubted she'd ever ride again; it was something she had only ever done to be close to Felipe, but she had another idea. She would continue to foster her father's love of polo and open the estate to retired ponies, breeding only a handful of new horses each year to ensure the bloodlines he'd been so passionate about weren't lost. And she would sponsor young riders who had the talent but not the finances to play polo, to make the sport accessible to all.

There were dark days ahead, with the war still raging through Europe, but her father would have been the first to tell her to look forward; to visualise a future after the darkest of days. She may have lost the love of her life, but her life was still hers to live, on her terms, with no man dictating to her what her future looked like.

And as she slowed to a walk when the stables came into view, giving her horse time to cool down, Valentina vowed to make the very most of her life.

She would never stop watching over her daughter, and she would never stop loving Felipe, but it didn't mean her life wasn't worth living. To the contrary, it meant she knew what true love was, and for that, she would always be grateful.

30

PRESENT DAY

Rose stared at the test in her hand. She'd thought it was scary when she'd first waited for a Covid test to show two lines, but seeing the two dark red lines on the pregnancy test was like nothing she'd ever experienced before, and she had no idea whether to be excited or terrified or both.

'Sweetheart, I thought you could use a coffee,' Benjamin said as he pushed open the door.

She looked up, her eyes meeting his as the smile on his face hovered into something resembling shock. Rose was surprised he didn't drop one of the two coffee cups he was holding.

'That's a, a—'

'Pregnancy test,' she whispered, curling her toes against the cold tiles as her stomach lurched.

'A pregnancy test,' he repeated, as if he wanted to say something but was at a loss for words so just repeated what she'd said.

'I'm pregnant.'

Benjamin started nodding. 'Right. I, ahh, I'm just going to set these cups down here.'

Rose was about to reach for him when he disappeared, and

she found herself dropping the test in the bin and staring into the still-full coffee cups he'd left behind. *I'm going to lose him.* Tears pricked her eyes as she placed both hands on the basin, turning on the water and running her hands beneath it for something to do.

Everything had felt as if it were falling into place, as if it was meant to be, and now she felt as if history was repeating itself. Only she had control over her own body and her own life in ways that her great-grandmother hadn't.

After taking a moment to gather herself, she picked up one of the cups, lifting the steaming liquid to her lips to take a sip. She couldn't see any point in letting the coffee go to waste.

But when she walked out of the bathroom, she was surprised to see Benjamin walking back into the room.

'Sorry, I—'

'It's fine, it came as a shock to me, too.'

'It's not that,' he said, as he came towards her and took the cup from her hands, setting it down beside the bed.

'Honestly, it's fine. I've only just come back and—'

'Rose, stop,' he said, taking her hand and shaking his head. 'Just stop and let me talk for a moment, would you?'

Rose pressed her lips together, seeing how serious Benjamin looked. But it wasn't until he dropped to one knee that she understood what was happening.

'Rose, this isn't how I planned this, but—'

'Stop,' she whispered. 'You don't have to do this.'

Benjamin sighed and stood up, letting go of one of her hands as he touched gently beneath her chin and lifted her face slightly, so she was looking into his eyes.

'Rose, I'm just going to say this before you interrupt me again,' he said, shaking his head. 'My father told me never to ask a woman to marry me unless I was certain I couldn't live the rest of my life without her, and from the moment you came back to

Argentina, I've known that I never wanted to know what it was like for you to leave again.'

Rose stared back at Benjamin, hardly able to believe the words that were falling from his mouth. She forced herself to stay quiet as he stared at her in the most tender way a man had ever looked at her in her life before.

'This is not what I planned, because I've been waiting for the perfect moment, but when I walked in on you before I realised that I just needed to ask you. That the perfect moment was now.'

'I don't want you to marry me just because I'm pregnant,' she whispered. 'I can do this on my own, you don't need to—'

'Rose,' Benjamin said, reaching into his pocket and holding a diamond solitaire on a band in the palm of his hand. 'Will you do me the honour of becoming my wife?'

She stared at the ring, before looking up at Benjamin.

'I've had this ring in my pocket since the day after you came home, so please, don't think that I've only proposed because of the baby. It's so much more than that, Rose,' he said, holding it out to her. 'I love you.'

Her heart started to beat a little faster, even though the voice in her head told her that he was only asking her because of what had just happened. But as he slipped the ring onto her finger, she also knew that he hadn't just rummaged up a ring in the last five minutes. *He bought this for me before.*

'What do you say?' Benjamin asked.

The weight of the diamond felt unusual on her finger. She barely wore jewellery, and if she did it was usually a necklace or a pair of earrings.

'I...' Rose wanted to say yes, but it all felt so soon, as if she was rushing head-first into something without giving it enough consideration. *For once in my life, can't I just say yes?*

She looked at the hopeful expression on Benjamin's face, saw the kindness within him, the love he had for her, and she couldn't help the smile that spread across her lips. 'Yes,' she said at last. 'Yes, I will marry you.'

He let out a whoop and scooped her up into his arms, swinging her around as she protested, before he dropped her onto the bed and flopped down beside her, still keeping hold of her hand.

'I've never been so nervous in my life,' he said. 'But this, *us*, it's going to be amazing. Being without you, coming back to this house when you were gone, I knew I'd made the biggest mistake of my life in letting you leave without telling you how I felt.'

'I need to be honest with you, Benj,' she said, rolling onto her side so she could look at him. 'The thought of a wedding without my mum right now, I can't even imagine it. But it doesn't mean I don't want to marry you.'

He leaned in and kissed her forehead, his lips lingering. 'We can get married quietly, just the two of us, or we can wait. We don't even need to tell anyone about the engagement until you're ready.'

'You're sure? I don't want to ruin this for you. I know how close you are to your family.'

He grinned. 'We're going to have our own little family now, and that's all that matters. When you're ready for us to tell the world, then we'll share the news. Until then, we can keep it all a secret.'

She sighed and wrapped her arms around him, wondering how she'd ever thought they weren't meant to be together.

'You're going to make a great dad, you know that?' she murmured, trying not to cry.

'You're going to make a great mum, too.'

Rose lay in Benjamin's arms, marvelling at how her life had taken such a wonderful yet surprising turn. Only weeks ago, she'd worried about whether she was making the right decision about her job, whether she was foolish to even travel to Buenos

Aires in the first place, and now she'd somehow stumbled into the future she was always supposed to have.

'I keep forgetting to tell you, but a letter arrived while you were gone. I put it in the top drawer in the kitchen.'

'Addressed to me?' she asked.

'Yes, addressed to you. It was handwritten, so I didn't open it on your behalf in case it was personal.'

They lay there a while longer, but curiosity got the better of Rose and she couldn't help going downstairs to take a look. The house was quiet, but when she found the letter and sat down at the kitchen table to open it, she saw the cat was sitting there, watching her. She'd taken to leaving one of the doors open a crack so he could come and go, and today he was blinking at her as if he wasn't quite sure about his new residence.

Rose turned her attention from him and slid her fingernail beneath the seal of the letter, finding two pages of cream paper folded inside, with a striking cursive writing covering the pages.

To my beautiful daughter,

I started writing this letter so many times, and didn't know how to start. In the end, I decided to simply start with the truth, so here it is. I have watched you your whole life, from when you were a little girl until you had your own daughter, and then a granddaughter after that. I never wanted to leave you, but at the time, I was barely an adult myself, and my life felt as if I didn't have a say in it. I was so determined to return for you, but fate meant that it wasn't to be. I want you to know that not a day passed that I didn't think about you.

One day I will leave everything to you, and I hope that you find a second home in Argentina, and that you feel as if you belong in the country I have loved so fiercely. You might have been born in London, but somewhere deep inside, you have

Spanish blood flowing through your veins, and a connection to Argentina that can never be erased.

Once, many years ago, I was forced into a marriage that I resisted with all of my heart, but that marriage gave me you, and I wouldn't have swapped those precious moments I spent holding you in my arms for anything. I only wish that things could have been different, and that I could have spent the rest of my life getting to know you.

If you've received this letter, then I am long gone. So please, breathe in the fresh air, explore the land around you and open your heart. And know that you were forever held in mine, until my very last breath.

Valentina Santiago

Rose stood, leaving the letter on the table as she walked out of the door and stood in the sunshine, tilting her head up to the sky and breathing in the air, just as her great-grandmother had instructed. Because she'd been right—somehow, despite everything, she did feel the connection to this property, to Argentina, to the legacy Valentina had left behind. And now she finally knew the truth.

'There you are.'

Benjamin's arms wrapped around her from behind, and she let him hold her, leaning back into him as she looked out at the landscape around them. Her world had been turned upside down more than once these past few years, but Rose had the most overwhelming feeling that she was at last, *somehow*, exactly where she was supposed to be.

31

ARGENTINA, 1995

When Valentina saw Felipe walking up to her porch, she was sitting in the front room, a book in hand, enjoying the late-afternoon sun as it bathed her chair in light. Her book fell from her hand, and her bookmark along with it, and she knew that this was a day she would never forget for as long as she lived.

Valentina rose and went into the hallway, checking her reflection in the mirror and smoothing down some flyaway wisps of hair. It had been a long time since she'd seen Felipe—back then she'd had a jet-black mane of hair that she'd preferred to wear loose and falling down her back. Now, that dark hair was streaked with silver, and she more often wore it pulled back into a soft bun. There was a gentle knock then, and Valentina took a deep breath, at peace with how she looked. She was a woman in her seventies now, but then Felipe also was a much older man than he'd been the last time they'd seen each other, but she guessed that he too still felt like the younger version of himself that looked nothing like the reflection staring back from the mirror.

She walked slowly down the hall, on the one hand not sure

if she was ready for this moment, but on the other, knowing that she'd been waiting for it since she was a girl of eighteen.

Valentina swung open the door. 'Felipe,' she said, as he took off his hat and held it bunched together in his hands. 'I was so sorry to hear about the passing of your wife.'

He nodded, his dark brown eyes meeting hers. His face was drawn with lines now, but his skin was still golden, weathered from years beneath the sun riding horses, and he was fortunate to still have a thick head of hair, albeit grey now.

'She was a wonderful woman,' he said, as tears shone from his eyes. 'She loved me and I loved her, and she was the most amazing mother to our children, and then grandmother to our grandchildren.'

Valentina stared back at him, neither of them daring to blink as they stood before each other, and when he dropped his hat to the ground and reached for her hands, she let him without thinking.

'But she wasn't you, Valentina,' he whispered. 'I've spent my entire life trying to be the best husband I could be to her, making her believe that there was no one more important to me in my life, and I did that. I almost made myself believe it. But after she passed away, I couldn't help it, I'd lie there remembering what it was like between us, and those feelings haven't changed in over sixty years.'

She wrapped her fingers around his, squeezing his hand. 'My feelings haven't changed, either,' she said. 'There have been others, of course there have, but I've always hoped that one day, if we waited long enough...'

'That the day would finally come for us to be together,' he finished for her.

Valentina didn't know what to say. 'Your family, it's so soon, and I don't want to show any disrespect to your late wife or your children.'

'Does anyone have to know, until we're ready?' he asked.

'Can this not just be something between us? A friendship that we're nurturing to see what might come of it? I'd be happy to just sit in your company and know that we're making the most of our time together.'

Valentina nodded, still holding his hand. 'Yes, Felipe. This can be something just for us, two people who have rekindled their friendship after many years. It doesn't have to be anything more.'

The hopeful expression in his eyes made her smile—that after all these years, he still wanted to be with her, that the love between them had never faded. She understood the pull he'd felt, knew what it felt like to pretend there wasn't someone else even though that person was still locked somewhere in your heart.

'Shall we begin by you coming inside and having a coffee with me?' she asked. 'We can even sit out here on the porch if you'd like, so we don't feel as if we're hiding.'

'I'd like that,' Felipe said. 'And Valentina?'

She waited for him to speak.

'I need you to know that I loved her, that what I had with my wife was sincere. I didn't love her in the way I've always loved you, but it was a love, nonetheless, and I don't want to pretend that she didn't mean the world to me. Because she did.'

'You don't need to explain yourself to me, Felipe,' she said, gesturing for him to come inside. 'We've both lived our lives, and now...' Valentina stopped and turned around, doing something she'd thought about doing for decades. She lifted her hand and gently placed it against Felipe's chest, feeling the steady beat of his heart as she leaned in and pressed her lips to his. It wasn't a passionate kiss, but it was a soft touch of her mouth to his that was filled with promise, a stirring of long-held memories. 'Now it's time for us to choose what we want. It wasn't meant to be before, but perhaps it is now?'

Felipe nodded, and she watched as he swallowed, his eyes

glancing down at her mouth as she smiled. She hadn't kissed the man in more than fifty years, and they weren't the same people they'd been then, but the chemistry between them was still there.

'I'm suddenly not so sure about coffee,' she said, turning away from him and heading into the kitchen. 'We might both need something stronger after all these years.'

She heard his footsteps behind her, and Valentina lifted her hand to her mouth, stifling a cry as the understanding of what had just happened settled over her. *Felipe is here, in my home.*

She'd waited her entire life for him, too scared to move on for fear that the moment she did, they'd lose whatever window they might have. And now here he was, with both of them free to be together. They'd both loved, and lost; they'd both lived full lives, with people they cared deeply about; but everything was changing now.

And she was ready for this next chapter in her life. With the man she'd always loved by her side.

Valentina straightened and took a deep breath, because when she turned around, she didn't want him to see her tears, only her smile.

———

Four weeks later, Valentina and Felipe sat together at the polo. Even though she'd very much been on the fringes of Felipe's life, she'd made sure to support his family in any way she could, never blaming him for the way things had worked out. And so she'd provided his son with a job and the very best polo ponies as soon as he'd shown an interest in the sport, but it had never surprised anyone, given the relationship her father had had with Felipe's father. It was also a natural continuation of her family's love of the sport, and she'd made sure to sponsor other riders and entire polo matches so that her support of Felipe's family wasn't obvious.

But today it was proving far more difficult to not be obvious. Every time Felipe moved, or his knee nudged against hers, or they glanced at each other, she felt like that teenager who'd run down to the stables to see the boy she loved, just to spend five minutes in his company.

'Felipe, would you have dinner with me tonight?' Valentina asked.

'I would love to,' he said, touching her hand for a moment before withdrawing it.

Part of Valentina wondered if his family would even mind—it wasn't as if she was a younger woman or after his money—but she was also conscious that it was his decision. Felipe needed to be ready to tell them.

'Is there a special occasion?'

'Did I tell you that I have someone keep an eye on my daughter and her family?'

He nodded. 'You did.'

'Well, that person just sent me a letter,' she took a deep breath, knowing her voice was shaking. 'My daughter has just become a grandmother.'

Felipe didn't hesitate in taking her hand then, and he kept hold of it, his eyes fixed on hers.

'So you're a great-grandmother now,' he said. 'Congratulations.'

'It breaks my heart not to know them,' she said. 'I've tried to celebrate all their milestones, telling myself that what I did was for the best, but...'

'There's no reason you can't make contact now,' he said.

'But after all these years? How would I explain why I've never come forward before? What would they think of me and the decisions I made?'

'Valentina, if they're anything like you, they'll find it in their hearts to forgive you. It was a different time then, society had different expectations of us all.'

'I keep thinking that if she wanted to find me, if she wanted to connect with me, wouldn't she have tried?' Valentina asked. 'And then I get so angry with myself, and I wish I'd left something more direct in that little box.'

Felipe didn't say anything.

'When I left it, I expected to come back within months for her. I honestly believed that I'd be able to get her back, that we'd have the rest of our lives together.'

'Valentina, it's not too late,' he said. 'It's never too late.'

He lifted her hand and held it to his cheek.

'Look at us. Five decades, and we picked up as if no time had passed at all.'

Valentina smiled; he was right, of course he was right. But she also knew in her heart that too many years had passed for her to come forward, that she had missed the opportunity to be in her daughter's life.

Felipe's family came towards them then, and he dropped her hand. But he didn't move away from her, leaving his knee touching against hers as his little grandson came running.

His son chatted and his daughter-in-law came forward to kiss his cheek, holding the hand of a little girl who was only a toddler. Valentina felt a pang of sadness as she watched them, the pain of never having had her own family a constant that she did her best to ignore, but at times like this it was almost impossible.

'Valentina, thank you for a beautiful afternoon,' his son said, before ruffling his own son's dark hair. 'This little one is already telling me he wants to be a polo rider one day.'

Valentina held out her hand to the boy, grinning when he confidently shook it.

'You come and see me when you're big enough to ride. I promise I'll have a horse waiting for you.'

The boy's eyes widened. 'Really?'

'My family has a long history of breeding the very best polo ponies, and yours has a history of producing the very best riders,' she told him. 'It would be a shame to break the tradition now.'

He beamed at Valentina, and she couldn't help but smile back.

'*Gracias*, Valentina,' Felipe whispered. 'You've made his day.'

'You're welcome,' she said, leaning in slightly to him for just a second when his son turned his back, and knowing in her heart that there was nothing she wouldn't do for Felipe's family. In fact, she intended on finding a way to provide for them even when she was gone. Her greatest hope was that somehow she'd bring her family and his together once she was no longer here, on the land that she loved, with the legacy that she'd fought so hard for.

Once, she'd given up everything to fight for what was right, and her only wish was that her family would discover just how much she'd loved them, despite her absence from their lives. She might not be there when they pieced together what had happened, but her greatest hope was that they'd one day come to Argentina and fall in love with their birthright, to live full lives made possible by the legacy she and her father before her had left behind.

'I love you,' Felipe whispered.

She met his gaze. 'I love you, too.'

For as long as we both live, for so many years to come, and for all the years we missed. I've loved you my entire life, Felipe, and I intend on treasuring every moment I have by your side.

32

PRESENT DAY

Rose sat cross-legged on the floor across from Jessica. They had takeaway coffee cups and the remnants of chocolate brownies between them, and they were surrounded by cardboard boxes.

'You know when I said I'd come back and help you pack everything up, this wasn't what I expected.'

They both laughed.

'If someone had told me how my life would change even a few months ago, I would never have believed them.' Rose had known there was little chance that her mum would beat her last round of cancer. She'd fought for so long, but they'd both known there was only so long she could keep going. But what Rose had never imagined was that there was happiness waiting for her after the darkness.

'I feel like it's been years since Mum passed,' Rose said, as she reached for her coffee and took one last sip. 'Sometimes it feels like I've only just lost her, and other times it almost feels like a lifetime ago.'

'I know what you mean,' Jessica said. 'So much has happened in the last few months.'

'I still can't believe you came all the way here to help me pack,' Rose said. 'You didn't need to.'

'I came because I wanted to, not because I needed to,' Jessica said. 'And besides, I had another reason to come.'

Rose's brow furrowed. 'You did?'

Jessica grinned. 'I wanted to meet Mr Tall, Dark and Handsome for myself.'

They both burst out laughing again, and Rose shook her head. 'You're coming to visit us in a few months in Argentina.'

'You're my best friend, Rose, I wasn't just going to let you run away with a handsome stranger.'

'What happened to following my heart and taking risks?'

Jessica waved her hand in the air. 'I just said that to stop you overthinking everything. The truth is, I want to set eyes on the man myself before I let you go.'

'I have this feeling that Mum would have loved him, you know?' Rose said, seeing Jessica tear up at the same time as her own eyes prickled. 'The way he looks at me, the way he treats me, it's all she ever wanted for me. She used to say that the only man worth having was one who looked at you like you were the only person in the room.'

'I remember her saying that,' Jessica said. 'In fact, I think she reminded me of that when I told her I was marrying Ryan.'

They sat a moment as Rose looked around the room, hardly able to believe that they'd almost packed up everything in the flat. Her personal belongings and some of her mother's things were all being sent ahead to Argentina, but the rest was going into storage for now. She'd found someone fantastic to rent the flat for the next six months, and after that, she'd decide what she was going to do.

'Knock, knock.'

Benjamin's voice calling out as he opened the door made Jessica's eyes widen.

'Mr Tall, Dark and Handsome is here,' Rose teased.

When Benjamin walked into the room, she stayed sitting while Jessica jumped to her feet, and Rose watched on nervously as the two most important people in her life met for the very first time.

'You must be Jessica,' Benjamin said, stepping closer and kissing her friend's cheek. 'I've heard so much about you.'

'And I you,' Jessica said, turning and giving Rose an arched brow as if to tell her just how much she approved. 'It's good to finally meet the man who swept my best friend off her feet.'

'Rose told me that if I didn't make a good impression on you, you might not let her move, so I've been a little nervous about meeting you.'

'Oh, she did, did she?' Jessica laughed. 'I can't say I approve of her moving countries, but I am looking forward to coming to visit. Advance warning, my girls are desperate to sit on an actual horse, so they may be expecting pony rides.'

Rose stood then, holding out her hand for Benjamin to help her to her feet. When she was standing, she slipped an arm around his waist, glancing up at him.

'Jess, we actually have some news to share with you.'

Jessica looked as if she were about to faint. 'Yes! I will be your matron of honour! I've waited years to be asked.'

Rose laughed, before placing both of her hands on her stomach and seeing the look on Jessica's face change.

'You will be, but we've decided to delay the wedding for a year or two.'

Jessica gasped. 'You're pregnant?'

'It wasn't exactly planned, and I wanted to wait until I'd actually seen a doctor—'

'But we're over the moon about it,' Benjamin interrupted, as Rose let go of him and embraced Jessica, who looked like she had no idea what to say.

'You're going to be a mum?'

Rose smiled through her tears as Jessica held her tight.

'I am,' she whispered back. 'And if I can be half the mum you are, I'll know I'm doing something right.'

'You look after this girl,' Jessica said when she finally let go of Rose. 'She's more special than you'll ever know.'

'How about I take you both out for lunch to celebrate?' Benjamin said.

'I'd love that,' Jessica said. 'I'm only here for two days, and I want to make the most of it.'

Benjamin excused himself then and Rose took hold of Jessica's hand. 'You like him?'

'Like? How could I not?' Jessica said, pulling her in for another hug. 'He's gorgeous, he's charming and he's the father of your child. Of course I love him.'

'Do you think Mum would have liked him?'

'I think your mum would have adored him. He's everything she could have ever wished for in a man for her only daughter.'

Rose smiled, glimpsing Benjamin through the open door that led into her bedroom.

'And you know what?'

'What?' Rose asked.

'He looks at you like you're the only person in the room,' Jessica whispered. 'I think the house could have fallen down around us, and he still wouldn't have been able to take his eyes off you.'

Rose grinned at Benjamin when he caught her eye, and she knew that Jessica was right. It might not have happened when she was expecting it, but somehow everything was falling into place.

'And you're going to be the best mother to this little peanut,' Jessica said, placing her hand over Rose's stomach.

'You think so?'

'Oh honey, I *know* so.'

EPILOGUE

ONE MONTH LATER

Rose lay beneath the ceibo tree, staring up at the thick green leaves swaying gently above her as Benjamin's fingers danced gently across her stomach. She laughed when he nudged her top up and pressed a kiss to her bare skin.

'Do you think Valentina and Felipe ever lay here like this?' she asked.

Benjamin lay down beside her, propped up on his elbow as he smiled down at her. 'Maybe. I'd say this tree has been here for over a hundred years.'

'I just keep thinking about them,' she said, rolling slightly so that she was facing him. 'It must have broken both their hearts to watch each other from afar, wishing they were together.'

Benjamin leaned down to kiss her, and she sighed against his mouth, loving the lazy way his lips moved against hers, as if they had all the time in the world.

'I think Valentina would have loved this,' he murmured when he pulled away, his lips still hovering over hers. 'Our two families, finally connected after all these years.'

Rose smiled up at him, hoping that he was right. But he was quick to distract her by placing his hand on her stomach.

'It's been a long time since a Santiago was born here,' he said. 'But it seems to me as if everything has come full circle.'

'Would you mind terribly if we used Santiago as the baby's middle name?' Rose asked.

'I think that's a great idea,' he said as he sat up, reaching for her and pulling her up to sit with him. 'It's the perfect way to honour your great-grandmother.'

Rose leaned into him, her head falling to Benjamin's shoulder. 'I just wish my mum was here to meet you,' she whispered, brushing away an unexpected tear from her cheek. 'To meet our baby when she arrives.'

'*She*, huh?' he teased, putting his arm around her and drawing her close.

Rose just laughed through her tears as Benjamin pressed a kiss to the top of her head.

'She's here with you, Rose,' he said.

'You truly believe that?'

He kissed her head again. 'I do, with all my heart.'

And so, they sat there, in no hurry to leave the most beautiful spot on the property, as Rose closed her eyes and remembered her mother, finally able to think about her without bursting into tears, even as she wished that there had been a way for her to meet Benjamin before she'd passed away. For her to see the magical property that Rose now called home. For her to know that she was going to be a grandmother.

But no matter what, in her heart she knew that her mother would have loved the man she'd chosen, and that there wouldn't have been a prouder grandma to ever live.

I love you, Mum.

'Do you want to stay a while longer?' Benjamin asked.

Rose nodded and lay back on the grass again, as Benjamin reached for her hand and lay back beside her. And as the wind blew gently against her skin and the sun slipped through the gaps in the leaves above, Rose knew there was nowhere in the world she'd rather be.

A LETTER FROM SORAYA

Dear reader,

Thank you so much for choosing to read *The Spanish Daughter*! If you enjoyed the book and want to keep up to date with all my latest releases (including the next books in the series!), just sign up at the following link. Your email address will never be shared, and you can unsubscribe at any time.

www.bookouture.com/soraya-lane

I do hope you loved reading *The Spanish Daughter* as much as I enjoyed writing it, and if you did, I would be very grateful if you could write a review. I can't wait to hear your thoughts on the story, and it makes such a difference in helping new readers to discover one of my books for the very first time.

This was the sixth book in *The Lost Daughters* series, and I'm looking forward to sharing more books with you very, very soon. If you haven't already read *The Italian Daughter, The Cuban Daughter, The Royal Daughter, The Sapphire Daughter* or *The Paris Daughter*, you might like to read those books next, and enjoy being swept away to Italy, Cuba, Greece, Switzerland and France, and falling in love with some truly unforgettable characters. There will be two more *Lost Daughters* novels published after this one, and I can't wait to uncover more family secrets before this series comes to an end!

One of my favourite things is hearing from readers—you can get in touch via my Facebook page, by joining Soraya's Reader Group on Facebook, or my website.

Thank you so much

Soraya x

www.sorayalane.com

Soraya's Reader Group:
https://www.facebook.com/groups/sorayalanereadergroup

facebook.com/SorayaLaneAuthor

ACKNOWLEDGEMENTS

I honestly can't believe that this is novel six in *The Lost Daughters* series—it feels like only yesterday I was writing the very first book! This story was a particularly special one to me (although I'm sure I've said that with every book, and I genuinely mean it at the time of writing!) because I was able to incorporate my love of horses into the plot. I've loved horses from the moment I first saw one as a very small child, and I always say that I begged my parents for a dog for many years, and the moment that I got a dog I started to beg for a pony! I'm pleased to share that my love for both dogs and horses has never wavered, and I now share my life with many four-legged friends.

Bringing this series to the world is a real team effort, from my editor through to design, sales and marketing, so I wanted to take the time to thank everyone who's been involved in this project. First and foremost, I must thank my editor Laura Deacon for sharing my vision for *The Lost Daughters* series and for being such a wonderful, encouraging editor to work with. Laura completely understands the type of stories I'm trying to write, and her guidance on this novel, particularly on character development, was second to none.

Huge thanks (as always!) go to rights extraordinaire Richard King who, along with the amazing Saidah Graham, is responsible for selling the series into more than twenty languages around the world. Having my book available in so many languages is truly a dream come true, and I thank both Richard and Saidah for their enthusiasm and dedication to selling my foreign rights.

Special thanks also to Peta Nightingale, Ruth Jones, Natasha Harding, Ruth Tross, Jess Readett, Melanie Price, and everyone else at Bookouture who has worked on my series so far, as well as copyeditor Jenny Page and proofreader Joni Wilson—I'm sorry if I've missed thanking you by name, but I appreciate you all!

Thank you to my long-time agent, Laura Bradford, who has been with me since the very beginning of my career, just before my first book sold almost fifteen years ago. Thank you for your dedication to my work, and for always being there for me and giving me such thoughtful guidance.

My list of people to thank became a lot longer with the publication of *The Lost Daughters* series, and I'd like to acknowledge the following editors and publishers for their support. Thank you to Hachette; to my UK editor Callum Kenny at Little, Brown (Sphere imprint); my New Zealand Hachette team, with special mention to Alison Shucksmith, Suzy Maddox and Tania Mackenzie-Cooke; Dutch editor Neeltje Smitskamp at Park Uitgevers; German editor Julia Cremer at Droemer-Knaur; editors Päivi Syrjänen and Iina Tikanoja at Otava (Finland); Norwegian editor Anja Gustavson at Kagge Forlag; and French pocketbook publisher Anne Maizeret from J'ai Lu. I would also like to acknowledge the following publishing houses: Hachette Australia, Albatros (Poland), Sextante (Brazil), Planeta (Spain), Planeta (Portugal), City Editions (France), Garzanti (Italy), Lindbak and Lindbak (Denmark), Euromedia (Czech), Modan Publishing House (Israel), Vulkan (Serbia), Lettero (Hungary), Sofoklis (Lithuania), Pegasus (Estonia), Hermes (Bulgaria), JP Politikens (Sweden), Grup Media Litera (Romania), Koncept izdavaštvo j.d.o.o. (Croatia) and Ucila International (Slovenia). Knowing that my series will be published in so many languages around the world by such well-respected publishing houses is more than I could have ever hoped for, and I still have to pinch myself when I see my name on international bestseller lists!

Then there are the people in my day-to-day life who are so supportive of my writing. I would be remiss not to thank my incredible family, who are always my biggest cheerleaders. Thank you to Hamish, Mack and Hunter for being so understanding of my career and for just making life so much fun—I'm so lucky to have you all! Thanks also to my parents, Maureen and Craig, and to authors Natalie Anderson and Yvonne Lindsay for the daily support. I also have to say a very, very special thank you to my assistant Lisa Pendle, who is in charge of many things behind the scenes. I honestly don't know what I'd do without Lisa, and my dogs also adore her, which tells me that she is, indeed, wonderful.

But as always, my biggest thanks go to you—my readers. I am so grateful for your support, and I truly hope you enjoy this book as much as I enjoyed writing it. I also love hearing from readers, so please don't hesitate to email me—hello@soray alane.com—and if you want to be connected on a regular basis I encourage you to join my Facebook Reader Group—facebook.com/groups/sorayalanereadergroup.

Soraya x

PUBLISHING TEAM

Turning a manuscript into a book requires the efforts of many people. The publishing team at Bookouture would like to acknowledge everyone who contributed to this publication.

Audio
Alba Proko
Sinead O'Connor
Melissa Tran

Commercial
Lauren Morrissette
Hannah Richmond
Imogen Allport

Cover design
Debbie Clement

Data and analysis
Mark Alder
Mohamed Bussuri

Editorial
Laura Deacon
Imogen Allport

Made in the USA
Las Vegas, NV
03 April 2025

20503152R00163